Bodhisattva
Blues

Bodhisattva Blues

a novel

Edward Canfor-Dumas

RIDER

LONDON · SYDNEY · AUCKLAND · JOHANNESBURG

1 3 5 7 9 10 8 6 4 2

First published in 2014 by Rider, an imprint of Ebury Publishing
Ebury Publishing is a Random House Group company

Text copyright © 2014 by Edward Canfor-Dumas

The Random House Group Limited Reg. No. 954009

Addresses for companies within the Random House Group can be found at:
www.randomhouse.co.uk

A CIP catalogue record for this book is
available from the British Library

The Random House Group Limited supports The Forest Stewardship
Council® (FSC®), the leading international forest-certification organisation.
Our books carrying the FSC label are printed on FSC®-certified paper.
FSC is the only forest certification scheme supported by the leading
environmental organisations, including Greenpeace.
Our paper procurement policy can be found at:
www.randomhouse.co.uk/environment

Printed and bound in Great Britain by
CPI Group (UK) Ltd, Croydon, CR0 4YY

ISBN 9781846044298

Copies are available at special rates for bulk orders. Contact the sales
development team on 020 7840 8487 for more information.

To buy books by your favourite authors and register for offers, visit:
www.randomhouse.co.uk

To Coralyn, Alexander and Emily – with love.
And laughter.

Chapter One

There is no such thing as coincidence – that's what a lot of people believe. For them, everything happens for a reason – it's God's will, or the movement of the stars, or karma – and what we call coincidence is just our failure to join the dots, or even to see them.

Maybe. I don't know. What I do know is that this story starts with a coincidence – or so it seemed at the time.

It was August. Hot. I was earning a bit of money teaching English conversation to twenty-seven gobby Italian teenagers at a summer school on the edge of London – St Catherine's Academy for Girls. It stood, solid and heavy, in acres of expensive lawn on top of a hill in Hertfordshire. From the hockey pitches I could pan, left to right, from Bentley Priory – once home of RAF Fighter Command – to the green and distant hills of Northwood. Away to the south, the sun flashed off planes gliding in and out of Heathrow.

I'd arrived early to swim in the school's empty pool. St Catherine's was like the *Marie Celeste* at this time of year. A gardener riding the tractor-mower across distant grass; from behind the chapel, the rhythmic hammering of the maintenance man fixing something; Tracksuit Wade, the trim and permanently tracksuited sports hall manager, who let me into the changing rooms. And that was it. My Italians were trawling round the Tower of London and I wasn't due to engage them in chat about Beefeaters, ravens and the Crown Jewels till they returned at half two.

I ploughed my laps, showered and changed, then ambled down the hill to the shops to buy some lunch, swimming gear in rucksack, pool-wet hair drying in the sun, birds tweeting in the blackberry-laden hedgerows. Down past the golf course, along the footpath through the overgrown churchyard, and out on to the high street opposite the bakery. A crusty roll was cut, buttered, stuffed with ham and tomato, and soon I was heading back to prepare for battle with the Italians.

I turned off the footpath and started up the hill, then stopped to pick a ripe, fat blackberry.

'Nice one.'

I looked round. Two youths – sixteen, seventeen years old, both black – were sauntering towards me on either side of the road. The speaker, the smaller of the two, was smiling. His mate wasn't. He just fixed me in his stare as he came closer.

Where had they sprung from? They must have followed me through the churchyard. Not good. This road led only to the school and a few large houses at the top of the hill. Not many people used it.

'Like blackberries, do you?' Smiler asked.

'Pretty much,' I said, trying to sound relaxed. I put it in my mouth – it was warm from the sun – and strode off.

'Can we lend your phone?' I looked back. They were still following me. 'Only we're meeting someone and he ain't turned up.'

Obviously bollocks. 'Sorry. Haven't got it with me.' I kept walking. But suddenly the bigger boy was in front of me – fierce, angry.

'You fucking stop, you cunt! Stand still!' He was tense, ready for a fight – and holding a large rock down at his side.

I froze. The moment I saw them I'd expected trouble but still – I was shocked. Lunchtime. Sunshine. A leafy lane. Hardly the place for a mugging. The surprise, the incongruity of it all, rooted me to the spot. Plus the threat of violence, of course.

'Don't move – cunt!' spat Big Boy. He lifted the rock.

My stomach lurched. I could die here, I thought. Bloody hell. He could bring that rock down on my head and ... An image of pink brain oozing through blood and shattered skull flashed before me. I blinked. I couldn't move. I was so stunned, so confused, so totally unprepared that standing stock-still seemed the only possible action. A rabbit in the headlights – on a sunny, summer's day.

'What's in the bag?'

I passed him the rucksack. As he unzipped it I saw that Smiler, still smiling, had closed in behind me, blocking any escape. Big Boy pulled out the ham and tomato roll in its paper bag, the damp towel wrapped around my swimming shorts and goggles, and gave them to Smiler as he felt inside the rucksack's main compartment. Empty. He methodically unzipped each of the side pockets. Nothing, except for my keys on a fob.

'Wallet?'

I shook my head. I'd locked it in my scruffy old Honda Civic while I swam. Ditto my phone.

He took the towel and ham roll from Smiler and stuffed them back in the rucksack, then jammed his hand into my pockets, front and back, searching for cash. Bloody hell, I thought, is this a violation or what? I started to get angry, and as I did, my mind began to clear. Fight them both? No – two against one and Big Boy especially looked fit and muscular. Leg it? No – probably faster than me. Shout for help? No one around to hear. Ergo – just take it.

Then I remembered something I'd seen on TV about moments like this: you had to try to note some detail about your attacker. Something physical, a piece of clothing, a way of talking, a smell – anything. Difficult, but it could be a game-changer for the police.

By now Big Boy had found the handful of change in my pockets and was looking disappointed: £2.35 and a set of keys obviously wasn't much return for a lunchtime's robbing. He handed back the rucksack and I noticed a diamond stud in his ear. Perhaps they'll leave me alone now, I thought. Big Boy had other ideas.

'Where you parked?'

Oh Christ – he's going to nick my car, the only thing I own worth any money; that and my laptop. How do I get out of this? Then something else popped into my mind: 'When the Buddha nature manifests from within, it receives protection from without.' Blimey. Where had that come from? I hadn't been around Buddhism for years, but I'd been a real enthusiast for a while, had even written a little book about it, and suddenly, almost as a reflex, I remembered the chant and said it in my head – just once. And bugger me – at that very moment a car appeared around the bend, climbing the hill.

Coincidence?

Big Boy dropped the rock. 'Don't move,' he muttered.

But this was my only chance. As the car got nearer I fluttered a hand down at my side, waving – willing – the car to stop. It did. Amazing.

The boys jumped as if they'd been zapped with a Taser. Smiler grabbed the keys from Big Boy, thrust them into my hand – how weird was that? – and without a word they sprinted past the car down the hill. A skidding turn at the footpath and they were gone. The attack had lasted less than two minutes.

'Ed?'

The driver was staring at me through the open window, astonished. My jaw dropped. It was my old boss, my old nemesis: Martin.

Now, *that's* what I call a coincidence.

I'd worked for Martin during the dot.com bubble, as a copywriter in a crappy online company called ItsTheBusiness.Com. We hadn't hit it off, to put it mildly, and things had turned really sour when the company went bust, owing me and a lot of others a lot of money. But Martin was a survivor, a ducker-and-diver. He fell on his feet with a rich investor friend and came up trumps in property development. The irony was that I helped him do it – with Buddhism. He thought I was an arrogant twat – and I loathed his Thatcherite guts – but he was that desperate he'd have tried anything. I taught him the little I knew – I was just getting into it at the time – and he staggered me by turning things around. He even paid me all the money he owed.

I hadn't seen him for a decade and here he was – a stone heavier, hair thinning, puffier and redder in the face (I guessed he liked a drink), but obviously doing well. He was driving a shiny new BMW 7 Series.

'Martin! Bloody hell.'

'What you doing here?'

'I just been mugged.'

'What – those bastards?' I nodded. 'You got a phone, want to call the police?' He found his mobile and offered it through the window.

'Cheers.' I was surprised to see my hand shaking as I called 999. I told the operator what had happened, then handed back the phone. 'They said to wait. They'll get a unit here as soon as possible.'

Martin grunted. 'What you doing here anyway?'

I told him about the summer school and the ham and tomato roll and the blackberry, and he told me he owned one of the large houses at the top of the hill – the one behind the tall trees and hoarding and razor-wire. He'd bought the original property just after Lehman Brothers tanked – the owner had needed 'liquidity' fast – then demolished it and built a much grander mansion on the site. The idea was to cash in as the economy picked up, but he'd hit a snag.

'What?'

'Oh, just one of the millions of bleeding bumps you get in the property game. Happens all the time. Anyway, can't sell it till that's sorted, so it's mothballed.'

'Uh-huh. So you're still in the property game then?'

'For my sins, yeah.' He glanced at his watch. 'Look, I'm meeting someone at the house. Hop in and I'll drop you at the school. You can tell the police to meet you there. If they want me as a witness or whatever I'll give you my number – OK?'

'Fair enough. Thanks.' I got in the car and sank into the soft leather seat. 'Mmm – nice.'

Martin smiled. 'Nought to sixty in 4.7 seconds. But it's a hybrid, so it's green too – just in case you're wondering.'

I wasn't, but I was impressed. We glided up the hill.

'Amazing coincidence, eh?' Martin seemed chuffed. 'Though I suppose you Buddhists would say it wasn't a coincidence at all, eh?'

'How d'you mean?'

'Well, you helped me out of a hole back then and I got you out of one just now. Cause and effect.'

'Guess so.' I hadn't seen it like that but it was an interesting angle.

He slowed as we passed his boarded-up site – no sign of his visitor – then gunned the BMW another fifty yards, turned into St Catherine's and pulled up alongside my Honda – the only other car there. He dug out a business card.

'In case the cops want a statement.'

'Thanks.'

'And what's your number?' I hesitated. Did I want him calling me? But I couldn't not tell him, not after what he'd just done. He tapped it into his phone. 'Let's not leave it another ten years,' he said. We shook hands, I got out, he gave a cheery wave and off he drove.

I called the police again and told them where I was, then sat in the car processing the last ten minutes. The mugging had shaken me up but so had Martin's sudden reappearance in my life. And the fact that he'd appeared just after I'd done that chant in my head – v-e-e-ery weird. I didn't conjure him out of thin air, obviously – he was en route to his meeting and would have turned that corner whatever I'd thought or done. But the coincidence of help appearing at that precise moment, and of it being him: that's what I couldn't get my head around.

What's more, this was my third summer at St Catherine's. In my first year that old house he'd bought was being demolished, and last summer the mansion was going up in its place. Then this summer I'd arrived to find everything had ground to a halt and razor-wire everywhere. So in all that time our lives had been a few yards apart and never crossed – until now. In a way that was as strange as bumping into each other. A different sort of coincidence perhaps?

Or was there really no such thing, only 'co-incidences': incidents that literally coincide, which we then try to fit into some framework of explanation that satisfies us? Martin had mentioned the Buddhist framework – the vast web of cause and effect that connects everything, as if his car coming along at that precise moment were the working of a kind of universal balance sheet. I'd saved him in the past and now – somehow, unknowingly – he'd been on hand to save me. Payback.

Hmm.

I remembered another great coincidence in my life. It had happened years ago, after university, when I'd decided to hitchhike across America – as you do. I knew only two people in the country – one on each coast – so flew out to California, spent a few days with Steve in San Diego, then he gave me a ride to the Interstate, I stuck out my thumb and off I went.

A few days later I found myself on the outskirts of a little town in northern Arizona, trying to hitch a ride to the Grand Canyon. A camper van slowed to a stop, but instead of picking me up it deposited a dark-haired, lanky guy who turned out to be a Brit: Nick, from Leeds, exploring the country for a few weeks before joining ICI's research department. He was heading for the Grand Canyon too, so we joined forces – hitching can be a lonely business.

Before long we got a lift and camped that night on the South Rim; Nick had a tent. Then we hiked down into the Canyon and camped by the Colorado River. After a couple of days of swimming and sunbathing, we hiked back up and hitched a ride out of the park.

But back on the main road no one wanted to pick up two male hitchhikers. So Nick and I decided to shake hands and try our luck solo. Almost at once, as he was walking away, a car stopped for me and off I sailed, waving to Nick as I passed. We hadn't even exchanged addresses.

The next week took me through New Mexico and Texas and – after some humming and hawing – to New Orleans. I didn't have much money and wasn't sure I could afford to stay in the city. But I tracked down the local YMCA, dumped my stuff and went out to explore the French Quarter. It was busy and vibrant after the empty spaces of Texas, heaving with tourists and jazz – and Nick. I bumped into him coming down Bourbon Street. He was gobsmacked. I was gobsmacked. It was gobsmacking. We were 1,500 miles from where we'd parted, we hadn't said where we were going – at the time neither of us knew – and the odds of meeting again were minuscule. Yet here we were.

But what did it mean? Nothing. We spent another couple of days together, sampling the pleasures of the Big Easy, then once again went our separate ways – and I've never seen him since. Now, if he'd been a girl and we'd ended up married with kids I suppose we'd be claiming that it had been destiny that our paths had crossed again. But as it was – nada. It was just a very strange *coincidence*.

So, remembering that, I was pretty chary about reading anything into my renewed acquaintance with Martin.

Except something was bothering me. And as I sat in the St Catherine's car park waiting for the police to turn up, I slowly realised what it was. Meeting Martin again was like looking back into the past. It had been a tough time – the dot.com bust, confusion, my life going nowhere – but I'd found someone and something … and lost them both. So I'd pressed on – face forward, don't look back – and all the regret had been buried, like a mine.

Meeting Martin again was like stepping on it. Suddenly, out of nowhere, there was pain in my chest, my lungs. A sharp stab in the throat.

Ah, Dora. My muse, the love of my life – once. She was a real grown-up: smart, sexy, beautiful. I'd met her through Geoff, the guy who'd introduced me to Buddhism, and I loved her toughness, her no-nonsense, no-bullshit attitude. Her clarity, determination, courage. Her refusal to be beaten. Her lack of sentimentality. Her energy. But it's a funny thing about relationships: what first attracts you can eventually become the very thing that drives you apart.

'The trouble with socialism,' said Oscar Wilde, 'is that it takes up too many evenings.' And so it was with Dora's Buddhism.

She was full on, dedicated. She held meetings, she went to meetings, she held meetings to plan other meetings. And when she wasn't at a meeting she was on a course. Or organising one. Or out visiting other Buddhists, supporting them, encouraging them, teaching them how to plan meetings and courses, and deal with the thousand natural shocks of their daily lives. Which was all totally noble. I admired and respected what she did, how much she gave to other people. And she insisted she got loads in return: vitality, satisfaction, a sense of always growing and developing. But it dominated everything. At times I thought: This must be what it's like to live with an elite athlete, whose whole life is built around training and performance, getting the right sleep and nutrition, all aimed at achieving one goal. And you either get with the programme or … you don't. And I didn't. I practised alongside her for a while but I just couldn't keep up.

Eventually, I stopped. The old me reappeared: cynical, booze-loving, lazy. And if there was one thing Dora couldn't stand it was someone not trying. 'Up to forty a man can get by on charm,' she'd say. 'After that it's strictly results.'

Stupidly, I didn't hear the warning – and a few days after my thirty-sixth birthday she kicked me out.

Fair enough – I deserved it. Even the charm had gone, such as it was. But looking back, what a twat I was. With her as a partner I was changing, growing. I even wrote a book, for God's sake. Actually finished it. How amazing is that? For me, very. But it was all thanks to Dora – she cracked the whip. If only she hadn't cracked it all the time.

My phone rang: Martin.

'Mart. Hi. What's up?'

'I'm looking at them.'

'Who?'

'Those bastards that took your £2.35.'

'Where?'

'Bus stop in the high street – by the baker's. Want to follow them, see where they go?'

'I'm waiting for the police.'

'Call them from the car. Should be there by now anyway, useless bastards.'

I checked my watch. One thirty. Still an hour before the Italians returned. I was supposed to be on site from two o'clock but ... 'Right – one minute.'

I fired up the Civic, hared down the hill, turned on to the high street and drove past the bus stop. Empty. Martin was standing on the corner opposite.

'They got on a 258 – come on!'

I slotted into a parking space, ran to his waiting Beamer and jumped in.

'Exciting, isn't it?'

'Will be if we can catch the black bastards,' he said. I winced. 'What?'

'Black bastards. Sounds a bit—'

'They're black and they're bastards. Just calling a spade a spade.' He grinned at his joke and pulled out into traffic. 'It's not racist, it's descriptive.'

I decided to let it pass. This wasn't the moment to challenge Martin's social attitudes. The bus was in sight, a dozen cars ahead, grinding up the hill.

'You're sure they're on it?'

'On the top deck, at the back. By the window.' He pointed.

There they were, sitting with arms stretched wide across the back of the seat, relaxed. I dug out my phone and called 999. The operator grasped the situation immediately.

'Stay on the line, caller, and keep the bus in sight. We'll direct the unit to you.'

I told Martin. 'More fun than property development, eh?'

He grunted. 'Except when a fat lump of dosh lands in your account.'

'How was your meeting?'

'Bastard blew me out.' He glanced at me. 'Ginger bastard this time. They're the worst.' He grinned again.

We followed the bus up the hill, then along the top and down the other side, pulling over to wait at a distance every time it stopped for passengers. The two youths didn't move till we got to the depot at Harrow Weald, end of the line. We stopped a few car lengths back as the bus disgorged everyone. The youths jumped off – and headed straight for us.

'Christ.' I got busy with my laces. Martin fiddled with the car mat under his feet. But Smiler and Big Boy walked past, oblivious.

We sat up again. Behind us they were crossing the road to a small park. I relayed the information to the police operator.

'Keep them in sight, caller,' she urged. 'A unit's on its way.'

'There's only one other gate, round the back,' said Martin.

'How do you know?' I asked as he pulled a U-turn.

'Grew up round here.'

We drove along the park perimeter, tracking the youths through the railings as they moseyed across the grass, then we turned down a quiet side street, pulled over and waited. I updated the operator and after a moment a young man emerged, bag slung over his shoulder, and headed away from us. A brief pause, then Smiler and Big Boy appeared – and followed him. I looked at Martin.

'You don't suppose …?'

He frowned, put the car in gear, and crawled forward. Ahead, the young man turned out of sight, followed moments later by Smiler and Big Boy. Martin pumped the accelerator, the Beamer surged down the road, then he eased off and we coasted towards the turning – the entrance to the car park of a small block of flats. He slowed to a stop. I lowered the window and listened. Silence. Then a shout – pain. Martin edged the car forward – and we gasped.

The young man was hanging on desperately to his shoulder bag. Big Boy was pulling at it, punching him repeatedly with his free hand. Smiler was riding on the young man's back, an arm round his neck.

'Hey!' Martin yelled and gunned the engine. The car leapt at the trio. Smiler and Big Boy looked round, startled. Martin stood on the brake, the car jolted to a halt and they dashed past us on to the street – just as a cop car appeared. Big Boy darted right, Smiler left. The cop car disappeared after him.

We jumped out of the Beamer. 'You all right, mate?'

Daft question. The young man was staggering around in a daze, blood pouring from his nose, one eye purple and swollen shut. I left him to Martin and ran to the street. To the right – nothing. Big Boy had obviously cut back into the park. But to the left – result. Smiler was spreadeagled on the bonnet of the police car, being handcuffed – and still smiling.

*

Fifteen minutes later Martin and I were heading back to St Catherine's. The police had taken our details and told me to get to my local nick as soon as possible to give a statement. I calculated I'd just about make it back to school for two thirty – I could pick up my car later – and all being well, no one would notice I'd not been there for two o'clock.

But all was not well.

We pulled into the school car park just as a stretcher was being loaded into an ambulance. Looking on were my class of Italians, oddly quiet, alongside Tracksuit Wade and the gardener – and Mrs Armstrong, the deputy head. She was fierce at the best of times – and this clearly wasn't one of them.

'Gawd. Now what?' I swallowed hard, got out of the car and went over.

'Ah. Nice of you to join us.' She looked daggers at me.

'Sorry, I was, um, I was mugged.'

'Mugged? When?' She sounded incredulous.

'Just down the hill. I've been with the police. We caught one of them.' She raised an eyebrow, righteous anger suddenly punctured by doubt, then glanced quizzically over at the BMW. 'Passer-by,' I explained. 'Came to my aid.'

The ambulance doors slammed. Inside was Valeria Adamoli, fifteen, with a split head, concussion and a broken arm.

'We're lucky it's not a broken neck,' said Mrs Armstrong through tight lips. The class had arrived back early and, thinking I was here, Tracksuit Wade had told them to go to the classroom. They'd got bored, turned up one of their iPlayers and Valeria, the class clown, had treated them all to a dance – on one of the desks. It tipped over, she fell . . .

'And now I shall have to call her parents in Milan to explain why we failed in our duty of care. Why there was no teacher present.'

'Just tell the truth,' I said. 'I'm sure they'll understand.'

'What – that you can't walk down the road the school's in without being mugged? Very reassuring. Anyway, I've asked Miss Wade to take the class for the afternoon. You and I need to make sure we have the facts absolutely clear – for the insurance. Or if the Adamolis decide to sue ...'

She left the implication hanging heavy in the air. A car horn beeped: Martin, wanting to get away. I waved, he signalled that I should call him and drove off. Mrs Armstrong's eyes narrowed.

'Very friendly for a passer-by – almost as if he knew you.'

I took a deep breath and started to explain about coincidences.

It was no good. I'd hardly closed my front door later that afternoon when my phone rang. It was the chair of the governors, no less, to say my contract was being terminated. Several of the kids had called home about Valeria, their parents had rung the school to find out what the hell was going on, 'And all in all we think it best if we just draw a line under the whole thing and find a new teacher.' I was outraged – I'd been mugged, for Christ's sake! But he wouldn't budge and even refused to pay for the two weeks left on my contract. I blustered about suing but he told me – politely and poshly – to get stuffed.

So that was that. Bye-bye to another beautiful relationship. Bye-bye to that lovely empty swimming pool. And bye-bye to a reference for a pile of job applications I was writing. *Sayonara* St Catherine's – *hola!* unemployment. Teaching English to foreigners was getting more and more competitive. Emptiness beckoned for the rest of the year – and beyond.

How the hell had I ended up here again? No job, no

woman, money running out, driving a beat-up car that nearly bankrupted me every time I filled the tank, and living in a poky little house whose mortgage I could only afford thanks to Chris the creepy lodger. He was a small, balding trainee actuary from Preston who kept weird hours and told the same joke whenever he met someone new: 'I'm training to be an actuary, which is like being an accountant – only not as exciting.' Sheesh. Friends who'd been with me through university had careers, families, wealth – fame even. So why not me?

I slumped on to the sofa. Karma – that's what Dora would have said. The same old thinking driving the same old action, leading to the same old dead-end. Groundhog Day, all over again. But what to do?

I knew what she would have said to that, too. Chant, challenge, change. Chant to reveal your wisdom, courage and compassion. Challenge your thinking and behaviour – and your situation *must* change. The oneness of life and its environment. But try to change your situation without challenging your thinking or behaviour and it'll just revert to a different version of the same thing. Simple – in theory. And easier said than done. Like losing weight. You know you just have to eat less but, the moment you start to cut down, your mind and body rebel – *we want food*! Put your whole life on a diet and the rioting's constant.

There was only one thing for it – a nice big glass of wine. It was early, not even six o'clock, but this was a crisis. I was uncorking the Shiraz when my phone rang: Martin again.

'Ed, mate, how are you?' I told him the news from the school. 'Shit, no – the bastards! But you were mugged, you were the victim!'

'Story of my life, Mart.'

'Well, at least you've got your Buddhism, eh? You know, for inner strength.'

'Mmm.' I didn't want to tell him I'd fallen off that wagon, disillusion him.

'Actually, that's what I wanted to talk about – if you've got the time.'

'Erm …'

'In fact, I was wondering if we might go for a drink or something.'

'What – now?'

'Well, yeah. Unless you're doing something?'

I put the cork back into the bottle of Shiraz. Might as well drink with him as on my own.

'OK,' I said. 'If you're buying. Only I'm a bit skint at the moment.'

Irony of ironies – so was Martin.

He confessed all over a pint. He'd sunk nearly two million quid into the house near St Catherine's and needed another million 'or thereabouts' to finish it. He reckoned he could sell it for five and come out two million ahead, but the bank wasn't playing ball and he couldn't raise the cash anywhere on terms he'd accept.

'A sniff of desperation and they go for the jugular,' he said bitterly.

'Why won't the bank cough up?'

He laughed at my naïvety. 'Because, my son, that way they get their hands on the place cheap and flog it themselves – plus everything else I own. It's all collateral for the loan.'

'You mean – you're looking at going bust again?'

He nodded grimly – 'That ginger no-show was my last chuck of the dice' – and took a pull at his beer.

'Blimey. Talk about karma.'

'Go on then.'

'Er, Groundhog Day. You know, the same situation keeps on coming round.'

'Yeah – that's me. Rise and fall with the bubble du jour.' Through another slug of beer.

'You married, family?'

He nodded. 'Two kids, six and eight. At prep school. Thing is' – he grimaced – 'the wife doesn't know about any of it.'

'What – you pledged your house without telling her?' He nodded glumly. I gave a soft whistle. 'Well, Mart, I got to say, for a man on the verge of bankruptcy you were pretty cool this afternoon. Wouldn't have guessed a thing.'

He barked a laugh. 'Piece of piss. I just pretended those bastards were a couple of banksters I know who all of a sudden aren't returning my calls.'

'Right. So the fact the building's taken so long …?'

'Cash-flow, planning. Original buyer pulling out. I only started cos I had a guaranteed sale – till he went tits up in Spain, property crash. Sodding euro.'

I shook my head. The disaster he was staring at put mine in the shade.

'So what can I do?'

'Well, unless you got a million under the bed …?'

'If only you'd asked me this time last week.'

He grinned, then went all serious.

'Thing is, Ed, when It'sTheBusiness went under you told me that Buddhist thing – *Kyo Chi Gyo I*, right?' I nodded. It was a principle Dora taught me, a variant on chant, challenge, change. 'Well, last time it worked like magic and this time it's just not. I'm getting closer and closer to the edge, and it's a million times worse than back then cos now it's my wife and kids involved too.'

'Right. So …?'

'So then it hit me – wham! Meeting you today wasn't a coincidence. It was fate. I turn up at exactly the right moment in your life – and you turn up at exactly the right moment in mine.'

'Because …?' I was starting to feel uneasy.

'To teach me how to do Buddhism – properly.'

'Eh?'

'It all makes sense now. I mean, you wrote a book, didn't you? You know! You got the knowledge, the nous, the direct line.'

'Me?'

'Yes! So I want you to teach me everything, the complete works. The chanting, the philosophy, the weirdo language. And I'll do it – hundred per cent.'

'Uh-huh …'

'Absolutely. I tried everything else to turn this shit around and, so far …' He drew a finger across his throat. 'You're my last hope, Ed.'

What could I say? I hadn't thought about this stuff for years. I gave him a weak smile.

'No pressure, then?'

That night I chanted for the first time in years. I made sure Chris wasn't in, then closed the door to my room, found my beads still in their silk pouch at the back of my sock drawer, sat in front of a blank wall and started. It was like getting back on an old bike. And very soon I was absorbed.

I had a disciple. Blimey. But how could I teach him when I didn't do it myself any more? OK, I owed him for rescuing me but what he wanted in return would mean commitment, spending time with him, being patient … And to be brutally honest, I still didn't like him. Part of me even thought he deserved his disaster. He'd been a huge fan of Mrs Thatcher, the market, deregulation – and it had turned round and bitten him. Hard. Twice. His wife and kids though – that was tough. It wasn't their fault and now they'd be on the street or in some grim B&B with a two-ring cooker and sharing a bathroom with four other families ...

As I chanted I saw in my mind's eye his car coming round the bend of the hill, and Smiler and Big Boy's reaction – their fear. They were going to get what they deserved, too. The police said it was only a matter of time till they caught Big Boy; he was probably already in their system some-where. And without realising it I'd rewound the mugging to its beginning: 'Nice one.' Only this time Big Boy ordered me to stop, showed me the rock in his hand – and I curled my lip in contempt.

'What you gonna do with that then?'

Before he could answer I karate-kicked it out of his hand, then thump, chop, punch, kick, elbow! And sud-denly they're both on the ground, groaning.

'How d'you like that! Eh, eh?'

I rewound the scene again. And again. And again. Playing and replaying it with slight variations, each time coming out on top, putting them to flight or leaving them in a bloody and battered heap. Threaten me, would you? Rob me, would you? Put the fucking fear of God into me, would you, eh? Hey – I'm talking to you, punk!

There was a knock at the door. 'You all right, Ed?' It was Chris.

'What? Oh, yeah. Fine – cheers.'

I'd hadn't realised it but I'd been running and rerun-ning this fight fantasy out loud. Gawd, how embarrassing. Perhaps I could pretend it was a play on the radio. I looked at my watch and got another surprise: I'd been chanting and muttering to myself for nearly an hour. Get a grip. But I felt better, strangely. Beating up Smiler and Big Boy in my imagination was venting all the anger and humiliation

I felt; regaining some power and control after feeling so helpless. And such a coward.

Then I remembered with shock something I'd censored from my memory of the event. When I'd seen that rock in Big Boy's hand I'd … begged. Yes, begged. 'Please don't hurt me.' That was my automatic reaction – animal fear. Cowardice. Pathetic pleading. It was so shameful I'd instantly buried it. But chanting had recovered it, remembered it, released it. Wow. Powerful ju-ju.

I chanted some more and quickly came to another realisation. There was no way I could look after Martin. There was no way I *wanted* to. I had to pass him on to someone else, some other Buddhist, and only one person came to mind. I texted Piers straight away.

Chapter Two

Two nights later I was sitting with Martin by the art nouveau fireplace in the front room of Piers's neat, terraced house in Kilburn. We'd just done gongyo, the basic practice – weird for Martin but for me like slipping on a pair of old sandals – and were settling down with half a dozen others to talk Buddhism. This was the locals' monthly discussion meeting, where they shared with each other – and anyone else who was interested – their understanding and experiences of the practice. Piers and I had lost contact when I'd split up with Dora, but he'd sounded genuinely pleased to hear from me and as soon as I mentioned Martin he'd invited us both to come along. So here we were.

Piers was one of life's nice guys – and awfully posh. Tall, lean, angular, with an accent only the best private education can buy, in another life he'd have been a captain in the Guards. In this one he was a landscape gardener. I'd met him soon after ItsTheBusiness.Com had gone under, when I was at rock bottom and desperate for a job. Dora used to run this little employment agency – that was how I'd met her – and she'd sent me along to him for a few days' hard labour.

At first he'd raised every left-wing hackle on my body

– his accent, mainly – but pretty soon my opinion changed. He was decent, sincere, hardworking and treated me not as an employee but an equal. We had some great chats as we dug and delved together and I came to see that my problem with him was just that: my problem. Hard to admit it but I was prejudiced – reverse snobbery.

Anyway, after a few days of toil and talk we became mates, and when Dora and I got together the friendship deepened. We saw a lot of each other – our local Buddhist groups were in the same part of north London – and we got especially close after the spectacular explosion of his romance with Kathy, a thirty-something American who looked like Michelle Pfeiffer, wrote for the *Wall Street Journal* and owned a flat in Islington. Cupid had struck while Piers was 'landscaping' her postage stamp of a garden. Kathy saw him as a sort of green-fingered Mr Darcy – which he was, I suppose – while Piers thought all his Christmases had come at once. After a few months he started to suggest that she might be 'a keeper'. A couple of times I even heard him murmur the 'M-word' – marriage.

Then one day, out of the blue, a Mr Kathy turned up from Boston and chucked a very large spanner in the works. Kathy had told Piers they were separated but apparently forgot to mention this to her husband, an investment banker who thought she was simply on a secondment to London. He yanked her back to the States, Piers was heartbroken, and Dora and I picked up the pieces. All very bonding.

But if Piers was unlucky in love (on that occasion) you could not for a moment say he was unlucky in women. They were drawn to him like butterflies to a buddleia. As proof of which witness Constanza, thirty-two, at this very moment kneeling serenely by his side. Constanza was from Barcelona and utterly, utterly gorgeous. Big doe eyes, masses of tumbling, thick brown hair, perfect white teeth and full pouting lips that looked as if they were permanently puckering for a kiss. Dear God, how did he do it? From Michelle Pfeiffer to Penelope Cruz without skipping a beat. He wasn't even that good-looking – a bit bony for my taste, but what did I know? It's said that men fall in love through the eyes, women through the ears; so perhaps it was the Eton accent that melted all these beauties.

As for the luscious Constanza, from the moment she opened the front door I was smitten. But absolutely no point in fanning that flame. Not only was she way out of my league, she was Piers's partner and clearly pregnant. They already had a mop-headed three-year-old, who had climbed on to her mother's knee, thumb in mouth, and was now scanning us, wide-eyed and serious, as Piers welcomed everyone with a smile.

'So – I'm Piers,' he said. 'I've been practising seventeen years, and I live here.'

He turned to his right: a tall black guy in his late thirties with big Afro hair, silver studs in both ears and rainbow-painted fingernails that matched his multicoloured chanting beads. 'Darren,' he said, with a hint of camp. 'I live down the road and I've been doing this for nearly three years now.'

Next was Jenny: mid-fifties, smock dress, thick grey hair pulled off her face into a severe ponytail. She lived near the park and had been a Buddhist 'for ever'.

I was next up. I said I'd met the practice – and Piers – in 2000 and that this was my first meeting 'for a while'. In fact, Dora used to hold gatherings like this when we were living together, but I'd never been a regular. Listening to a bunch of strangers banging on about their problems never appealed to me as a fun way to spend an evening, so I used to go down the pub or to the cinema – another node of conflict with Dora. But with Martin sitting next to me, keen and curious, this wasn't the time or place to confess to that or my lapsed practice. Too complicated.

Then Martin introduced himself – and opened a can of worms. He explained that I'd worked for him till the dot. com bust and had really helped him when he went under; that we'd lost touch but, completely by chance, he'd been able to return the favour a couple of days ago when he rescued me from a mugging. Everyone perked up. Drama.

'What happened?' asked Jenny, alarmed.

I'd spent most of that morning reciting the story in forensic detail to a young PC at Watford police station, so I just sketched a brief outline, which prompted caring sighs and tuts and shakes of the head. Except from Jenny.

'You should chant for them,' she declared.

'Eh?' Martin's brow furrowed.

'People cause suffering to others because they're suffering themselves,' Jenny explained. 'You have to break the cycle by bringing out their Buddha nature. And yours.'

Martin looked unconvinced. 'Or you could maybe bang them up for a few years.'

'That just perpetuates things,' said Jenny, smiling sweetly. 'The karma.'

Martin opened his mouth to object – I thought I could see the words 'Hippy crap' forming – but Piers jumped in.

'Let's finish the introductions, then we can get the discussion rolling – OK?'

Martin clamped his jaw shut and all eyes swivelled to the young woman on his right: Rachel, mid-twenties, plain and mousy-haired. She explained with a laugh that she was Piers's 'assistant-cum-apprentice-cum-slave' and had been so impressed with how he handled problems at work that she'd decided to 'give Buddhism a whirl' about a year ago.

'I've been doing it religiously ever since.' She giggled. Everyone smiled – it was an old joke – except Constanza, who lasered a cold stare at her. Interesting, I thought. Surely she can't feel threatened? But women see things differently – and different things.

Next in the circle was a squat, burly bloke with a beard. I recognised him as an old friend of Geoff, my mentor.

'Stevens – Bernie,' he barked in a broad London accent, throwing a military salute. '476712, builder and Buddhist, twenty years and counting, sah!'

This time it was Jenny who didn't smile. More tension there?

And finally it was the lovely lady of the house. 'Constanza. I leeve here with Pierce. I start to chant at Spain since ten years. And this is Bella.' Who continued to suck her thumb and watch us with serious eyes as Constanza ruffled her curls.

So there we were: the magnificent, er, eight. Piers and Darren, Jenny, me, Martin, Rachel, Bernie and Constanza. Eight and a half if you included Bella.

'Goodo,' said Piers. 'The theme tonight is human revolution and Darren's going to tell us what it's all about.'

'Take it away, Gay-Boy.' All heads snapped round to Bernie.

'Don't mind him,' Darren explained with weary tolerance. 'I call him Lout-Boy, so it's all evens.' Bernie smiled. Martin looked bemused, Jenny as if she'd just sucked on a lemon. She drew a deep breath through her nose and fixed her attention on Darren.

'So, human revolution,' he said. 'Basically, it's another way of saying we're all the Buddha, or all trying to become the Buddha.' He turned to Martin. 'Do you know about the Ten Worlds?'

'Er ...'

'Well,' Darren continued, 'this form of Buddhism says we all have ten basic life states, and human revolution means trying more and more to base our lives on the higher ones and not one of the lower states like anger or hunger or animality. So what that means, basically, is that everything that happens to us, or every decision we make, we have the choice to continue our karma by reacting from the same life state we always do, or to challenge it by responding from the higher ones, especially Buddhahood, which means wisdom, courage and compassion. So human revolution basically means positive transformation of the self.' He smiled broadly.

'OK ...' Martin sounded cautious. 'So is this like mindfulness or...?'

'Well, to be honest I don't know much about that,' said Darren, 'except I think it's based on Buddhism.' He looked to Piers, who nodded. 'But *this* practice is based on chanting, to bring out and strengthen your Buddhahood.'

'Right.'

'Thank you, Darren,' said Piers. 'So – anyone got an experience?'

'Ooh, me, sir!' Bernie stuck his hand up, squirming like a schoolkid. Piers looked wary but nodded. 'Well,' said Bernie, 'I used to hate gays. In fact, in my Nazi youth I even went queer-bashing, as we used to call it in the good old days. But now, thanks to Buddhism, I love 'em – don't I, Gay-Boy?'

He spread his arms wide towards Darren and puckered up. Darren sighed and turned to me and Martin.

'You'll have to excuse him – he's got a very particular sense of humour.'

'Mmm – that's not funny,' said Jenny.

Piers stepped in again. 'Has anyone got a real experience?'

'That was a real experience,' Bernie protested. 'I did use

to hate gays, I did used to beat them up and now I think poofs like Gay-Boy here are truly wonderful.'

'Then why do you use such vile language about them all the time?' Jenny's face was taut with disapproval.

Bernie struck a pose, reciting. '"Before the multitude they seem possessed of the three poisons or manifest the signs of heretical views. My disciples in this manner use expedient means to save living beings." Lotus Sutra, chapter eight. Which means, Jenny my darling, that my function in your life is to help you do your human revolution.'

'I am not your darling.'

'Not yet.' He fluttered his eyes at her. She scowled.

'An experience, anyone?' Piers pleaded, looking round the room. Rachel shook her head. Darren looked at Constanza, who looked at Jenny, who opened then closed her mouth. 'Jenny?'

'As long as Lout-Boy doesn't make fun of me.' Bernie outlined a cross on his heart. Jenny scrutinised him closely, then decided. 'All right.' She took a deep breath – and told a sad story about her cat.

Zuma was a lively and very friendly tabby she'd had since he was a kitten. He had an incredibly loud purr and used to follow her around like a puppy. They were very close. Then last week, on Monday, Zuma went missing. He didn't come in all day or that night and she got really worried. When he did eventually appear, on the Tuesday evening, he was very subdued and just wanted to sit and sleep under the coffee table in her sitting room.

'He used to eat like a horse,' Jenny said, 'but he was totally off his food, so I knew something was wrong.'

She took him to the vet, who said they'd have to do some tests, which cost hundreds of pounds but luckily she had pet insurance.

'That was last Wednesday and on Monday they had

the results back, which showed cat cancer.' Rachel gave a concerned moan. 'The vet said he'd be able to treat it but it would cost maybe a thousand pounds, which wasn't covered, and there'd be no guarantee it would work – but did I want to go ahead anyway?' She started to well up with emotion. 'So I went home and chanted the rest of that evening and decided ... I had to let him go. And next morning I went along and said goodbye to him. He was just sitting quietly on the examination table with such ... trust.' Her voice cracked. 'And then I left him and just burst into tears. It was the hardest thing I think I've ever done in my life.' She dabbed her eyes with a ball of tissue she'd fished from her sleeve as Darren rubbed her back in sympathy.

A moment of silence as we absorbed the tragedy – broken by Bernie.

'And?' We all looked at him. 'The theme's human revolution, right? So you're saying what – you had to do human revolution to have him put down? If you hadn't chanted he'd still be meowing under your coffee table?'

'You promised not to do this,' murmured Darren.

'I'm not making fun of her. All I'm saying is – what's that got to do with what we're supposed to be talking about?'

'It was very painful for me!' Jenny's face was taut with anger again.

'And the chanting helped,' Rachel offered helpfully.

Bernie shrugged, bemused.

'You're such a ... a ... disgusting man!' Jenny was almost choking with indignation. 'I don't know why I come here and listen to your... your disgusting ...' She stopped, then abruptly gathered her things and started to get up.

'No, Jenny – please.' Piers reached out a hand to restrain her. Jenny pulled away.

'I can't bear being in the same room as him!'

'Hey, lovely people!' Constanza made a T-sign with her hands – time out. 'We have a guest, eh?' She nodded towards me and Martin, who looked a little shell-shocked, then turned on Bernie. 'I theenk you should apologise.'

'What the fuck for?' Bernie was genuinely surprised. 'All I asked was what her cat has to do with human revolution.'

'And don't swear!' Constanza put her hands over Bella's ears.

'Don't bother,' said Jenny with contempt. 'Swear words are all he knows.'

'For fuck's sake,' said Bernie, as if to prove her point. He raised his hands in surrender at Jenny. 'All right – you sit down and talk about your cat. If I can't say what I think I'm off.' He gathered up his beads and headed out of the door. Piers went after him.

'Bernie ...'

Another moment of silence, broken by their muffled voices in the hallway. Jenny sat down again, honour restored. Martin looked around the room. 'So,' he said. 'Buddhism's all about peace then?'

Darren sighed. 'It is actually. Except you've got to bring out the poisons – to really see them, transform them – to get there.'

'Tell him your experience,' suggested Rachel.

'Not that again,' he said, waving a dismissive hand.

'But there's been a development,' she said. 'Today. You told me.' We all looked at him.

'Oh, all right.'

As he was collecting his thoughts Piers came back in. 'Sorry about that.' He sat down again and addressed Jenny. 'You all right?' She nodded.

Darren turned towards me and Martin, and began.

'Just over three years ago I was in this really good job in this big, famous company as senior catering manager, looking after all their events, receptions, corporate hospitality. It was well-paid, lots of responsibility, about fifty people under me. One day my alarm went off, usual time, six thirty – and instead of jumping up and getting ready for work like I always did, I looked at it and thought, No. I can't. I won't. I pulled the duvet back over my head and at nine o'clock I called in sick. And when I put the phone down I knew at that moment I'd never walk into that company again. Because for years I'd been putting up with verbal bullying about the fact that I'm a gay black man. Or a black gay man. Whatever. Endless comments and "jokes". I was Queen of Spades, Chocolate Tart, Bog Brush – because of my hair – and a lot worse. And I'd just smile and pretend it was funny or I didn't mind, but it really bugged me, and after a time it built up and up till in the end I couldn't take it any more.

'So I was signed off with severe stress, put on anti-depressants and advised to get some legal advice, which basically said I had a case to sue for harassment in the workplace. The company, the directors, should have had policies in place that made it clear this sort of thing wasn't acceptable – but sometimes it was the actual directors doing the bullying! The problem was I didn't have any money for lawyers, so I was stuck.

'Anyway, it was then I met the practice through this woman at the CAB who'd gone there for help, and eventually I pitched up here and met the lovely Piers and Constanza, thank God, and started to chant. And when I did all this anger just blew to the surface, like striking oil. And I thought, I'm not going to let those bastards get away with it! So I decided to take them to an employment tribunal and represent myself. Which is what I did and I've been fighting all this time, on and off, against this top QC and the management, who've said some horrible lies about me not being good at my job and being really unpopular with everyone – which is total rubbish, basically. And anyway, last Friday I got the judgement.' He paused for effect. Rachel took the bait.

'And?'

'I lost.' Her face fell. 'No compensation, no job and according to the rules I have to pay their costs – thirty-seven grand.'

Jenny looked appalled, Rachel incensed. 'Well, that's ridiculous!'

'Sorry, Rache – no fairy tale this time.' Darren smiled. 'But the funny thing is I'm OK. I don't feel like I've lost at all. The fact that I took them on – that's huge to me. I was such a scaredy-cat, wouldn't say boo to a goose, and I found this strength I never knew I had. In fact, after the final session their QC took me aside and said he thought I'd done a brilliant job for someone who's never been trained. And en route I've made some great friends who are men – and not gay! That's a first, I can tell you. And Piers and Bernie have been fantastic, chanting with me, giving me advice, encouragement. Sometimes telling me off, things I didn't want to hear, like what a wuss I'd been to take all that crap for years without standing up for myself.'

'You mean – this Bernie?' Martin pointed at the space where he'd been sitting.

Darren nodded. 'And – cherry on the cake – this morning I got a call from one of the directors, who'd actually been a friend while I was there and was my secret spy during the whole thing, feeding me titbits about what the board were going to do and how they were thinking.'

'Protection,' said Constanza.

'Exactly,' said Darren. 'Anyway, she called this morning to say they're not going to claim their costs.'

'Gosh,' said Rachel, perking up. 'Why not?'

'Well, the thing is, the case showed they really do have a problem with their anti-harassment policy – as in, it doesn't exist, except on paper. And there are other staff muttering about taking them to a tribunal, because the bullying's everywhere, and they'd be outraged to hear that I didn't just lose – I'm going to be forced to pay thousands of pounds for the privilege! So my friend's persuaded the board to bite the bullet and turn over a new leaf: no more homophobia, no more racism, sexism, zero tolerance throughout the company.'

'That's some result.' Martin was impressed.

'Yes, well – I haven't got a job or any money but I feel, you know, good. So I suppose that's human revolution – from scaredy-cat to tiger. Continuing the feline theme.'

He nodded to Jenny, who smiled her thanks.

'Just one thing, though,' said Martin. Darren looked at him quizzically. 'Well, she said it earlier' – nodding at Jenny – 'about the language used here towards you. Why isn't that homophobia?'

Darren looked at where Bernie had been sitting. 'Good question.' He thought for a moment. 'Bernie's really helped me, supported me. So I think part of my human revolution has been learning to see what's actually in someone's heart, not just what comes out of their mouth.'

I glanced over at Jenny. From the look on her face she clearly didn't agree.

'Well – that was different.'

It was about an hour later, Constanza had just shut the front door on us and Martin and I were standing on the pavement outside the house. The discussion had rolled on, Martin had asked lots of questions – about the practice, what the chanting meant, if there was a joining fee – then the structured part of the meeting had ended and we'd chatted in twos and threes over tea and coffee. Now it was over he didn't know quite what to make of it all.

'Not what you'd expected?'

Martin shook his head. 'Not exactly Woodstock, was it? You know – peace, love and understanding.'

I laughed. 'Well, you get that too – sometimes. But Buddhists have been arguing with each other, debating, pretty much since the word go.'

Martin smiled. 'Look, you in a hurry? Only I fancy a pint.'

I hesitated. The whole point of this evening was to start weaning Martin on to someone who'd be able to teach him the Buddhist ropes. The longer he spent with me the less likely that was to happen.

'You OK to drink and drive?' He'd given me a lift here but I was hoping we'd head straight back.

'Ah, come on – it's only a pint. And I saw a nice boozer at the end of the road. I'll buy.'

I couldn't really say no, could I?

Buddhism and beer: an inextricable part of my karma, I thought, as we walked past the gaggle of drinkers standing outside the Oak & Saw and into the half-empty bar. I'd had my first lesson in the teachings over a couple of pints with Geoff in a London pub.

It was a warm summer evening and most of the punters were in the garden at the back or chatting on the pavement out front. Most – but not all.

'Hurrah.'

Bernie was sitting by himself between the unlit fireplace and the large, frosted front window. He pointed to the half-finished pint of Guinness and whisky chaser on the table in front of him.

'Same again, there's a good chap,' he said in passable

imitation of a 1950s BBC radio announcer. Martin raised an eyebrow but went to the bar while I plonked myself on a stool opposite Bernie.

'How's the cattery then?'

I grinned. 'You were sorely missed.'

Bernie took a gulp out of his Guinness and wiped the foam from his moustache. 'They go in threes, those meetings,' he said. 'One month it's all lovely and cosy and inspiring. Then the next month you wonder why the crap you bothered, it's so sodding boring. And about twice a year it kicks off, like that. Ha! Usually manage to stay in the same room, though. But tonight I thought, Sod this – I'll create more value down the pub.'

'And have you?'

'Been waiting for you two, haven't I?'

'That's amazing, because we didn't know we were coming.'

He grinned. 'Wise men can perceive the cause of things, as snakes know the way of snakes. Hurrah.'

He raised his whisky glass in a toast and downed the contents as Martin arrived with a refill and two pints of bitter. 'They'll bring the Guinness in a bit,' he explained, nodding back at the bar.

'You, sir, are an officer and a gentleman.' Bernie waggled his fresh glass of whisky in salute.

'And you, Bernard,' said Martin, sliding on to the bench-seat next to him, 'are not my idea of a Buddhist at all.'

Bernie leaned towards him. 'Call me that again,' he murmured, 'and I shall have to kill you.' Martin looked startled. 'Bernard. Last warning.' Martin tapped the side of his nose to say he'd got the message. 'So what is your idea of a Buddhist then, Mart? It was Mart, wasn't it? Mart the Tart?'

'Well, that's a good example – Bernie.' He said the name

with deliberate emphasis, making the point that he'd show respect even if Bernie didn't. 'I thought Buddhism was all about wisdom and inner peace, and I don't mean to upset you but—'

'You won't.'

'But you seem to be very … confrontational.' Bernie nodded. 'And aggressive.' He nodded again. 'And you swear a fuck of a lot.'

'I like swearing,' Bernie said. 'Stops me hitting people. Cheers.'

This last word was to the pretty barmaid who had brought his Guinness. He gazed in appreciation at her bottom as she returned to the bar.

'And this is after twenty years of Buddhist practice?'

'Saved my life, mate.' Bernie's attention snapped back to us. He drained the last of his Guinness and started on the next pint.

'How?'

'That stuff about being a Nazi – people think I'm joking, but when I was about twenty I was in the National Front.'

'Oh?'

'Mmm – cos I bought all their crap about immigrants. My dad was a labourer – Irish, the irony, ha! But he was out of work a lot and these black bastards were taking our jobs, right?'

Black bastards – but Martin didn't react.

'Anyway, we used to have fights with the Anti-Nazi League most weeks, if we were lucky. We'd have a march through some immigrant area, like Brixton, they'd pitch up to take us on, we'd kick the shit out of each other, then all run away and do it again next week. Till one day some fucker stabbed me and I wound up in A&E. And would you believe it – in the bed next to me was this ANL bastard who'd been in the same ruck and I couldn't fucking get to him! I was hooked up to a drip and monitor and all that bollocks and couldn't move. So we called each other names for a couple of hours till we got bored of that, and on the ward we actually started to talk. And – to cut a long story short – he let me see the error of my ways. Hallelujah. Opened my eyes to the evils of capitalism, how it uses nationalism to keep the workers down. So I jumped ship, joined the ANL and started fighting the fascists, my old mates in the Front. Ha!'

He swallowed some more Guinness.

'Only I got stabbed again and found myself back on the same fucking ward, almost the same fucking bed – only longer this time cos it'd missed a kidney by a gnat's whisker. But as I lay there watching the dribbling geriatrics all around me, it slowly started to sink in that if I went on like this I'd be dead soon. So I started to ask myself what I was really doing with these arseholes – all of them, Left, Right – and I realised I didn't actually believe any of it. I didn't even like them much, the people. I just liked fighting – and how sad was that? So when I got out I walked away from it all. But wanting to smash people's heads in – that didn't go. It kept coming up, especially after a few of these.' He picked up his whisky and downed it in one.

'So why Buddhism?'

Martin was intrigued. So was I. Bernie was an acquired taste for a lot of people, even Buddhists, and Dora had never acquired it, so I'd not seen much of him when I was with her and had never heard his story before.

'My old mate Geoff – your mate, too, right?'

I nodded. 'Diamond geezer.'

'He was. Anyway, I used to work for him on and off; he was a builder and I was a brickie in them days. Then his business hit the skids and he hit the bottle. But when I saw him again it was like he was a new man. Buddhism. And cos I trusted him I gave it a go.'

A builder whose business went bust: I could see that chimed with Martin. 'Simple as that?' he said. Bernie nodded. 'And the effect was ...?'

'I stopped hitting people. Just swore at them instead. Progress!' He raised his glass and laughed. Martin frowned and sipped his beer, obviously still bothered. 'If it's any help, mate,' said Bernie, 'I'm nowhere near the worst Buddhist there's ever been.'

'No?'

'Not even close.'

Bernie grinned again and started telling the story of Angulimala, a disciple of the Buddha – and a serial killer.

'The name means "necklace of fingers", cos he used to chop a digit off his victims and string 'em round his neck.'

'Charming.'

'Very. The story goes he was told by this priest – who had a grudge against him –that if he killed a thousand people he'd be reborn in heaven. And the dork believed him. So off he went a-murdering, and he'd done nine hundred and ninety-nine when he met the Buddha and tried to top him, too – you know, to get the full set. But the Buddha figured Angulimala had been tricked, so he put him straight and converted him to Buddhism.'

'And let me guess – he gave him community service.'

Bernie grinned. 'Velly good, Glasshopper – you are rearning.' He clinked Martin's glass. 'Yeah, he told Angulimala he'd have to make up for what he'd done through good deeds, and brace himself that everyone would try to get him whatever he did. That's cause and effect – don't go away just cos you say you're sorry. Anyway, compared to him I'm a choirboy. A bit sweary but so what?'

As Martin was taking this in I saw my moment. 'You

two've actually got something in common. Mart's in the trade – property development.'

It was a total change of subject but if they hit it off maybe I'd be able to slide him into the builder's arms, so to speak, and escape. But Bernie just roared with laughter.

'Ha – you poor sod! How much you lost?' Martin looked stunned at his guess – an expression Bernie didn't miss. 'Don't worry, mate – you and me both. All in the same bubble, eh? Or were.' He started to sing.

> I'm forever blowing bubbles,
> Pretty bubbles in the air,
> They fly so high,
> Nearly reach the sky,
> Then like my dreams,
> They fade and die.
> Fortune's always hiding,
> I've looked everywhere,
> I'm forever blowing bubbles,
> Pretty bubbles in the air.

'Pretty much sums it up,' said Martin.

'Don't be shy, Mart,' I said, getting up. 'Tell him your tale of woe while I pay a visit.'

I glanced back en route to the Gents. Bernie was listening with interest as Martin started to unburden himself. So – how to cement their new friendship?

'Sorry, guys – I got to shoot off,' I announced on my return. 'My lodger's locked himself out of the house' – I pointed at my mobile to indicate I'd had a message – 'and I've got to let him in.'

Martin started to stand. 'I'll give you a lift.'

'No, you finish your conversation. It's only thirty minutes on the Tube.' Martin didn't protest. I could sense he already felt a connection with Bernie. 'So, thanks for the beer.' I drained it. 'And don't lead him astray, Bernie – all right?'

'As long as he keeps buying ...'

I grinned at them, waved goodbye and walked out feeling pretty pleased with myself. I'd taken Martin to a meeting, introduced him to the wacky world of Buddhism and left him in safe hands. Well, safe-ish. But if Bernie screwed up – and I didn't think he would, from what Darren had said about how he'd been supported – there was always Piers. Or Darren himself. Anyway, as far as I was concerned he was someone else's responsibility now. Job done.

The universe had other ideas.

Chapter Three

Seven fifty-eight.

I hit the snooze button on my alarm but the ringing didn't stop. Then I realised it was the doorbell. Postman? I dragged on my dressing gown, stumbled groggily down the stairs to the front door – and there was Martin. He looked surprised.

'Didn't you get my voicemail? Or text?' I shook my head – news to me. 'I said I'd be round at eight unless I heard from you.'

'What for?'

'Morning thingy – you know. The chanting thing.'

'Gongyo?'

'That's it,' said Martin, clapping his hands together. 'After talking to Bernie last night I thought, No time like the present. So I called you on the way home, then texted …'

I dug into the pocket of my jacket, hanging by the door, and pulled out my phone. It showed an unread message and a missed call. 'So you did.'

'Right. So how about it? Now I'm here.'

No. This would definitely not do. I was not going to let him park his bloody life in mine. Besides, he'd twig in about ten seconds that I wasn't practising because I didn't have any of the Buddhist gear he'd seen at Piers's.

'Sorry, Mart, but it's not exactly convenient right now – you know?'

He looked blank. Then a smile grew on his face. He glanced up towards the bedroom window. 'You old dog,' he said, aiming a playful punch at my shoulder. His fist froze in mid-air as he caught sight of something behind me. I turned to see Chris heading to the galley kitchen – barefoot, sleepy-eyed and tightly wrapped in his shiny, Chinese red silk dressing gown. Martin's eyes flicked back to me.

'My lodger,' I blurted. 'He's an actuary.'

Martin nodded. And then a look of curious fascination grew on his face. I knew why: I'd erupted into one of my sudden mega-blushes, which explode when I'm ambushed by unexpected embarrassment. I start to turn pink and sweat, the person staring at my rapidly drenched features makes me even more self-consciously mortified – and before I know it I'm trapped in a perspiration death spiral. Bloody hell, I hadn't suffered one of these for years.

'Actually, to be accurate, he's a trainee actuary.' It was no good. Sweat was already running into my eyes. 'Anyway . . .'

'Look, I didn't mean to disturb you, Ed. If you're busy.'

'No, no – I'm not. It's just ... Look,' I said, trying to regain control of the situation, 'we could do it this evening. I could come to you or—'

'Evenings are tricky – kids' bedtime, supper, all that.'

'Or later this morning?'

'At mine?'

'Only if it suits.'

He checked his watch, weighed things up – and surprised me. 'All right. Half ten?'

'Perfect.'

'I'll text you the address,' he said and, with an uncertain glance over my shoulder, turned away.

I shut the door on him and joined Chris in the kitchen, stirring a cup of tea in his ludicrously camp dressing gown. 'Who was that?' he asked in his flat Lancashire vowels.

'A friend,' I said, irritated. 'But shouldn't you be at work?' He was normally long gone by now.

'Why – am I in the way?'

'Course not. Just surprised you're still here.'

'Exam.'

'Oh.'

He was always taking exams, or retaking them.

'You all right?' he asked, studying me with concern. 'Only you look a bit … hot.'

What was the problem here – really? I mulled it over as I dragged a razor across my face. Martin needed my help and I didn't want to give it. Yes, he was a painful reminder of what I'd lost, but there was something else. What? I couldn't put my finger on it.

By the end of the shave I realised the only way I'd get to the bottom of this was by chanting. I was pretty resistant to that, too, but I knew from experience it did have a way of clearing the fog. It was like sending a truffle hound to root around in the leaf-litter of my subconscious and dig up what was bothering me.

My phone beeped: a text from Martin with his address. It'd be good to identify the problem before I saw him again – if I could.

Chris was still swanning around – his exam wasn't till two – so I shut myself in my bedroom, grabbed my beads, sat on my bed facing the blank wall and started to chant under my breath.

At first there was the usual interference: the doubt, the 'Why am I doing this?', the thoughts drifting off to what I could have for lunch … And then Big Boy's face burst into my mind. I was back on that lane, the rock was in his hand – and suddenly I grabbed his wrist, pulled him towards me and kneed him in the balls, whirled round and caught Smiler with a karate kick to the head; he reeled backwards, I pulled Big Boy to the ground and started battering his frightened face with my fist. 'Take that, you—'

Whoa – stop! Stop right there! I was breathing hard, heart racing. Phew. Still lurking just below the surface, eh? But why not? It was only three days ago. Post-traumatic stress. Sounds dramatic but it *had* been a trauma. Not as much as going to war, obviously, but still. Best to know it's there and needs to be sorted. But how?

I wiped the images of Big Boy and Smiler from my mind and tried to focus on Martin. Why didn't I want to help him?

As I chanted I saw him sitting next to me as we drove up the hill to the school, then us arriving, Valeria being loaded into the ambulance. Valeria. How was she? Perhaps I should send her a card. Or flowers maybe? No, the others would tease her, even think there was something going on between us. So how could I find out how she was without going through the school? Ah – Tracksuit Wade. Her number was in my phone; I'd taken it to check when she'd be around for my swims. I'd ring and ask about Valeria, try to find out how the school was dealing with her parents, the insurance ... Lawyers.

Martin. I still wasn't chanting about him. Come on, Ed – focus. I gave my beads a determined shake and smiled at Martin's surprise as he caught sight of Chris in his shiny silk dressing gown. I'd have to put him straight about that when I saw him later. Though I did sometimes wonder about Chris. The bathroom was crammed with his 'grooming products': pre-shave cream, after-shave lotion, body scrub, shower gel, *moisturiser*. At least he didn't wear an earring. Or a stud, like the diamond in Big Boy's ear. Left or right? I hadn't been able to answer when the police asked that. I closed my eyes and ... left. The left ear, definitely. Amazing that a detail like that was lodged in my memory somewhere – a truffle, just waiting to be snuffled out of the earth.

Dora used to bang on about that: how everything that happens to us, everything we do or think or feel, is all imprinted on our lives and adds up to make us what we are. Nothing is ever lost but will emerge when the time and conditions are right. Karma ...

Damn. I *still* wasn't chanting about Martin. Every time I tried to focus on him my mind would skip off elsewhere. It was like trying to push the same pole of two magnets together: they just jump apart. Was there something I *really* didn't want to look at?

OK, I thought, I'm going to have to get tricksy here. Point my mind in another direction, distract it and – tra-la! – the answer will pop up when I least expect it.

So, what to chant about? Constanza's face swam into view. Ah, how lovely. Just the thought of her made me smile. What a beauty. What a lucky chap that Piers was. And what were my chances of ever finding a partner like that? Zero. Because that's exactly what I had to offer.

And there it was. Even as I was dreaming about Constanza a word rose into the light, like a bubble from the inky depths of my subconscious. Martin didn't just remind me of what I'd lost – he reminded me that I'd *failed*. Failed at my relationship with Dora, failed at Buddhism, failed to achieve anything significant in my life. And worse, deep down I believed I always would fail. I didn't want to hold Martin's hand on his journey of self-discovery because that meant I'd have to go with him – and fail again.

Dora used to say that if I wanted to change my world I

had to change myself. 'You're the body, Ed,' she'd say, 'and your world's the shadow. You bend, your shadow bends. You think your shadow's going to bend if you don't? Dream on.' The problem was ... I just couldn't bend. It was as if my muscles and joints had seized up. And Constanza crystallised everything. I see a woman like her and think, Not for me – ever. What's the point in even trying when failure's written through me like a stick of rock?

Another bubble floated up from the inky depths. If failure was in my DNA, had I destroyed things with Dora *deliberately*? Everything was going to fall apart sooner or later, so why wait for later? Give it a good kick now and get it over with. I was programmed to fail, programmed to sabotage anything that looked like succeeding ...

Jeez. What a thing to see on a wet Thursday morning.

But then the strangest thing: a rush of anger surged through me. At myself. 'How pathetic,' it said. 'Look at you. Where did all this failure crap come from? You used to *win* – at school, college. You played football, swam, passed your exams – good exams. Where did that go? Where did you *let* it go? "Failure's in your DNA"? What total tosh.'

What drama can go on in your head. It wasn't even nine in the morning, I was sitting on my bed in my shabby little house in Watford, still in my dressing gown, and it felt as if an elemental struggle were being played out in my psyche. Weird.

Angry Ed continued. 'Get a piece of paper – now!' I grabbed a blank card and a pen from my desk. 'Good. Now write this down. *Enjoy life. Win.*'

I wrote, then stared at the card. Three words – very simple, very direct, very ... well, what did they mean exactly?

'Enjoy life.' Well, I thought I did. I certainly enjoyed a drink. And *Match of the Day*. And a good book, a good conversation, swimming, walking in the countryside. Sex when I could get it, which was hardly ever these days – with someone else, anyway. Food? Up to a point, but not like people who make a fetish out of it.

So was that it, the sum total of my enjoyment of life: alcohol, football, reading, conversation, swimming, walking, occasional sex and food? Seemed pretty ... thin.

And what about this little word: 'win'? Win what? The girl? The job? Fame, fortune? At something? Over someone? Over oneself? And if I won did someone have to lose? The more I looked at those three letters the more complicated they became.

But as I started to chant again I felt I was on to something. I'd forced open a rusted door and was peeking through the crack into a dim, mysterious interior: the dark basement of my life, where the fuses hummed and the boiler rumbled.

I'd forgotten that chanting could take me down here. It had happened once before when Dora had insisted on a really long session – a whole hour! I'd gone along with it to please her, silently complaining for the first twenty minutes about how tedious it was. And then something had happened. I'd slipped through this same door, this crack in my consciousness, to a part of me that I'd only ever vaguely sensed before. And here I was again, warily flashing my torch around and getting my bearings.

Incredible, really, that chanting could do this for me. One minute a truffle hound, digging up the earth, the next minute Indiana Jones, leading me down to the treasure chamber. At least, that's how it felt. I was going to discover something valuable. It might be guarded by booby-traps and scary monsters – but the more protected, the more precious ...

Still chanting, I looked again at the three words I'd written: *Enjoy life. Win.* I turned the card over and listed my enjoyments: booze, football, reading, conversation, swimming, walking, sex and food. I studied them; they really were quite limited. In fact, apart from the reading and conversation, everything was quite animal ...

Whoosh, zap, flash. A rush of realisation as everything clicked together in a great, long line.

Animality: the state of being driven by instinct, urges, impulses; never thinking things through properly; the law of the jungle, the strong preying on the weak; fear, foolishness, ignorance. And I was dominated by it.

This was what was stamped so deeply into my life; in me and all around me, as natural as the air I breathed. The impulsiveness that drove me to chase after Smiler and Big Boy – and hang the consequences. The rabbit in the headlights when they attacked me. The very fact that they were drawn to me as prey.

And then, of course, there was the big one. Dora had told me time and again that the whole point of practising Buddhism was to reveal and strengthen our Buddha nature, and if we stopped we wouldn't be able to do that. Yeah, yeah, I remember thinking. But wisdom, courage and compassion aren't exclusive to Buddhism. You can generate them in all sorts of ways – look at all the wise, courageous and compassionate people who don't practise anything. And at all the Buddhists who aren't wise, courageous or compassionate. Not that I could see, anyway. So Dora's words didn't stop me stopping; if anything, they had the opposite effect: I wanted to prove her wrong.

But I didn't. My animality just crept back into pole position. It had to. I could see that now. It was like riding a bike, Dora said: stop pedalling and you coast for a while. Then you fall off.

What a prat I was. I'd seen this about myself years ago, when Geoff had been around. Seen it, assumed I'd changed it, even written about it – then I stopped pedalling. No wonder I was stuck.

I should call Dora, I thought. Apologise, eat humble pie, say how she'd been right all along. Except I didn't know where she was. Last I heard she was in the West Indies – Barbados – but I didn't have a number. Maybe Piers did, though.

Then another thought struck me. OK, you stop pedalling, you fall off. But it wasn't like falling off a mountain – *splat*. You've fallen off a bike. And there was nothing to stop you getting back on and starting to pedal again.

I smiled, suddenly cheerful, as if a light had come on. OK, I thought, let's go on this journey with Martin. Who knows where it might lead? I remembered another Buddhist saying: 'Light a lamp for another and your own path will be illuminated.'

But, as I soon discovered, only one step at a time …

Martin lived in Radlett, a short drive from my place but almost another world. Once a quiet village, the coming of the railway had linked it to London's financial heart, the City. It became a commuter town, growing ever richer on a mainline of money, and its estate agents now gleefully punted it as one of the most expensive places in the UK to buy a house. You couldn't go to the greengrocer's without tripping over a millionaire.

Martin's FBH[1] was at the end of a long and sinuous private road flanked by high, dark cedars and guarded by an undulating line of speed bumps. The limit was 10mph, presumably so you could admire at leisure all the other FBHs to left and right. Each was fronted by a cricket pitch of verdant lawn, across which sprinklers waved back and forth

---

[1] Fucking Big House.

in a languid fan dance. Each was adorned with at least one Jag or Merc or BMW, or the occasional Porsche or Ferrari or Aston Martin. And though each house was different, they all looked as if they'd been styled by a crack team from *Country Life* – because these houses were always on show, always in the shop window. I was probably bringing down their value just rattling past in my crappy Honda, its loose exhaust scraping on every speed bump we vaulted.

I pulled into Martin's neat, block-paved drive and parked in the shade of one of the cedars, next to a smart VW Golf. At first glance the house seemed nothing like as grand as its neighbours. It was on three storeys, the topmost built into the roof, and I guessed it dated from the 1930s; the brickwork was deeply weathered and the roof tiles tinged green with moss and lichen. A mature wisteria, heavy with plump, purple racemes, wound up over the porch and under the first-floor windows. All very homely, I thought, and surprisingly modest. But the narrow frontage was deceptive. Once inside, the house opened up like the Tardis.

Martin showed me through to the kitchen, bright white and as big as a five-a-side pitch. A massive island work-station, topped with white marble shot through with delicate black veins, dominated the room like a huge monochrome Stilton. Work surfaces of the same marble ran along three of the walls, punctuated only by the double sink, the walk-in fridge and a large white Aga radiating unneeded warmth into the room. A long oak table and ten chairs stood parallel to the far wall, just about the only objects that weren't dazzling white. Everything was top-of-the-range and completely, utterly spotless.

'Coffee?' Martin reached for the cafetière.

'Please.'

I looked out of the window. The back garden was a small

park, the stripes of the manicured lawn leading down to a shimmering blue swimming pool. In it, two impossibly cute children – both blond, a boy and a girl – were shrieking with delight as they splashed a sturdy young woman in a one-piece bathing costume that came almost up to her chin.

'Wife and kids?'

Martin glanced out of the window and snorted. 'Ha! Do me a favour. Au pair and kids. And the wife chooses her – know what I mean?' I looked blank. 'So there's no competition.'

'Ah. Where is she?'

'Fiona? Out with her trainer. Comes twice a week. If the weather's good they go for a run, take the dog.'

'Right.'

Martin handed me a cup of black coffee. 'Milk, sugar?'

'Cheers, no – this is good.'

'OK, let's go up.'

I followed him back into the hall and up the stairs to the top floor. Jack Vettriano prints hung on the walls. In each corner on the half-landings stood large glass vases full of coloured marbles. Cream carpet was everywhere – spotless, again. The entire place felt like a show home.

'You must have very well-behaved kids,' I said, as we reached the top landing.

'Why's that?' Martin was panting from the climb.

'All this cream carpet. Doesn't normally go with young kids.'

He grunted. 'Tell Fiona.' A sore point, obviously. 'Now, this is where *I* live.' He pushed open the door to his office.

It was a complete mess. Letters, papers and architect's plans covered a large black desk. Piles of trade mags were stacked against the wall alongside copies of the *FT* and *Daily Telegraph*. Framed prints of buildings – past projects,

I guessed – adorned the walls. And everywhere were samples: bricks, cladding, a selection of taps, light switches, sections of plastic pipe, various door handles, a radiator control, metal brackets, a burglar alarm and more.

'Opening a DIY store?' I asked.

Martin smiled. 'You got a project like Hillview and the world and his wife wants to flog you something.'

He nodded at a drawing Blu-tacked to the wall – an artist's impression of the mansion that I'd glimpsed behind the razor-wire. It was set in an idyllic, imagined garden and looked totally des res; whereas it was actually a half-finished monster that threatened to drag him and his family into poverty.

'Hillview? It wasn't called that before, was it?'

'No. I changed it.'

'You don't think it needs something a bit grander? Only Hillview sounds …'

'What?'

I shrugged. 'You know – suburban.'

Martin scowled. 'It's on a hill and it's got a view. And that's what your Arab or Russian or Chinese squillionaire wants to know – right? Cos they're the only ones with any bloody money in this climate, so—'

'OK, just a thought.'

'You stick to writing, Ed, and I'll stick to property – OK?'

'Fine.' Coo – touchy or what?

Martin glared at me. 'How's that going, anyway?'

'Oh, you know. The writer's lot—'

'Is not a lot.'

I forced a laugh – *my* sore point. Martin held me in his stare, then he suddenly smiled and gave me a friendly slap on the arm.

'Come on, maestro – let's get spiritual.'

'Gongyo?'

'Yeah. You want to clear a space or what?'

I looked around at his building supplies. 'Actually, Mart, have you got somewhere, you know, a bit quieter – visually?'

He thought for a moment, then his face lit up. 'Follow me.'

I did – back down to the ground floor, around behind the staircase, along a short passage, to a plain white door. He took a key from a hook on the wall. 'No one ever comes in here.' He grinned, unlocked the door and ushered me in. 'Our very own sports centre.'

It was an austere room, containing a rowing-machine, weights, exercise bike, treadmill, mats and a padded bench. One wall was a large mirror, above which a long, shallow window let in a strip of daylight. Martin flicked on the spots.

'We keep it locked because of the kids,' he explained. 'Don't want them damaging the equipment – or themselves. So – quiet enough? We won't be disturbed.'

'No, it's good.'

I pulled the bench to face one of the blank walls and sat at one end. Martin looked at me. 'You want me to sit next to you?'

'So I can take you through the book.' Gongyo involves reciting a couple of passages of the Lotus Sutra – in ancient Chinese. Pronounced according to medieval Japanese. It can be a bit tricky at first.

Martin sat on the bench, snuggling deliberately close. 'Sure your friend won't mind?'

'What friend?'

'At your place.' He was trying hard not to smirk.

'Oh – you mean my *lodger*. Who pays rent for a room – his room. No, I don't think he'd mind.'

'So what happened to that black bird?' Martin asked, as I fished my beads and gongyo book from my pocket.

'Blackbird?'

'Your squeeze.'

'Dora?' Martin nodded. 'We split up.'

'Oh. Sorry to hear it.'

'It's OK. Long time ago now. Shall we start?'

'Fire away.'

Once you've got the hang of it, cantering through the sutra passages takes a few minutes but Martin couldn't grasp even the basics. He stumbled over every word, the rhythm of every line, then insisted on repeating everything till he got it right. I was practically eating my knuckles with frustration by the time we staggered to the end, twenty-five minutes later.

'Excellent.' He beamed. 'I enjoyed that. And now we chant – right? About anything we like.'

I nodded, giving silent thanks the ordeal had finished, and started to chant. Martin joined in and, to my pleasant surprise, was in rhythm. He even harmonised.

Bang. We jumped and whirled round to see Martin's daughter framed in the open doorway, the door swinging back on its hinges. She was wrapped in a large pink towel, blonde tresses dripping wet from the pool and big blue eyes wide with bewildered surprise.

'Daddy's chanting, Puddle,' said Martin. 'Close the door. Go on – shoo.' He waved her away. She stared for a moment, then turned and fled, leaving the door open. Martin got up to close it. 'That's Amelia,' he said. 'Takes after me – won't do what she's told.'

He rejoined me on the bench and we started chanting again. A minute later I heard a soft click and looked round. Amelia and her brother – also wrapped in a towel, head full of wet curls – were peeping through the crack in the door, hands clamped hard over their mouths and shoulders heaving as they tried to gag their giggling.

Martin sighed deeply, then leapt up and yanked the door wide open. The children jumped but stood their ground, grinning, unafraid, as if a tickle were more likely than a smack.

'Scram,' Martin growled. 'Or I'll tell Mummy you've been in the house – with wet feet.' He made a threatening lunge, they squealed with mock terror and ran off. Martin took the key from the hook outside, closed the door and locked it.

'I'll thrash them later,' he said, taking his place beside me for the third time.

'How old again?'

'Six and eight.'

'Cute.'

'Yeah. Best pickle them before they get any older.'

I smiled and started to chant, and we quickly got into a nice rhythm. This was all very new for me. The first time round, with Geoff and Dora, I'd been the novice – always following, learning. I'd never had to take responsibility for anyone other than myself. And here I was teaching what I knew to someone who, ten years ago, I wouldn't have given the time of day. It was bizarre, especially in these surroundings. Although it did occur to me that a gym was oddly fitting as a venue. This was a place to exercise physical muscles, while chanting was supposed to strengthen your Buddha muscle – Buddhahood.

The door handle rattled hard. Martin sighed again, irritated this time.

'Go away!'

'I want to come in!' It was a woman's voice, a soft Irish accent.

Martin jumped as if shot and unlocked the door. A striking blonde in black running gear – she looked like a pint of Guinness – took a step into the room, breathing heavily. She seemed familiar but I couldn't place her. Martin smiled nervously.

'Fiona – Ed. Ed – my wife, Fiona.'

'Hi.' I smiled and nodded. She glanced at me, then back at Martin.

'We were just doing some chanting,' he said with forced brightness. 'You remember, I said—'

'I want to warm down.'

'In here?' Martin sounded surprised.

'Where else? It's the gym.'

Martin seemed flustered. 'Well, we'll only be—'

'Now. Jackie's worried I'll get a cramp.' She crossed to the treadmill, flicked the plug at the wall and beeped the control panel. The track started to roll with a low rumble. Fiona stepped on to it and beeped the control panel several more times. The track gained speed and she started to jog, her blonde ponytail swinging with each stride against her black T-shirt.

Martin turned to me. 'Looks like we're done.'

I followed him out and he closed the door. 'Sorry about that,' he said. 'Doesn't usually warm down – not in there, anyway.'

'No problem. You can always do more chanting by yourself.'

Martin nodded but seemed embarrassed by what had just happened. 'Probably some instruction from Jackie. She's the new trainer. Anyway, thanks for that. Feels … well, hard to say really. Good – sort of. Not sure why, but anyway – what's next?'

What indeed? I suggested he tried to chant twice a day, morning and evening, for as long he liked; the phrase I remembered was 'to your heart's content'. In the meantime I'd get a gongyo book and some beads for him, and maybe

Piers would have a CD he could borrow to practise with. Martin seemed disappointed.

'But you'll come round again, yeah?'

'Yeah, sure.'

'Great.' He smiled, satisfied, and showed me to the door.

But to be honest it was a relief to be going. I didn't feel comfortable being there and when I got to my car I realised why. The Golf had gone – the trainer's, I supposed – and a note was stuck under my windscreen wiper: 'Do not park here again'.

Nice. And no prizes for guessing who put it there. I sensed trouble ahead …

Chapter Four

Despite his apparent enthusiasm, Martin promptly went silent on me. I sent him a couple of texts suggesting another session. I left a message on his mobile. I even ordered a gongyo book and CD to be delivered straight to his door. But no response. It was as if he'd ceased to exist.

I was disappointed. I'd warmed to the idea of our climb up the mountain of enlightenment together and felt miffed that we'd fallen at the first hurdle. I was assuming he'd crumbled at opposition from Fiona, because from the short time I was there I'd sensed that she was the 'swing personality'. This is my theory that every family has one member whose mood above all sets the general atmosphere. In mine it was my dad. If he was happy, my mum and I were. If he was depressed, we were gloomy. If he was angry, we were fearful. But *our* moods simply bounced off him. If my mum was down and he was up, for instance, he'd gently tease her out of it or just ignore her till she cheered up.

The swing personality doesn't have to be a parent. Screaming newborn babies, toddlers going through their terrible twos, sulky and intransigent adolescents: any family member can set the tone for all the others. If the others allow it, of course. If they don't – well, let battle commence.

Dora explained this – and all relationships, in fact – as a battle of life states, the Ten Worlds: your own and other people's, inside and out. When we were together her Buddhahood drew out mine, but it also challenged my animality. The more my wisdom, courage and compassion struggled to get out, the more my stupidity dug in its heels. And when, in the end, stupidity triumphed and I baled out of the practice, her Buddhahood finally gave way to anger, she lost patience and kicked me out.

That's why I persisted in trying to contact Martin. Fiona's note had left me feeling distinctly queasy and I guessed he might need reinforcements. But before long my own worries started to eclipse concern for him.

The first wobble came when I called Tracksuit Wade, who shook me with the news that Valeria was still in hospital. She'd caught an infection after an operation to reset the bone in her arm and was really quite ill.

'How ill?' I tried to keep the panic out of my voice.

'Well, I don't think she's going to die or anything,' Tracksuit said breezily, 'but she could be in there for some time. Unless they fly her back to Italy, of course, cos the family's not too thrilled with the NHS right now.'

'Uh-huh. And, er, how's the school reacting?'

'Hunkering down with the lawyers, I think.'

'Right …'

My mind leapt forward to the county court, standing in the dock as the judge stripped me of all my worldly goods to compensate Valeria and her family. Not that they'd fetch much. But poor Valeria.

There was one, tiny upside to this news: I lived a hop, skip and a jump away from Watford General, so at least I could visit her and say sorry in person. A small gesture, maybe, but it might make her feel a bit better. And me. Unless I gave her another infection.

The hospital had thought of that. Handy dispensers of anti-bacterial gunk were positioned at the doors to every ward – a quick squirt, a rub of the hands and I was safe to enter.

Valeria was in a small side ward, in a bed by the window, asleep. A few days before she'd been a rosy-cheeked picture of plump good health. Now she was pale and gaunt, breathing deeply through an oxygen mask, a drip stuck in her arm and hooked up to a monitor. I was shaken.

I'd bought her a chocolate orange – a little something to brighten her recovery, I hoped – and was putting it on her bedside cabinet when she opened her eyes. To my surprise she broke into a broad grin.

'Hey, Prof,' she mumbled weakly through the mask. '*Ciao. Come stai?*'

'Never mind about me,' I protested. 'What about you?'

She shook her head and pulled down the corners of her mouth. '*Stupido.* I am *idiota.* And I make you lose your job. *Mi scuso!*' She smiled a sad apology and squeezed my hand.

'No, it's me who should—'

'*Eh – cara bambina!*'

An expensively dressed woman in her fifties, with big hair, big bosom and big handbag, stood in the doorway. She swept in, bent to kiss Valeria on the forehead, then looked up at me from across the bed.

'*Chi è questo?*' she asked Valeria.

'*Il mio maestro, Mama.*'

Bam. Signora Adamoli went rigid, shocked, as if she'd been slapped on the arse. Her expression darkened, the thunder clouds gathered – and all at once a tsunami of angry Italian engulfed me, with lots of finger jabbing, shoulder hunching and hand waving. After a good two minutes she stopped for breath, her ample chest heaving with indignation as she sucked in air. Valeria turned her face to me and lifted her mask, worried.

'She no 'appy.'

Signora Adamoli was glaring at me. 'Yes, I think I got that, Valeria. Thank you.'

I retreated to my lair, shut the door and waited for the lawyer's letter to plop on to the mat. For the next few days the only time I went out was to buy milk and red wine from the corner shop. I brooded and drank, and sank into a fight with the insistent voice of negativity in my head.

'Failed at the first fence with Martin. Failed in your duty of care to Valeria. And soon to fail in all these job applications you should be emailing but aren't – because there's no point, is there? St Catherine's are going to sue you, and when that gets out …' The voice mocked loudest when I chanted. 'Look at you – desperate, clutching at straws. Sad really. Still, I suppose you've got to pass the time somehow.'

Then the police called; they'd caught Big Boy. Ha! Some good news, a spark of light in the gloom. I'd stopped getting flashbacks whenever I chanted, but still found myself looking round every time I left the house. I had a lurking fear that I might bump into him in the street somewhere; or worse, that he might actually be tracking me down as revenge for coming after him and Smiler with the cops.

There was a sting in the tail, though: an ID parade to formally identify each suspect. I agreed, though the thought of having to walk down the line and touch Big Boy on the shoulder didn't thrill me. Or did they do it all behind plate glass nowadays?

I needn't have worried. At Harrow cop shop a young female PC, short and round, led me along a dim, yellowing corridor and down a flight of stairs to the ID Suite – a windowless, neon-lit room that housed three chairs and a

wooden desk, on which stood an ancient computer terminal with a grubby keyboard. This was their VIPER system,
she explained as I sat at the desk – Video Identification
Parade Electronic Recording. I was going to be shown
video clips of possible suspects, and if I recognised my
attackers I should write down the numbers on the form
she put in front of me. She pointed to a high corner of the
room; a video camera would record this 'parade' as the suspects' lawyer was not present. Any questions? I shook my
head, she went through some official stuff for the camera,
then tapped a button on the keyboard.

The terminal sprang to life. A black youth of about
sixteen stared out of the screen at me, impassive. He was
sitting in front of a grey panel and turned his head first left,
then right, then back to the centre. So we're starting with
Smiler, I thought – but it's not you, mate. The screen went
dark, then No. 2 appeared. He looked a lot like No. 1 and
went through the same routine. But he wasn't Smiler either.
Nor was No. 3. Or No. 4.

I started to tense up. What if I didn't pick him out?
Would he get off? Another failure …?

No. 5? No. Or was it? Hard to tell. I hated to admit it
but these guys all looked pretty similar to me. So either
the cops had chosen the lookalikes well or … was I a closet
racist? I didn't see black people as individuals but simply as
black – was that it?

No. 6? No. More self-doubt. No. 7? No. My anxiety grew.
Then No. 8 – and my stomach turned over. Smiler, definitely. The recognition had been instantaneous, visceral
– literally a reaction in my gut. I wrote down the number,
amazed again at my life's mysterious ability to remember
stuff at a level deeper than my conscious mind, and started
the second set of clips. I'd pick out Big Boy, no problem.

I didn't. I ran through the nine clips, twice, without so

much as a twitch, let alone a churning of the guts. No. 4 was a strong contender but No. 7 also looked familiar. Very. What to do? Would he walk free if I didn't pick him out – and maybe come after me? Or hadn't they got him after all?

Then I remembered: the diamond ear-stud. None of the youths in the clips was wearing one but Big Boy must have a little hole in his ear. Which one? I closed my eyes, pictured the scene, remembered. The left. His left ear.

I asked to see No. 7 again. The screen went black, then No. 7 appeared, staring straight at me. 'Go on, then,' he seemed to be saying. 'Identify me. I dare you.' He turned his head first to the left, then the right – and there it was, a tiny hole in his left earlobe. 'Thanks,' I said to the policewoman. 'Got him.'

I left the cop shop feeling pleased with myself, even though the policewoman wasn't allowed to say if I'd picked the right guys. But I was also puzzled. Why had I reacted so strongly to the clip of Smiler but not Big Boy, even though he was by far the scarier of the two? Why could I recall some things and not others? And exactly where in me was this 'basement' of my memory? It was all very puzzling, one of those everyday things that gets stranger the more you look at it. Perhaps I should read my book again – that might tell me. If I could remember where I'd put it. But then, if everything we've ever thought and done is imprinted on our lives somewhere, why the hell couldn't I remember what I'd written? There was only one thing for it: ask Piers. He was good on this sort of stuff.

Then, without warning, Martin resurfaced, in a breathless, excited text message. 'Unbelievable. Stunned. Totally effing unreal. Call me asap.' I tried but kept getting his voicemail. I texted him back – no reply. Finally, around lunchtime the red light on my phone started to blink: a text from Martin apologising for his slow response 'but the morning's been nuts'. Did I want to come over for a sandwich and update? I texted back with a reference to 'parking problems' at his place, he replied with 'WTF??'. I sent 'Ask Mrs?' and quickly got 'Ah. Hang on.' Twenty minutes later he texted with 'Change of plan. Yours for gongyo @ 6pm?' Gongyo? He'd been learning all this time? But if he came here my guilty secret, my five-year lapse, would be out. There again, if he thought something 'unreal' had happened perhaps that wouldn't matter. What the hell – in for a penny. I tapped out a reply: 'OK. But going out at 7.30.' Martin's text winged back to me. 'Done. C U then.'

I wasn't actually going anywhere at seven thirty but Chris usually got home around eight and I wanted to avoid any possible awkwardness. Yes, it was my house and logically I could invite anyone I wanted, at any time I wanted. But Chris had been living there for nearly a year and in all those months neither of us had had anyone over for so much as a cup of tea. He was very private and basically used the place as somewhere to change his clothes and sleep. He was out at work most of the day – when he wasn't taking an exam – and disappeared most weekends, 'seeing friends'. Which suited me fine. Since splitting from Dora I'd got used to my own company. I wouldn't call myself Johnny-No-Mates, exactly, but – well, actually that's what I was, pretty much. I never put in the effort necessary to keep friendships going, so eventually people dropped me. When I was with Dora we'd relied on her friends for our social life, and before that it'd been the same with my previous girlfriend, Angie. There'd been the Buddhists, of course, but once you've left a club so much of what bound you together – the shared culture and assumptions, the regular contact – just doesn't work any more. Which can be quite painful. Better avoided. The only long-term friendship was with my old mate Derek the muso, who called me up once or twice a year between tours – I was a fixed point in his constantly moving world. Fixed as in unchanging, immobile, stuck in a rut …

Anyway, as I tidied the house ahead of Martin's impending visit I realised that Chris and I had an understanding – which, in a typically male way, we had forged by nothing other than habit – that 15 Bladon Street was a kind of functional no-man's-land, where we coexisted at a minimal level of interaction. Both of us could come and go at any time secure in the knowledge that when we returned our space, literal and metaphorical, would be waiting for us precisely as we'd left it. Bringing other people into that space – friends to one but strangers to the other – would be a violation of our unspoken pact.

So as six o'clock crept closer I could feel myself growing steadily more anxious, as if I were seeing someone behind Chris's back. How ridiculous was that? Even the thought of him walking in on me and Martin chanting together made me cringe with embarrassment. As it was, if he was in the house I chanted like a member of the French Resistance hiding a radio from the Nazis, because it's – well, strange, isn't it? Not the thing most people do. Martin's kids had thought it hilarious the moment they saw us chanting and his wife obviously had a problem with it. But so did I for a long time. In fact, if Dora hadn't been holding my hand throughout I don't think I'd have given it a go.

No. I had to get Martin in and out before Chris's return and leave the place looking as it always did: unloved.

The best-laid plans. It was nearly six thirty and I was about to call it off when the doorbell rang. Martin, full of apology.

'Sorry, mate. Forgot the traffic backs up this time of day.

That bloody ring road …' He stepped through the doorway.

'No problem. Just tell me what's happened.' I was dying of curiosity.

'Let's do gongyo,' he said. 'I'll tell you after. And thanks for the stuff, by the way.' He pulled his gongyo book and beads from his jacket. 'How much do I owe you?'

'Present,' I said, in a fit of largesse.

'Ah. Cheers – good of you.'

'And you can do me a quid pro quo.'

'What?'

I told him about the ID parade and what to look out for if the police called him.

'Totally,' he said. 'Sooner those toe-rags are banged up the better.' He looked round the sitting room. 'So, where's your gubbins? You know, your Buddhist doo-da.'

I took a deep breath – time to confess. As Martin listened a frown deepened on his forehead. 'You mean, you only started again after I asked you to teach me?'

I nodded guiltily. ''Fraid so.'

He suddenly brightened. 'That's a relief.' He saw my surprise and laughed. 'Well, you're not exactly an advert, are you, if you've been at it for years.'

Ouch. Crushing or what? But accurate. I forced a smile. 'Glad you see it that way.'

'Cheer up, mate; if I can do it, you can.' He laughed again. 'So – gongyo?'

I pointed to a space I'd made opposite a blank piece of wall, drew up a couple of chairs and off we went. To my surprise Martin had made great strides since his first, stumbling attempt and we finished the whole shebang, including a good chunk of chanting, in twenty minutes flat.

'Blimey. You've come on some,' I said. 'Especially as I wasn't sure your missus approved.'

'Ha!' Martin snorted. 'She doesn't. Catholic, you see.

Lapsed but still *tinks Oi bin cot boi de Debble.*' It was quite a good Irish accent.

'Meaning me?'

'You're the Debble's Spawn. Or was – till this morning.'

'So what's happened?'

'Well, I've been doing this since you came round, right? And getting the book and CD helped, so cheers for that. But I had to do it in my office or when Fiona was out of the house. And you were totally banned, mate.'

'Mmm, sussed that – the parking ticket.'

'Yeah, sorry. Anyway, all this time I've been chanting about this fucking house—'

'Hillview.'

'Yeah. And how'm I going to get the money to finish it, or get rid of it, or find any way on God's earth to stay out of the black hole of bloody bustness?'

'Again.'

'Yeah. Once is unlucky, twice is—'

'Karma.'

'Well, it's certainly starting to look like a habit, yeah. Which means your credibility's pretty much screwed with the bank, suppliers and, well, everyone basically.'

'So?'

'So I'm chanting and doing *Kyo Chi Gyo I* and making loads of causes – cos last time I remember you banging on about how causes make effects, yeah?' I nodded. 'Anyway, I'm giving it the full hundred and ten per cent, cos to my mind, you want to test something you got to do it properly, right? And – you got a coffee or something, by the way?'

I got up and headed for the kitchen. 'Go on.'

Martin followed me. 'Well, there I was, giving it both barrels – and I just ran out of causes. I'd chanted about everything, done everything I could think of … and nothing.'

'No effects?'

'Sweet FA. So I thought, Now what? It's not working so, what – jack it in, carry on, what?'

'And?'

'Well, the thing is, even though nothing was coming back, I felt better – in myself. Like sleeping. I been getting the 4 a.m. wake-up, you know: my life's shit, I'm useless, we're all doomed?' Yup – been there, done that. Was still doing it, in fact. 'Well, it stopped being every night. Maybe every other night now, but at least I'm getting some sleep, you know?' I nodded again and gave him his coffee, waiting for the punchline. 'And after a couple of weeks I even started to think, if the worst happens maybe it's not the end of the world after all. Maybe we could start again, as long as I keep the family together somehow. I mean, I didn't start off with anything. Fiona's family were piss-poor till not so long ago. And kids adapt. We could start again.'

'Hope.'

'Exactly. But then this morning, out of the bleedin' blue – a text.' He waggled his phone. 'From the bloke I was going to meet when I bumped into you.'

'The ginger bastard?'

'Self-same. Full of apologies, wife's been ill, delays at the bank, dog's been sick on his homework, blah-di-blah – whatever. Long story short, he's got a buyer, got the finance, wants to do the deal, and as soon as it's signed I'm home and dry.' He spread his arms and beamed exhilarated, bemused delight. I was stunned.

'Bloody hell, Martin. That's fantastic.'

'Yep. With one mighty bound Jack was free.' A gleeful grin split his chops. 'Which means that you have gone from being the Devil's Spawn to the Archangel Gabriel himself.'

'With Fiona?'

He nodded. 'Who I'd like you to meet properly, over supper. She's got a lot of questions.'

'Oh?' That sounded ominous.

'Well, she can't rubbish this now, can she? Or stop me doing it. So come round, we'll do gongyo, some chanting, then have a bite and few glasses of wine. Could be a celebration.'

'So you're going to keep on with the chanting?'

'You joking? It's a no-brainer, mate. Legions of bloody banana-skins between here and selling that fucker.' I was relieved. I sensed that as long as he kept going I would, too. 'So – supper?'

'Mmm, sounds good.' As in bad.

'Great. I'll find some dates and get back to you. Any no-go evenings – you know, when you do macramé or tae kwon do, double-entry bookkeeping …?'

I pretended to search my mental diary. 'No … I think the evenings are pretty clear for the next little while.'

'Great.' He checked his watch and gulped down a mouthful of scalding coffee. 'Got to go. And you're out soon too. See you at Piers's tomorrow? Only I can't give you a lift – sorry. I'll be coming from town.'

'No problem.'

A key scraped in the lock and the door opened – Chris, unusually early. He looked surprised to see a visitor in the house but at least we weren't chanting, thank God. I introduced them again.

'Martin, Chris. You met the other week?'

'Oh yes,' said Chris. 'Ed's friend.'

'That's the one,' said Martin, shaking Chris's hand. 'And you're the trainee actuary.'

'Yes,' said Chris, beaming at the open goal. 'It's like being an accountant, only not as exciting.'

*

Twenty-four hours later I was in Piers's sitting room. We'd finished gongyo and were settling down for the discussion meeting – but tension was in the air. This was the first time Bernie and Jenny had been in the same room since the blow-up at the last meeting and no one knew how they'd react.

The cast was as before: those two, Piers, Constanza (sigh), Darren and Rachel; minus Bella, who was on a sleepover, and Martin, who'd sent me a text saying he'd been delayed; but plus Aidan, who'd been on holiday in August. He was a clean-cut, handsome guy in his early thirties, wearing tight jeans and a white T-shirt that clung to his tanned, toned physique – muscles on his muscles, pecs of steel, washboard stomach. Just looking at him made me feel fat, unfit and in my forties – which I was, all three.

Piers welcomed everyone, then announced that this month we'd be discussing respect, for oneself and other people – a challenging concept at the heart of Buddhist practice and human revolution. At once the tension tightened a notch. People glanced at each other. Bernie looked at Jenny, who stared down at the carpet in front of her. He spoke.

'All right, before we start: elephant in the room. Last meeting, Jenny, what I said about your cat – out of order.' She looked up, surprised. 'I apologise. I should have been more considerate. All right?'

Jenny didn't know quite how to take this. She cleared her throat. 'Well, yes, you should have been but . . . Apology accepted.'

Bernie grunted. Not quite peace breaking out – a 'Well, perhaps I overreacted' would have been nice, something like that – but at least the tension had relaxed. A bit. Piers smiled.

'Excellent. Thank you. So—' The doorbell rang. 'Excuse

me.' He got up to answer it and the room fell into an awkward silence. It was broken by Darren.

'Nice tan.' He smiled at Aidan. 'Where'd you get it?'

'Greece. Corfu.'

'Oh, I love Corfu.'

'Mmm, I used to. Half dead right now.'

'Why?' asked Rachel, surprised.

'Economy's tanking.' Rachel looked blank. 'The euro crisis. There've been riots in Athens, people killed.'

'Oh.' She didn't sound any the wiser.

Constanza looked amazed. 'That was in May. You no watch TV?'

'Not much, to be honest.' Rachel pulled an apologetic face. 'I mean, I knew there were problems, but—'

She stopped as Piers came back in with Martin, who gave a smiling nod to the group, winked at me and found a place to sit. Aidan finished his story.

'Anyway, tourists aren't coming, especially the Germans. Which means nice empty beaches—'

'And empty sun-loungers,' Darren added. 'Plenty of towel space.'

'Yeah,' said Aidan. 'But half the restaurants and bars are closed.'

'Spain next,' said Constanza. 'You see. Boom!' She mimed an explosion with her hands.

'What we talking about?' asked Martin, his ears pricking up at the mention of Spain.

'The euro,' said Constanza.

'Respect, actually – that's the theme,' said Jenny forcefully.

Constanza flashed her a glance. Piers saw the danger and deftly intervened. 'Well, maybe there's a link we can explore in the discussion?' Constanza frowned but said nothing. Piers pressed on. 'Excellent. So first off we're going to hear about a chap called Bodhisattva Never Disparaging, who's absolutely key to the theme. Jenny?'

She flashed a tight, tense smile and opened a large, battered paperback, her hands shaking slightly. 'He appears in chapter twenty of the Lotus Sutra,' she said and started to read.

The story tells how the monk Never Disparaging bows in respect to everyone he meets because, he tells them, one day they will all become Buddhas. But instead of thanking him, the people reply with angry words, some of them pelting him with sticks and stones. How dare he presume to make such a prediction, they cry. Never Disparaging doesn't give up, however. Each time he's assaulted he runs off to a safe distance and continues to shout out to his attackers that he respects them because one day they will all become Buddhas.

'And because he always spoke these words, the overbearing arrogant monks, nuns, laymen and laywomen gave him the name Never Disparaging.' Jenny stopped reading and looked up, avoiding Bernie's gaze.

Martin raised a hand. 'Bodhisattva?'

'Someone who helps others,' said Darren. 'Especially helps them become a Buddha.'

'Ah, right,' said Martin, and pointed at me. I shook my head – not me.

'Basically, Never Disparaging is in 'ere,' said Constanza, thumping a fist against her chest. 'In my 'eart I fight to respect – Pierce, Bernie, Jenny, you, you, you,' pointing around the room. 'To respect *everyone*. Becoss *everyone* have Booddha nature. *Everyone* can be Booddha. So I can bring out Booddha from you – *if* I am Booddha in my 'eart. Like the Bodhisattva Never Disparaging.'

'Except he didn't, did he?' said Martin. 'He showed them respect and they chucked things at him.'

'Yes – is 'ard,' said Constanza. 'Becoss life is full of eediots, eh?' She laughed.

'Well, that's the funny thing about Buddhahood,' said Darren. 'It brings out the best or the worst in other people. But even people who are really hostile form a connection, and one day they'll become Buddhas too.'

Martin frowned. 'Eh?'

'It's like with love,' Darren said. 'The opposite's not hate, it's indifference. With hate there's still a connection. You hate cos you care.'

Martin opened his mouth to respond, then closed it again, stumped.

'For me,' said Jenny, putting down the paperback, 'the important thing is not to slander, even if I don't like someone.' She turned to Martin. 'Slander's the opposite of respect – it's *always* disparaging, looking down on people. Always undermining them, looking for their faults, weak points, making fun of them, trying to hurt them, dismissing, discouraging them. I hate that, so I really try not to do it. Including animals, because you can slander them too.'

'Especially when you kill 'em, eh?' said Bernie. He knew – we all knew – that her speech had been directed at him. Jenny flashed him an angry glance.

'Putting an animal out of its misery is not slander. It's respect.'

'You want to end their suffering,' said Bernie.

Jenny hesitated, suspecting a trap. 'Yes,' she said.

'Right,' he continued. 'So respect int just being nice to people. It's doing what you think they need to end their suffering – or the suffering they're causing. Especially when they're idiots, like what Constanza said. What's that quote: "If you lack mercy to correct your friend ...?"' He looked at Piers, who took the battered paperback from Jenny and started to leaf through it.

'Here we are. "If one befriends another person but lacks the mercy to correct him, one is in fact his enemy." And then: "The consequences of a grave offence are extremely difficult to erase. The most important thing is to continually strengthen our wish to benefit others."'

'Exactly,' said Bernie. 'And mercy – or compassion, same thing – is shown in two ways, mother love and father love. Mother love's "There, there", kiss it better, "You can do it, darling." Encouragement. And that's what Never Disparaging shows. Father love's tough love. It's telling an idiot, "You're an idiot." Because you want them to FUCKING WAKE UP!' Everyone jumped, startled. 'To stop being idiots and hurting people, or themselves. Or both.'

Jenny's expression hardened. 'So you're foul to me because you think I'm an idiot?'

Darren groaned. 'People, no …'

Bernie frowned, irritated. 'I think you're basically a mother love person but you showed father love when you had to – like with your cat. My default's basically father love, so I'm very shouty and sweary. But I can do lovely, soft mummy love too, sometimes. Depends what's needed.'

Our attention snapped back to Jenny, like at a tennis match. But she simply sniffed, folded her arms and looked at Piers, who seemed nonplussed that war had somehow been averted. Martin raised his hand again.

'So what about the bastards who mugged Ed? We gotta respect them?' Good question – I was wondering about that.

'Father love,' said Aidan. 'Compassionate correction.'

'*Si*,' said Constanza. 'Boodha is like parent – father, mother, both – and you, me, everyone are the children. So a child is bad – you don't just throw away, if you are parent. You are angry, yes, but you think very much how … how I make this child gooder – *si*? And you try and try and try. You don't just throw away.'

Not a bad answer, I thought, but something was niggling me. Piers must have noticed.

'Ed, what do you think?'

'Well, it's a question, really. If we all have mother love and father love, and from what Bernie was saying I'm guessing we're all biased towards one or the other, how do we know we're using what the person actually needs and not just our default?'

Constanza looked straight at me and puckered up – at least, that's what it looked like. 'Weesdom, Ed. Your Boodha weesdom, from your chanting. Weesdom is daughter of compassion. And then, with Boodha courage, you take action.'

Ah, Constanza. You could give me guidance all night.

The rest of the meeting went pretty well, not least because Martin recounted his miraculous news – he'd been having trouble for months with this property deal, but since starting to chant it had all fallen into place and he'd just signed the contract – and everyone perked up. Nothing like a positive experience for lightening the mood. No one walked out, Rachel played a tune on her flute, and Bernie and Jenny even managed to exchange a couple of polite words over tea and biscuits at the end. I also asked Piers about why I couldn't remember stuff I'd written if everything we've ever done is supposed to be imprinted in our lives somewhere, and he dug out an article for me to read on something called the nine consciousnesses. So all in all I left feeling more cheerful than I'd been for quite a while.

The mood lasted until I was just climbing into bed and my phone rang. I didn't recognise the number, but perhaps it was the police – they call at strange times. I pressed the button.

'Hello?'

'Ed?' It was a familiar, gruff voice.

'Bernie?'

'Yeah. Sorry to disturb, m'darling, but Piers gave me your number.'

'Oh?'

'Yeah. We went out with your mate Martin after the meeting and he's offered us a job on that house near you.'

'What, Hillview?'

'That's the one. We're taking a look tomorrow first thing, wondered if you wanted to come along.'

'Er ...'

'You said you was curious about it.'

I had, during my tale of the mugging. But I was surprised – and puzzled. Why would they want me there?

'Ah, yes, I am curious but I don't quite ... Does Martin know?'

'No, we just thought of it. No reason he'd mind though, is there?'

'Not that I know of.'

'Well then – you on?'

'Er, yeah, OK. Why not?'

'Right. Half eight then. See you there. Sleep tight.'

And he rang off. I got into bed and turned off the light.

Piers and Bernie working for Martin – that was an interesting development. Positive, spreading the good fortune around. But I felt uneasy. It sounded like a spur-of-the-moment idea that had occurred to Martin over a few beers. And I wasn't too sure how he'd take me turning up unannounced in the morning. Would he think I was fishing for a job too – or just being nosy?

Well, whatever; it'd be good to get a look inside, satisfy my curiosity after all this time. And perhaps there might be something in this for me, too; something mystic, the universe giving with one hand what it's taken with the other. I save Mart, he saves me, I save him again, he saves me again and so it goes, on and on. I drifted into a circle of speculation – and off …

But I didn't sleep well. I dreamed that Big Boy was following me, down on to a Tube train in the rush hour and pushing through the commuters, closer and closer, trying to reach me – with a stiletto in his sleeve. I was trying to get away but the people wouldn't move, wouldn't let me through … I looked round. Big Boy was there, he jabbed with his hand—

I woke sweating. It was almost four o'clock.

Chapter Five

It was hammering down when I pulled up outside Hillview. Bernie and Piers were already there, sheltering in Bernie's white Escort van under the trees. I flashed my headlights, they tooted back – and then I waited. The rain beat on the car roof, the wipers swept across the windscreen every six seconds (I counted), the *Today* programme chattered away on the radio.

It felt odd to be up here again, familiar yet strange. St Catherine's was a few yards down the road, known but off-limits now, while Hillview, hidden behind its dirty white hoarding and razor-wire, was about to reveal its secrets.

Time passed, *Today* finished, we had the pips and the news, and then a programme started on how, since the crash, the world of finance and economics was in disarray – no one could agree on anything any more.

I must have dozed off, because when I next looked it was nine twenty. Still no Martin. I was about to dash over to consult with Piers and Bernie when a sleek BMW appeared in my mirror, glided past and stopped with its nose hard against the padlocked hoarding at the entrance to the site. Martin got out, swaddled in what looked like a trawler-man's outfit, all bright shiny yellow, and beckoned Bernie and Piers to approach. I wound down my window and shouted through the rain.

'Can we park inside?'

Martin looked round, surprised to see me, and shook his head. 'On foot!'

I killed the radio, pulled the hood of my kagool over my head, and got out. The rain was getting even heavier, the wind was gusting and it was bloody cold. I ran over to the gate, where Martin was struggling with the padlock.

'Problem?'

'Fucking thing,' he muttered, his irritation rising with every thwarted twist of the key. 'Opened yesterday ...'

'Give it here, come on.' Bernie had snuck up behind us with Piers. He was wearing a heavy donkey jacket, Doc Martens and a beanie in West Ham claret and blue. He pushed Martin aside, took a can of WD40 from his jacket and squirted some of the magic oil into the padlock keyhole. He slid in the key and the lock fell open. Martin just grunted, then pushed back the hoarding far enough to squeeze through – and disappeared. Bernie, Piers and I exchanged a look.

'No fucking manners, some people,' said Bernie. 'No thank you, no "Sorry I'm late", no—'

'Bernie, please – not now,' said Piers. Bernie scowled but bit his lip. Piers nodded. 'Good man. Don't want to blow it before we start, eh?' He squeezed sideways through the gap and out of sight.

Bernie looked at me. I gestured at the gate.

'After you.'

He turned sideways, sucked in his ample belly – and got stuck. He sighed, then gave the hoarding a mighty shove. There was the sound of splintering ... and he was in. I followed – and at once saw why we'd had to leave the cars on the road.

The area in front of the house was jammed with building materials: giant sacks of topsoil, bags of builder's plaster turned rock-hard by the weather, a mountain of sand, bubble-wrapped panes of glass stacked in the porch, and pallet piled on pallet of new bricks and roof tiles. Puzzling, as the roof and brickwork looked complete.

Stacked against the hoarding under the trees to the right of the house were four cargo containers, painted white. The top two had been converted into a site office – a wooden staircase led to a door at the far end – while the bottom pair were as they came; storage space, I guessed. Opposite them, to the left of the house, stood a cement silo some thirty feet tall. But what most surprised me were the diggers. One was parked by the silo and the other had been reversed almost up to the gate to block any vehicles getting on to the site. How long had they been sitting there, I wondered, and at what cost?

'Come on, get inside!' Martin was calling from the open entrance to the house – there was no door yet. Piers splashed over to him as Bernie surveyed the detritus with a professional eye. I followed, picking my way through the mud. It was only a few yards but I entered the house with my shoes caked in the heavy clay soil.

'Should've worn boots,' said Martin as I stamped around trying to dislodge it. 'If I'd known you were coming I'd have warned you.' He didn't seem at all put out by my presence.

'Bernie invited me,' I said. 'I've always been intrigued by this place.'

'Jesus – nice weather for ducks or what?' Bernie joined us in the lobby. 'How long's the site been idle?'

'Since spring,' said Martin.

'That silo's going to be fucked then. Any cement in there'll be like – well, concrete.' He laughed.

'I know,' said Martin.

Bernie pushed past us into the house proper. The lobby led into a circular atrium, fronted by a huge window that rose from just above the lobby entrance to the roof. Four doorways led off the space and a curve of concrete steps swept up to the first floor. This was mirrored by another curve that dropped out of sight into the basement – the house was on four storeys, not the three that I'd thought. As we joined him Bernie pointed at a large opening high in the wall above the first-floor landing.

'More rooms up there?'

Martin nodded. 'There's a spiral staircase from the first floor. And that space'll have a railing.'

He led us through one of the door spaces into a large open area that ran all the way around the house. This would be partitioned into a kitchen, dining room and lounge at the back, he explained, with a TV room and a study at the front. Although the interior was still just a grey shell of breeze blocks and concrete, thanks to the many windows the space was surprisingly light and airy, even with the rain lashing down outside.

'The roof's done and dry?' Bernie asked. Martin nodded. 'And all the windows are in?' Martin nodded again. 'So what's with all that glass out front?'

'Over-delivery,' said Martin. 'But as it turns out it's a good mistake.' He saw the puzzled look on our faces and smiled. He crossed to a set of french windows leading out into the garden and pointed. 'See that?'

We joined him and looked out. It was another park, even larger than Martin's, sloping away to a copse of beech and birch trees at the bottom. Halfway down the overgrown jungle of lawn a large hole had been cut out of the slope and the spoil piled to one side in a mountain of mud.

'What is it?' asked Piers.

'Swimming pool,' said Martin. 'Except the new client wants it inside.'

Bernie barked a laugh. 'Bit fucking late!'

'It's what turned the deal,' said Martin. 'We stick up a conservatory, here' – he waved his hand at the area just outside the french windows – 'using all that glass. But instead of plants, we put in a pool. Simple. And meanwhile, we shove that crap back in the hole' – he pointed to the mountain of mud – 'turf it over and Bob's your uncle.'

There was a moment of silence as we took this in. Piers broke it.

'What about planning permission?'

'Retrospective,' said Martin with easy confidence. 'Done all the time.'

Bernie sniffed. 'How big's this pool gonna be?'

'Twenty metres.' Martin caught Bernie's look of surprise. 'He wants to swim laps.'

'He can go down the road for that,' I said, jerking a thumb towards St Catherine's. Martin ignored me, his eyes on Bernie, who had unlocked the french windows and stepped out into the downpour. 'Or if he's training for the Olympics he could get one of those endless pools,' I continued, as Bernie started pacing out the distance. 'It has a current, so you swim on the spot. Like a sort of liquid treadmill.' Martin wasn't listening. Bernie came back in, beard and beanie running with water.

'Twenty-metre pool, plus your surround, depth of wall – that's three-quarters of the back of the house gone, easy.'

'The customer is king, Bernie,' said Martin.

'The customer's a fucking idiot if he wants that. It means you got to look out through the pool-house to see the garden.' Martin gave a resigned shrug. Bernie shook his head, scandalised.

'You're sure he's got the money?' Piers looked worried.

'All agreed,' said Martin. 'The first tranche should be in my account by close of play today. If it's not, all bets are off.' His phone rang. He checked the caller – 'Talk of the devil. Colin, how are you?' – and strode off out of earshot.

Bernie, Piers and I grouped into a huddle.

'Well, that's one way to fuck up a nice house,' said Bernie.

'Yes,' said Piers. 'The Golden Rule triumphs again.'

'What's that?' I asked.

Bernie laughed. 'Oh, sweet innocence! He who has the gold makes the rules.'

'Ah.'

'*If* he's got it.' For some reason Piers directed this at me.

'Well, you heard him,' I said. 'He'll know today.'

Piers glanced at Martin, deep in conversation in a front corner of the house, and made a decision.

'Going to look at the garden.'

He pulled the wide brim of his bush hat down hard on to his head, pushed open the french windows and waded out into the monsoon. Bernie secured the door behind him, dug out his tobacco tin and started to roll a cigarette.

'You know, Bernie,' I said, 'I'm still not entirely clear what I'm doing here.'

'Tell you later,' said Bernie, concentrating on his roll-up.

'How about now?'

He shook his head and nodded a warning. I looked round to see Martin bearing down on us with a broad smile. '*Alles in ordnung*,' he said, clapping and rubbing his hands together in satisfaction. 'So I'll give you the full tour, and then you can decide if you want the job or not – all right? Maybe get you involved too, Ed. You want to call Piers?'

Through the french windows we could see him peering into the pit that would have been the swimming pool, rain running off his hat into the hole.

'He's more interested in the great outdoors,' said Bernie, licking the gummed strip on his almost-made cigarette.

'Right then,' said Martin. 'Follow me.'

An hour or so later, Bernie, Piers and I were sitting in the warm fug of Snax R' Us on the high street. The smell of fried bacon hung heavy in the air and the plate-glass window had misted up, obscuring the bakery across the road where I'd bought my ham and tomato roll on that fateful afternoon a few weeks back.

Bernie and Piers were trying very hard not to get excited. For all the nutty vandalism of the pool extension, Hillview would be a big deal for them. Since the financial crash house-building had slumped to a hundred-year low and landscape gardening wasn't featuring high on many must-do lists either. But they didn't know what to make of Martin and confessed they'd asked me along to fill in the gaps, if I could.

I hesitated. Martin had told me about his financial predicament in confidence, but now he'd done the deal I guessed that was all history. I gave them a brief summary. Piers looked troubled.

'Crikey. All or nothing, eh?'

I nodded. 'But it looks like he's pulled it off.'

'If he has actually *got* the moolah,' said Bernie, his hands wrapped round a steaming mug of tea.

'Well, if you don't trust him,' I said, 'ask for a copy of his bank statements. Or a down-payment or something.'

Piers and Bernie looked at each other across the table. 'Sod it,' said Bernie. 'Let's do it. We negotiate a price – each – get cash up front for materials and contingency, then get paid weekly for labour. All with pukka contracts. So if he goes belly up we lose a week's money – max.'

'Well, I'm going to jolly well chant about it,' said Piers.

'Because I'll have to take on at least two more chaps for something that size.' My ears pricked up.

''Course,' said Bernie. 'I'll be subbing too. But beggars can't be choosers, eh?'

'Talking of which,' I said to Piers, 'if you're looking for a guy who's not afraid of hard graft, getting his hands dirty, who's local ...'

'You know someone?' Piers was poker-faced.

I opened my arms wide. 'Dude!'

Piers smiled. 'Funny thing, karma.'

It was a throwaway remark, a gentle dig, but it rankled. Once upon a time I used to think that karma was a sort of hippie punishment, something the universe doled out for 'bad stuff' you'd done in previous lives – or in this one if the heavens moved fast enough. Then I met Geoff and Dora – who couldn't have been less like hippies if they'd tried. They explained that karma's not just about what we've done in the past that's produced this effect now; it's also about what we're doing *now* that will produce more effects in the future. Easy enough to understand – in theory. But Piers's remark set me off on another unexpected truffle hunt to discover how it actually related to my life.

It was the evening of the day after our visit to Hillview and I'd been chanting for about half an hour, hoping Piers would call to say he'd taken the job and wanted to employ me. But I was also feeling pissed off because I couldn't understand, ten years on, how I might be working for him as a labourer – again. How, despite all that had happened in between, I had somehow made the causes to find myself out of work, short of money and desperate enough to actually want the job. In short, the same old complaint: how the hell had my life turned out like this? It was almost as strange as bumping into Nick in New Orleans or Martin turning up in his BMW, as if some vast, unseen hand was moving me around an invisible, multi-dimensional chessboard. Except, according to Buddhism, it wasn't. Everything in my life was a result of my own thoughts, words and actions. Cause led to effect led to cause to effect ... to here, and now. My life was my karma, my karma was my life. And in the end it all came down to the choices I made – consciously or, perhaps more often, unconsciously. Some gentlemen prefer blondes – because their karma tells them to?

Not that I did prefer blondes. I preferred ... what? I was stumped. And seamlessly, before I knew it, I was away on the truffle hunt, riffling through the significant women in my life to identify what had attracted me to them – and them to me. There were four – Dora, Angie, Kimberley and Sharon – but they seemed to have nothing in common at all. So was the attraction random or was there some deeper, karmic pattern?

There was only one thing for it: a thorough, systematic review of my love life, such as it was. If there was a pattern maybe I'd see it and even how I might change it. Because whatever I'd done up to now clearly hadn't worked.

As I chanted I lined up my past girlfriends in chronological order, trying to remember their faces and what the attraction was. There weren't that many so it wasn't too difficult. The brief flings were easy: lust that quickly palled on one side or the other, or both. But the Fab Four continued to stump me – they were so different.

Dora was black, Angie a Jewish brunette, Kimberley a curly-haired, blue-eyed Canadian and Sharon a freckle-faced redhead. Two were older than me, two younger. Dora and Angie were both ... how can I put this? Well, not afraid of letting you know what they thought. Assertive. Combative, even. But Sharon wasn't like that at all. She was in the year above me at Queen Eleanor's, our sister school, and in the three years we were together there wasn't a cross word between us – until I went off to university and 'that bitch' Kimberley got her claws into me. From the moment they met Sharon was convinced that Kimberley was after me and, more to the point, that I fancied her too. The more I pooh-poohed both ideas the more certain she became, until we were having so many blazing rows about it we split up – and Kimberley picked up the pieces.

The irony was that only half of Sharon's suspicions were true: Kimberley *was* after me but I didn't really fancy her. I thought she was funny and attractive and exotically different – Canadian is almost American, right? But if Sharon hadn't been so jealous and paranoid, or Kimberley so determined, I would never have swapped.

Pow. That's when it hit me – another of those eureka moments. I hadn't pursued, wooed and won *any* of these women: it was totally the other way round.

Sharon had spotted me during a joint school production of *Oh, What A Lovely War!* and asked me out. I'd been so surprised and impressed at her boldness – the confidence of the older woman – that I fell for her on the spot.

Kimberley had singled me out because we shared a sense of humour. She was alone in the UK and we bonded over comedy CDs and TV shows: *The Young Ones*, *Blackadder*, Robin Williams; all sorts of stuff that we played to each other late at night in our rooms in hall. She knew I had a girlfriend at home but had a couple of aces up her sleeve: proximity and ten-week terms. She later confessed to me that she'd 'smelled' Sharon's insecurity the first time she came up to visit – the non-university girl surrounded by all these clever, confident students – but she always denied playing on it. I'm not so sure, though, looking back.

Angie had been even more brazen. I'd met her during a job for a PR agency in the West End – I was scraping a living as a copywriter for promo literature – and thought she was sharp and sassy and sexy. A bunch of us from the agency went out a few times – lunch or a drink after work – but, like Constanza, I'd automatically classed her as out of my league.

Then one of her workmates had a dinner party one Friday night out in the suburbs somewhere – six of us, all single – which didn't end till past midnight. Two got a minicab back into town, the hostess pointed Angie and me towards the spare bedrooms, then whisked her target off to bed – I later learned she'd planned the evening precisely for that result.

I was just falling asleep when there was a crash and a hissed cry of pain close by my ear. I sat bolt upright to see a shadowy form stumbling around in the dark.

'Angie?' I whispered.

'Can I get in?' she whispered back.

OK, I know it sounds like every schoolboy's dream but it did actually happen like that. She didn't get out again, so to speak, for two and a half years.

Dora ambushed me, too. I'd been going to her agency looking for work but also, after a while, to get her advice about Angie; this was not long after we'd split up and I was trying to get her back. Dora didn't just have a female perspective on things – she had a Buddhist angle, too, which I found fascinating. But I had no idea she saw me as anything other than a client, until the fateful lunchtime I told her Angie and I were over for good – and she kissed me. On the mouth. A moment on the lip …

It was so obvious: I'd never been in the driving seat of these relationships. They'd lasted only as long as the women wanted, and as soon as they'd had enough of me we were done. Sharon had told me to 'go to that bitch, then!' And I had. After graduating Kimberley had gone back to

Canada, with hardly a glance over her shoulder. I later discovered she'd had a boyfriend there the whole time. Angie had walked out. And Dora I've already explained.

I remembered something Geoff used to say, that 'the future is a vacuum waiting to be filled with reality.' It's determined by the strongest input and if we don't make it, someone else will. So if that was true for these relationships, what about other areas of my life? When the going got tough did I just roll over and give up? Was that why I found myself on the point of labouring for Piers again – my life had been shaped by my passivity as much as by my animality? Tranquillity, the Buddhists called it, one of the basic life states – but its real name in my case was laziness. Lazy thinking, lack of effort, of purpose, willpower, backbone. That's why I taught English to foreigners (more accurately, English *conversation*, since basically I just turned up to chat): not because I loved it but because it was easy.

There was no way round it. If character is destiny, and mine was weak and pathetic, I was … doomed.

My thoughts ran on like this for a couple of minutes, my spirits sinking lower and lower as I continued to chant. Then something odd happened: I caught sight of my *Enjoy life. Win* card and Angry Ed kicked in again.

'Woah!' he snorted. 'Doomed? Not true. What about when you wrote the book? That took effort, backbone. So did supporting Martin when you didn't want to. You're just in a trough, and you've got to push through the troughs to get to the peaks. *Chanting* plus *action* equals *result*. You've done it before so you can do it again. Why not? Like that thing Dora used to say: "From this moment forward." Don't obsess about what you've done in the past, the mistakes. Focus on what you're going to do *now* to make a new future, a better future.'

89

It was as if a switch had been flicked. Hope sprang up out of nowhere – and my phone rang. Piers offering me a job? But as I reached for it another thought flashed through my mind: if it was, should I take it? Wouldn't that be reinforcing the same old karma? Then again, I needed the money ...

It wasn't Piers. It was Martin, calling to make good that invitation to supper – tomorrow night? I said thanks, that would be lovely, and asked if he'd heard from the dynamic duo.

'Oh yeah,' he said. 'Piers called yesterday afternoon to say they're onboard – both of them.'

My spirits crashed again. No need to decide whether to take the job. If Piers hadn't called in more than twenty-four hours he obviously didn't want me.

All next day I battled with my negative thoughts. 'The bastards. The fuckers. You help Martin but does he help you? No. He helps Bernie and Piers. Then what does Piers do? Makes some snide joke about karma and employs someone else. Light a lamp for another and he pisses off with it and leaves you in the dark.'

I couldn't keep that up for long, though. Anger takes too much energy and mine was ebbing away as despair tightened its grip.

Strong word, despair. And perhaps I wasn't there yet. But I was definitely paddling round the edge of the Slough of Despond. Of hopelessness. Desolation. The bleak certainty that nothing I did would ever make a difference. I couldn't even get a labouring job. I thought of calling Piers to ask why he hadn't given it to me, but why put him on the spot, embarrass him? He didn't have to employ me. He probably wanted someone with skills, who could do labouring *and* other stuff – planting, pruning, whatever. Someone better suited. Fair enough. Stupid, really, to make such a big deal of it. It was just a silly, crappy little job.

I almost didn't go to Martin's. What was the point: to sit and listen to his flint-faced wife slag off Buddhism? But come five o'clock I found myself walking down to the corner shop for a bottle of wine. And not just any old gut-rot – I spent the best part of a tenner. That's my problem: too well-mannered. Or was it that turning him down would be just too much emotional effort – passivity strikes again? Frankly, I was too tired to care. I'd go along, smile coldly if Fiona decided to attack, say how nice the meal was and be back in time for *Newsnight*.

Guilt struck as I left the shop. It was right opposite Watford General and I hadn't so much as thought of Valeria since my visit. I hesitated, then marched across the road and into the hospital. Doing good would lift my mood: wasn't that what Buddhism taught? You make a cause for someone else's happiness and the effect's lodged at once in your own life – supposedly. But Valeria was long gone, the nurse said, whisked back to Italy the day after I saw her – by air ambulance. I could see the bill climbing with the plane.

So I was still feeling pretty negative as the Civic scraped up and down over the speed bumps towards Martin's front door. I'd decided that if Fiona gave me any grief about parking I'd simply turn round and come home. Of course, I knew I wouldn't – that was all fantasy bravado, like me beating up Big Boy and Smiler. And anyway, when I arrived Martin opened the door to me and batted away my concern.

'Ah, don't worry about it,' he said. 'She must have been due her period or something.' As he ushered me in a shaggy black dog tore round the corner, tail wagging furiously, and immediately buried its nose in my crotch. 'That's Dave. Don't worry – he won't bite.'

'Dave?' I said, fighting him off.

'The kids named him.'

'Right. What breed?' I couldn't identify it.

'Labradoodle,' said Martin, pulling Dave away from my groin. 'Cross between a Labrador and a poodle. He's totally harmless. Bit soppy really – aren't you?' He grabbed Dave by the chops and waggled his head to and fro, then straightened up and took the wine. 'Pushed the boat out, eh?' He smiled. 'Come on – gongyo, then we'll get stuck in.' He led me towards the gym, Dave in tow.

'Shouldn't I say hello to—'

'She's in the shower,' he said. 'Oh – and no money talk at supper, OK?'

I tapped my nose. '*Omerta.*'

Amelia and her brother were in the gym, sitting primly on the bench, which was already placed opposite the blank wall. Martin addressed them with mock sternness.

'Right: Amelia, Oliver – this is Ed. Say hello.' They got up, shook my hand and said hello in turn, all very formal.

'Pleased to meet you,' I said, with a little bow.

'Amelia and Oliver have decided they want to become Buddhists too,' Martin explained, 'so they've been learning gongyo – haven't you?' They nodded, and held up their beads – Martin must have bought them a set each. 'Well, Ed here is an expert, so listen very carefully to how he does it and we'll all learn something, all right?' The children nodded again. 'But any giggling and you'll be straight out. Understood?'

He shouldn't have said that because at once their faces cracked. They slapped their hands over their mouths to hide the incriminating signs but Martin gave me a sly wink, pretending not to see. He gestured to the bench and we sat down, me at one end, then Martin, Amelia and Oliver. Dave sniffed around, looking for action, then lay down at Oliver's command. Martin turned to me. 'Nice and steady,' he said.

I was expecting another painful stumble through the book but the kids didn't just keep up, they had the rhythm and pronunciation better than Martin. I was seriously impressed and told them so when we finished ten minutes later. They swelled with pride.

'They've been listening to the CD,' Martin explained, ruffling Oliver's hair as we stood up to leave.

'And doing it,' protested Amelia. 'Every day.'

'Yep, been keeping me on track.' Martin smiled.

'He doesn't want to do it,' said Oliver. 'He comes home and says, "Oh no, leave me alone, I'm tired."' He gave an exaggerated yawn, mimicking his dad.

'But we make him!' squealed Amelia, whacking Martin on the bottom. He grabbed her hand and pinned her tight against him.

'See what I have to put up with?' he said, as she giggled and wriggled. 'Two dictators!'

'Make that three.' The words came from Fiona. She was in the doorway, in slacks and a yellow cashmere jumper, her blonde hair gathered in a French twist. Oliver ran over and flung his arms round her waist. 'Finished?' she said to Martin, not acknowledging my presence. He smiled and nodded. 'Come on then,' she said to the children. 'Bed.' They let out a moan of protest.

'Go on,' said Martin. 'Or no story.' Reluctantly, theatrically dragging her feet, Amelia joined Oliver and Fiona, then turned to give me a cheery wave before the three of them disappeared through the doorway. 'Right,' said Martin with a jovial clap of the hands. 'Drink.'

*

He was filling my second large glass of red when Fiona joined us ten minutes later in their hangar of a kitchen. He'd been chatting away about Hillview without the slightest hint that he was going to follow up on the vague 'maybe get you involved' he'd muttered when we'd looked round the house. Perhaps he thought this meal was thanks enough for saving his nuts. Again.

Fiona's entrance was Martin's signal to see to his paternal duties, which left the two of us awkwardly alone. She turned her back on me to fiddle with a pan steaming on the Aga. Dave was curled up in his basket, so no help there. Silence.

'You've got a lovely home,' I said. A lame gambit but needs must.

'Thank you.' She continued to stir the pan. More silence.

'Your work, I'm guessing.'

'Why?' She sounded curious, back still towards me.

'Well, I've been in Martin's office and he seems a lot less …' I hesitated.

'What?'

I'd wanted to say 'anal' but suspected she might – just possibly – take offence. 'Stylish,' I said.

Fiona turned her head to study me – was I being sincere? 'You know about interiors then?'

'Not really.' I smiled. 'Just know what I like.'

It was enough. Fiona perked up and for the next quarter of an hour we talked interior design. She'd been 'sort of' in that line before she knew Martin and since getting married had helped 'kit out' several of his developments.

'It's how we met, actually,' she said in her soft Irish brogue – a touch wistfully, I thought. I wanted to ask her the details – I was slowly warming to her, not least because she was more attractive than I remembered from our first meeting; I'd not noticed her green eyes, for example – but Martin came bustling in. He gave her a loud kiss on the cheek, grabbed his glass of red and drained it with a smack of satisfaction.

'Now,' he said, 'where's my dinner?'

It passed off almost without incident. We got through the first two courses easily enough and the conversation was all very polite and safe: life in Radlett and Watford, the local schools, my mugging and its aftermath. Martin hadn't been contacted yet – police inefficiency, we decided – and was keen to know the latest. But neither of them mentioned Buddhism, which was OK by me as I was feeling increasingly fuzzy as the wine slipped down. Fiona didn't say much at all, in fact, and whenever I looked over I seemed to find her cool, green eyes gazing back – sizing me up, I guessed.

The wheels came off when we got to the cheesecake and raspberries. By then Martin and I had polished off the best part of two reds and a white – Fiona drank maybe one glass the entire evening – and we'd 'relaxed' really quite a lot. I looked at Fiona through a mist of alcohol as she cut the cheesecake and decided to ask the question that had been bugging me all night.

'Have we met somewhere? You know – before?'

'No,' she said. Simply, clearly, definitely. I ploughed on.

'Only you look really familiar.' She shook her head. 'You haven't been on television, have you? Or a film?'

'Nope.' She added raspberries to the plate and passed it to me.

'She was in a brochure once,' said Martin, trying to help. Fiona's eyes flashed – a warning sign. 'A long time ago.'

'Not that long. Just before I met you!'

'Ah – he doesn't want to hear about that,' she said,

staring daggers at Martin. He didn't seem to notice. And I certainly didn't.

'No, sounds interesting,' I insisted.

'It was a holiday brochure – I've got it somewhere.' Martin pushed himself up from the table, swaying slightly.

'Martin, no – let's not. Martin, please. Martin …' Fiona's protests died away as he clumped out of the kitchen.

'So how did that happen?' I slurred. Fiona gave me a basilisk stare.

'I used to do a bit of modelling.' She made it sound on a par with juvenile shop-lifting.

'Ah. Well, perhaps I've seen you on a hoarding somewhere.'

'A *hoarding*? No – not ever.' She spat it with such cold disdain that, even inebriated, I finally realised she didn't want to go there. Too late. Martin swayed back in, brochure in hand.

'Got it. *Riviera Wales 2002.*' He handed it to me, open on a double-page spread of a deluxe caravan park set among the dunes of the Llyn peninsula. Fiona featured as the young mum of an archetypal nuclear family: having a barbecue by the caravan, exploring rock pools together on the seashore, cycling with the kids while dad plays golf; and the whole family splashing about in a water park and in the surf. It was the last two pictures that I suspected Fiona didn't want me to see.

'Fills that bikini, doesn't she?' Martin leered over my shoulder. 'Now you know why I married her, eh?' He grinned at Fiona. She was stony-faced. 'Ah, come on, Fi – it's nothing to be ashamed of. You got a lovely body.'

Fiona leaned over, snatched the brochure from my hands and slung it into the corner of the room. She nodded at my cheesecake. 'Will you be having cream with that?'

*

The evening did not recover. Fiona completely blanked Martin and when he finally tried to steer the conversation round to chanting – supposedly why I'd been invited – all she asked was whether every Buddhist drank as much as I did. I wasn't ready for that. I began to burble about how Buddhism comes in different forms and my one was about transforming desires rather than eliminating them, but she held up a hand.

'It's OK,' she said. 'Do what you like. I just wanted to know what he sees in it.' She jerked her head towards Martin, wished me goodnight and strode out.

Martin sighed, then got up and brought a bottle of brandy to the table. 'Armenian. Churchill's favourite.' He broke open the cap. 'And apologies for that.'

'Ah, don't worry,' I said as he poured generous slugs into two balloon glasses. 'We're a temperamental bunch, artists.'

'Sorry?' He handed me a glass.

'You know – moody.' Martin looked confused. 'Moody artists. We can be moody.'

'Who's "we"?'

'Me and Fiona.' Martin looked even more bewildered. 'Writer, interior designer …?'

'Fiona? She's not an interior designer. Where'd you get that from?'

It was my turn to be confused. 'Didn't she do all this?' I waved my arm vaguely at the house. 'And your—'

Martin gave a hollow laugh. 'Fiona shops,' he said. 'She spends money. Show her a room – any room – and she can spend five grand like that.' He clicked his fingers. 'Though this lot' – he waved a drunken arm at the kitchen – 'came in at more like eighty.'

'I misunderstood,' I said. I was pretty sure I hadn't but there was no point pouring more petrol on to their argument.

'What did she tell you?'

'Well, what you said, only I got the wrong end of the stick.'

Martin didn't look convinced. We sipped our brandies.

'So how'd you meet?' I was intrigued now. Had Fiona been spinning me a bit of blarney?

'Booth babe.' I looked blank. 'You know – trade show. Totty on one of the stands – waste water management. When I want to wind her up I remind her I rescued her from the bog – in both senses.' He laughed, then saw my pained smile; I was remembering what I didn't like about him. 'No, she's great, Fiona. Fantastic. Keeps my arse in line, that's for sure.'

He changed the subject. If Fiona didn't have any questions about Buddhism he certainly did, and I tried my best to answer them as we worked our way through the brandy. When I next looked at the kitchen clock it was past midnight and I was far too stewed to drive home. No problem, said Martin; the au pair was out for the evening so I could crash in her bed. Which I did – and had a weird dream.

I dreamed that I woke up in the middle of the night and saw Fiona standing by the bed, looking down at me. She was wearing a silk robe but somehow I could tell that underneath it she was naked. I said something like, 'Can I help you?' – something crass – but she didn't answer. I closed my eyes and when I opened them again – whether it was moments or hours later I don't know – she'd gone. That was it. Next thing I knew it was morning and I had a stonking hangover.

I took it into the shower, then gingerly downstairs to the kitchen. Dave greeted me by diving straight for my groin again.

'Dave – down!' He looked round to see Fiona's green

eyes glaring at him. He hesitated, then decided it was best to obey. He retreated to his basket, disappointed.

'Hello,' I said.

Fiona nodded a greeting, then turned to see to the kids, who were in school uniform, chomping through breakfast. If she *had* come into my room she was playing it very cool.

'What time did you call it a night?' she asked, more polite than friendly.

'Midnight,' I said, then gave her my quizzical 'Is there something I should know?' face. She looked puzzled.

'You OK?'

I wasn't – the smell of coffee was turning my stomach – so I said I had to get back, thanked her for the lovely meal and headed for the door.

Martin appeared just as I was leaving, padding down the stairs in a towelling robe, fresh from a bath. He'd drunk even more than me but looked pink and perky.

'You OK to drive?' he asked. 'Only you're probably still over the limit.' I said I'd risk it, thanked him for his hospitality and left.

It's a good thing I wasn't stopped on the way back. I had trouble focusing and had to wind down all the windows to clear my head with a blast of cold, wet air; it was raining yet again. God knows how much alcohol was still sloshing around my system. When I reached home all I wanted was bed; this hangover was an unpleasant reminder of a period when getting blotto was a regular event. So I pulled the bedroom curtain, stripped off and crawled under the duvet. Bliss.

I was just dropping off when my phone rang. I was going to kill it, then saw the caller and answered.

Piers – offering me a job.

Chapter Six

What a klutz. All that heartache, rage, self-pity – based on what? An assumption. False perception. A rush to judgement. While the reality had been completely different.

During the call Piers reminded me that he and Bernie had agreed to accept Martin's offer only if they got proper contracts and some of the money upfront. These had both just come through, so now he felt able to take on a couple of extra bods and I was first in the queue. I was so surprised – and choked with gratitude and relief, and remorse that I'd done him such an injustice – that I couldn't speak.

'Hello? You still there?' He sounded concerned.

I coughed. 'Yeah. Just got something stuck in my throat.' I coughed again. 'That's better. Gone now.'

'Goodo. Well, I want to get cracking asap so if you're up for it I could see you there at noon today. Got a couple of things to do first.'

'Sure.' Hangover or not, I'd be there. 'And thanks, Piers – really appreciate it.'

He laughed. 'Oh, don't worry, old man. I intend to work you into the ground.'

*

My head was still thumping when, three hours later, I pulled up outside Hillview. More wind and rain. I'd been able to grab some sleep but knew from painful experience that time was the only healer for my hangovers. This one would be with me till evening.

During the short drive I'd started musing on how I'd misjudged Piers – how I'd reacted to what I'd *believed* rather than what actually *was* – which led to another of those mini-realisations I seemed to be specialising in recently. It went like this.

A policeman comes to the door and tells me that my beautiful girlfriend – let's call her, ooh ... Constanza – has been killed in a car accident in, say, Barcelona. I feel shock, I weep and wail, spiral into a depression. Then the copper comes back a bit later and says oops, sorry, the Spanish authorities mixed up the ID and Constanza is, in fact, alive and well and on the next flight home. I perk up at once and rush to meet her at the airport, where I smother her in kisses – to her great surprise, as she doesn't know she's returned from the dead – then hurry her home to make mad, passionate love till we both fall asleep, exhausted. Say.

But the point, I realised, as I pulled the kagool hood over my head and got out of the car, is that my reaction would be the same whether the news of Constanza's death were true or false – as long as I believed it. So perception + belief = reality? Perhaps this was what Buddhism meant by 'reality is illusion' – that it's 'made' by us, consciously and unconsciously. Perception feeds belief and belief shapes perception: they support each other. And perhaps this is what it means to live in a 'parallel universe'. It's not that there are billions and billions of alternative universes existing side by side on some unseen astral plane, but that those parallel universes are *us*. We inhabit, in parallel, a shared reality that is constantly being created and re-created by our beliefs and ever changing perceptions.

Quite a thought for a short drive. No wonder I still had a headache.

I found Piers and Rachel bent over one of the diggers, wrestling with its innards. Neither machine would start, Piers explained, and Martin had gone to get new batteries. I'd just missed him.

'So what do you want me to do?'

Piers handed Rachel the spanner and led me back out to the road, where his van was parked. 'You know what bramble looks like?'

'Of course – blackberries. It was just round that bend that I was mugged.' I pointed down the hill. 'I can show you the exact bush if you like.'

'Ah, it was here, was it? I hadn't put that together, sorry.' He smiled sheepishly and unlocked the back of the van. 'Anyway, I want you to take these and chop down every last bit of bramble you can see.' He pulled out a pair of secateurs, a machete and a pair of heavy-duty gloves.

I took the tools and gloves. 'And then what?'

'Then we lay down a barrier of old carpet, so the roots will be starved of light and eventually die away. In fact, we're covering all the areas where we clear out the really tough stuff.'

I frowned. 'Won't that look odd – carpet everywhere?'

Piers laughed. 'Don't worry – we'll cover it with tons of mulch. And we only use wool carpet, so that rots away too. It's really very eco-friendly.'

'I'll take your word for it,' I said. 'But I actually meant "and then what" should I do with the stuff I've chopped out?'

'Just pile it up. We'll have a big bonfire at some point.'

So that's what I did for the rest of the day. I hacked and

slashed and chopped and yanked, as the rain lashed down, the wind dashed it into my face and the thorns found any bare patch of skin to fight back and draw blood. But in a masochistic, man-against-bramble sort of way I actually enjoyed it. It took the edge off the hangover and the rhythm of hard, physical work set my mind free to wander – and wonder. About that dream, for example. Assuming Fiona hadn't actually come into my room – and I couldn't think why she would have – I concluded that it must have been prompted by three things. First, remembering in that chanting session how Angie and I had got together. Second, seeing Fiona in her bikini in that holiday brochure. And third, Chris's silk dressing gown, which for some obscure reason was obviously still preying on my mind.

But what did it mean? Nothing, I decided. It was just a mish-mash of impressions and feelings. You could read into them whatever you wanted, like tea leaves at the bottom of a cup. Something niggled, though – a feeling that I couldn't pin down. I'd have to send out the truffle hound the next time I chanted …

I chopped out another armful of bramble and hauled it across to the pile I was building near the trees at the bottom of the garden. As I dumped it I looked back up the hill to the house and whoosh – out of nowhere, completely unbidden – I was hit by a surge of inexplicable happiness. It was cold and wet, windy; my head hurt and I was covered in scratches; and yet, without warning or explanation, this … joy – there was no other word for it – just burst inside me. Even weirder, at that exact moment the sun broke through the gusting clouds and a pencil of golden light hit the house. I looked up at the sky. The clouds were already scurrying across the gap to choke off the sunlight, as if it had somehow struggled free and had to be brought back under control. And then it was gone, like the door to a house full of warmth and life slammed shut against a cold, black night – with me outside.

But I didn't mind; quite the reverse. The moment had been all the more intense for being so brief. Dora had talked about how she sometimes had these random attacks of inexplicable happiness but I'd never really understood what she was on about – until now.

As I stood there absorbing the experience, hugging it to me, a figure in shiny yellow waterproofs appeared at the top of the hill: Martin. There was something in the way he was staring that said he was surprised to see me there. I waved cheerily and after a moment he waved back, then turned and disappeared. Did Piers tell him he was going to offer me a job? Did it matter? I decided I was in too good a mood to worry about it and returned to the battle of the bramble.

Soon I was waist-deep in a massive thicket, hacking a path to the main stem and reflecting on my sudden rush of happiness. It had passed as abruptly as the shaft of sunlight but its glow still lingered. And the more I thought about it the more I saw that it wasn't inexplicable at all. In that moment, looking up at the house, I'd sensed that my life had broken out of its little box. I was out of my comfort zone, being battered by the elements, but working hard and revelling in the effort. Enjoying life meant appreciating all of it – the bad weather as much as the good. Winning meant helping to create something real and tangible, and looking around me I could actually see the progress I was making against the brambles. It wasn't my garden, I'd probably never get the chance to sit in it and take pleasure from its finished beauty, but I was helping to create something of value and that made me feel good.

Up on the hill behind me I could see the buildings of St Catherine's. I'd come only a few short yards but it felt as if everything had changed. Not long ago I was in a rut, completely stuck, but since the mugging all sorts of possibilities, connections, relationships had opened up. I'd stopped walking round and round in a circle and had struck out on a journey. Quite where, I didn't know – yet. But I sensed that I would find out.

So that was it. I felt, somehow, that I was turning poison into medicine. It wasn't inexplicable at all. It was just a matter of joining the dots.

The site came alive over the next couple of days. The gardening crew was joined by Luis, a handsome, nut-brown Portuguese in his thirties, with jet-black hair pulled back in a little ponytail and permanent stubble. He looked like Jesus and spoke hardly any English. Not that his language skills mattered much for the first two weeks, as we did nothing but clear away the jungle that had colonised the garden in the three years it had lain undisturbed. We made short work of the remaining brambles, plus the nettles, hogwort, vetch and dandelions. The ivy was more of a problem, as was the blackthorn. But the real enemy was a huge ash tree in the grounds next door that had seeded everywhere. The seedling looked innocuous at first – just two oval leaves on a wiry stem – but it grew like a triffid. Some were already the size of small trees. Its taproot had the grip of a python and each one had to be almost quarried out of the muddy ground, sometimes by all four of us.

'*Ichinen*,' grunted Piers, as we grappled with a plant almost as tall as he was, whose slender trunk belied a sinuous, unrelenting root that seemed to reach down for ever into the sticky clay earth.

'Remind me,' I gasped, breaking off to catch my breath.

'Determination. Direction. Focus. The thing that drives your life, deep down. And this bastard' – he gave the plant a frustrated kick with his boot – 'just wants to survive. They all do.' He cast a despairing eye over the two dozen or so saplings poking up around the garden, knowing that many more smaller ones were hiding among the uncleared vegetation.

'Nuclear bomb,' suggested Rachel.

'Nuclear ...?' Luis frowned, not sure if he'd heard correctly. Piers slapped him on the shoulder.

'Don't worry, Luis. Just a small one, to loosen the root.'

Rachel laughed, her eyes sparkling, cheeks rosy-pink in the cold. Luis smiled shyly, confused. Only a matter of time before fancy blossoms there, I thought. Like Piers and Constanza but the other way around – very Latin male and very English female. Classic.

'Come on,' said Piers. 'Let's get this chap out and have a nice cup of tea.'

While we were waging war on nature Bernie had started on the house. He'd recruited a gang of five: four Poles, all cousins, for the plumbing and electrics; and natty Norris, a cheerful black guy of about my age, who'd been a professional boxer till a bad beating had convinced him it was time to take up the less perilous trade of carpentry. Bernie had graduated from bricklayer to all-round builder and pitched in wherever he saw the need. Right now he was doing the studwork with Norris, as the Poles laid the pipes and wiring throughout the house.

Martin tried to call in at least once a day but we saw him less and less. At first he was running around for digger parts; the new batteries didn't do the trick and it wasn't until the Monday of the second week that the machines fired up. Then seemingly endless meetings – with the planning people, the client's people, the money men, the architect – conspired to keep him away. But Piers and Bernie were in regular contact and, most importantly, we all got paid on time, in full.

I managed to speak to him only twice. The first time he said how surprised he was to see me working for Piers;

he'd had no idea I'd be interested in that sort of job. I made a feeble joke about doing 'on-the-ground' research for my new book, but he didn't get it.

'You're writing another book?'

'No. Actually, I'm trying to change my karma.'

But he didn't get that either. So I just came clean that Chris's rent barely covered the mortgage and I needed to eat.

The second time, I asked about the buyer and his swimming habits. I could understand wanting to swim laps uninterrupted – I'd tried a couple of public pools since losing access to the one at St Catherine's but they were always rammed with … well, the public. Swimming without bumping into a flailing child or an aged breaststroker was practically impossible. But ruining this fabulous house for that, presumably at vast cost – it didn't make sense. Martin looked at me as if I'd just flown in from Planet Naïve.

'What makes sense, Ed, is he's going to take this place off my hands. The rest? Couldn't give a shit.' Fair enough. Not how I saw it but it wasn't my problem.

'So who is he – some ginger multimillionaire?'

'No, Ginger's the agent. The rest' – Martin tapped the side of his nose – 'confidential, sorry. But if you want somewhere to swim, use my pool any time – feel free. Or the gym. Shift some of that tum, eh?' And with a friendly pat on my belly he'd driven off to another of his many meetings. Cheeky sod.

I didn't take him up on his offer. There was something about the thought of being around Fiona that I found disconcerting. Which also made it difficult getting together with Martin for Buddhist stuff. I texted him a couple of times but he found various reasons for not coming to me, and I didn't want to go there – so it didn't happen.

*

'This world is the domain of the devil king of the sixth heaven. All of its people have been under the rule of this devil king since time without beginning.'

Darren paused and looked up from the book. It was the monthly discussion meeting and all the usual suspects were there: him and Aidan, Piers and Constanza, Bernie, Jenny, Rachel and me. But no Martin. A 'business thing' had come up and his absence had diverted the discussion from 'gratitude' – what we were meant to be discussing – to 'negativity'. We were still nine though (with Bella tucked up in bed), because Piers had invited Luis, who'd obviously come along (a) out of politeness – don't offend the boss – and (b) because of Rachel. Why else sit through an hour-long meeting on an abstruse subject you know nothing about, in a language you don't understand? Constanza was translating everything into Spanish, which possibly confused him even more. Darren continued to read.

'To deceive the true mind of the Buddha nature, he causes the people to drink the wine of greed, anger, and foolishness, and feeds them nothing but dishes of evil that leave them prostrate on the ground of the three evil paths. When he happens on persons who have turned their hearts to goodness, he acts to obstruct them. He is determined to make believers in the Lotus Sutra fall into evil.'

'So the fact that Martin's not here, Ed, and you haven't been able to get together with him,' said Darren, 'is absolutely classic from a Buddhist point of view. It's the devil king having his wicked way.' He laughed, then stopped abruptly. Luis was muttering darkly in Portuguese, red in the face, shifting around as if getting ready to jump up and run. Constanza laid a restraining hand on his arm.

'Hey – *calmarse. No es así.*'

'What's up?' asked Piers.

''E say that if 'e want *o Diabo – Diablo*, devil – he would stay with Holy Mother Church. He think in England we do not go with this rubbish. *Si?*' She turned to Luis, who nodded brusquely.

'Tell him it's just a metaphor,' suggested Jenny.

'Meta ...?' Constanza looked lost. I was about to explain – the English language being my thing, of course – when Rachel reached forward and grasped Luis by the hand. Their eyes locked.

'We don't believe in the devil or demons or anything like that, Luis.' Constanza started to translate. 'Buddhism just used those words, in a different time, different culture, to explain how negativity works within our own lives. Because it's all inside here.' She patted her chest. 'Understand?' Luis held her gaze with his dark eyes, then smiled and nodded.

'I sorry. I think ...' He trailed off, embarrassed.

'Don't worry about it, sunshine.' Bernie had been watching the exchange closely, stroking his beard. 'I was raised with all that crap, too – hellfire and demons. But we're just talking about positive and negative, stuff that creates value and stuff that destroys it, or blocks it.' Constanza translated and Luis nodded again, apparently pacified.

'In fact, it's all on the Gohonzon,' said Jenny, pointing to the scroll that was the focus of our chanting. It was covered in hieroglyphics – actually ancient Chinese and Sanskrit – and housed in a little cabinet that Piers opened for gongyo. 'That squiggle down the middle,' she said, 'the big, bold one – that's Buddhahood, and the devil king of the sixth heaven is ... um ... one of the other, smaller squiggles. Do you know which one, Piers?'

'Actually, I don't – sorry. Should do.'

Constanza raised an eyebrow, unimpressed, and didn't translate. Jenny looked enquiringly at Bernie. He leaned forward.

'It's that bad boy there,' he said, pointing to a squiggle.

'Thank you,' said Jenny, with a clipped politeness that suggested they'd buried the hatchet – for now. 'The point is,' she continued, 'him being there on the Gohonzon indicates that negativity exists even in the Buddha's life. She is not a perfect being, like a god.'

'Or goddess,' said Bernie. Jenny 'smiled' at him.

'But she has learned how to transform the negativity in her life – whether it's inside her or outside, in the environment – moment by moment into something positive.'

'Poison into medicine,' said Rachel.

'Poison into medicine, the beautiful lotus flower growing out of the muddy swamp, "earthly desires are enlightenment": they're all different ways of saying the same thing,' said Jenny. 'So in the Buddha's life, fundamental darkness, negativity, actually has a positive function. It's like the grit the oyster uses to make a pearl.' And she turned to Bernie with a sweet smile.

I hadn't much warmed to Jenny before now. To my shame I'd written her off as Cat-Lady, the bitter, childless spinster trapped in a life of frustration and regret. But her speech suggested there was more to her than met the eye – my eye, that is. And I couldn't know it then but what she'd said about the devil king would soon become intensely relevant, because life was about to deliver me a bundle of big surprises.

The first was Chris. I'd been seeing more of him recently, as I had to be up earlier every day to get to Hillview and we bumped into each other in the little galley kitchen. Evenings were much the same: he got in late and quickly retired to his room, and he always disappeared at the weekend, sometimes not returning till the Monday evening.

This particular weekend, though, he announced he was going to a concert on Saturday night and would be back late 'so please don't chain the door'. No problem. All I had planned was a Chinese, a bottle of red and *Match of the Day*.

And there wasn't a problem – until I was woken at about 2 a.m. by the unmistakable sounds of vigorous rumpy-pumpy next door. Chris's room.

I was shocked – he didn't do that sort of thing. Then I was embarrassed – I felt like an eavesdropper. Then curious; every now and then I heard Chris mutter something but his partner seemed to be completely silent. And then, because it went on for quite a long time, I got really bloody irritated. This wasn't just inconsiderate: it broke all our unwritten, unspoken rules. Finally, around three o'clock, silence; though I then spent another half-hour fretting over how to tackle him about this transgression, dreading the inevitable morning moment when I'd meet his *inamorata* in the kitchen and have to pretend I'd snored right through their mattress mambo.

I woke at just before nine and listened: the house was quiet. Maybe if I got up now I could sneak down, grab some tea and cereal, and scuttle back to my room till the coast was clear.

Or maybe not.

I walked into the kitchen to find a burly, hairy-chested bloke waiting for the kettle to boil and crunching toast. In Chris's red silk dressing gown.

He jumped when he saw me, wiped his buttery hand and held it out. 'Hi,' he said with a friendly smile. American. 'I'm Scott.' We shook hands. 'Just making some tea and I'll be outa your way.'

'OK …' I wandered next door, turned on the television and started flicking through the channels. I never watch morning TV, ever. But I was in shock – again. No wonder I hadn't heard Chris's partner last night – I'd been listening for a female voice.

Scott emerged from the kitchen, a steaming mug in each hand – 'All clear!' – and headed for the stairs.

'Thanks,' I muttered.

I made myself some tea and toast and beat a retreat to my room, where I stayed till I heard them both go out, an hour or so later. The entire time my head was reeling. Chris's *inamorata* was an *inamorato*. Who'd have thought? Well, me, but only in an idle, speculative sort of way. And here was the reality: two grown men shagging in the room next to me. In *my* house. I knew I should be cool and accepting and think, hey, what's the difference, we're all just people. But I wasn't. I was disgusted.

I got down to gongyo, turning the scenario over in my mind, trying to chant through the emotion to understand my reaction. Was I not just a closet racist but a homophobe as well? Would I feel differently if it *had* been a woman with Chris next door? Be honest, Ed.

Yes, I decided, I would feel different, but only up to a point. It was the surprise, plus the lack of consideration, plus the sheer animal physicality of the thing that added up to bother me. The fact that it was two men at it just intensified those three issues. The bottom line, I concluded – and yes, I saw the pun – was that sex should be private, and kept private.

I finished my chanting feeling a bit better – at least now I knew what I thought and why – and waited for Chris's return. It might be really awkward but there was no way we could not talk about this.

It was late afternoon and already dark when he bounced in, flushed from the cold and carrying two large shopping bags; he'd bought some new clothes. 'So,' he said, hurrying over to the radiator to warm up, 'what did you think?'

I looked up from the Sunday paper. '*De quoi?*'

'Scott!' He sounded surprised that I wasn't bursting to

give an opinion. But why would I? We hardly ever spoke, and never about anything personal. I struggled to find the right response. 'Careful.' Chris wagged a finger at me. 'Because I think he might be The One.'

Eh? In less than thirty seconds he'd told me more about himself than in the whole of the previous twelve months. What was going on? I decided to play it neutral. 'How long have you known him?'

'Since June. He works over at Leavesden – you know, the studios – on *Harry Potter*. They're finishing the last one. And he lives in Hemel.'

It was a few miles away. 'Uh-huh. So is that where you've been spending the weekends?'

'Some of them, yes. But it wasn't till just recently that I thought it'd be OK to bring him back here.'

'Oh?'

'Mmm, you know – when I met Martin.'

'*Martin?*'

'Yes. Before that I, you know, *wondered* if you were, you know, gay. But when he started coming here and you went—'

'Whoa, whoa – Chris. I am *not* gay.'

His face fell. 'But you spent the night at his place.'

'I had dinner, with him and his wife.' Chris blinked, stunned. 'He's got two kids.'

'Well, that doesn't mean anything.'

'Actually, Chris, in this case it does. It means he's straight. And so am I.' He stared at me, frozen with shock, then swallowed hard.

'Last night. D-did you …?'

'Hear you?' He nodded. I nodded. He groaned and covered his face with his hand. 'It's OK. No harm done.' He shook his head, still hiding his face. 'Really, Chris, it's OK.' Because suddenly it was. All the offended, self-righteous judgements I'd been nursing since the early hours had evaporated the instant I saw the bright, cheerful man who'd breezed in a few moments ago crumble before my eyes.

Chris uncovered his face, took a deep breath and mustered a tight smile. 'Sure,' he said. He scanned the room as if desperately searching for some way to regain a scrap of dignity. 'Right, well – work tomorrow.' He picked up his shopping bags and ran upstairs.

I never saw him again.

He didn't reappear that evening and next morning had left before I got up. When I came home after work his key was on the mat, all his stuff had gone and a handwritten note was propped against the kettle.

Dear Ed,

Sorry for the short notice but I've decided to move in with Scott. He's been on at me for ages and now seems a good time. Please keep the deposit in lieu of a month's notice. Hope this is OK and you find some-one soon. Good luck with everything.

Chris

Another surprise, and one I didn't feel good about. I saw again the look on his face, standing by the radiator, when he realised he'd shown me who he truly was. Horror, fear, humiliation. How sad that he felt he had to live a life so closed and hidden, even now, when attitudes had changed so much. Or perhaps they hadn't, given Darren's experience – or my initial reaction. I wasn't proud of that. He had as much right to happiness as anyone else and I had no right to judge him. But I'd helped to drive him away. I sent him a text.

Hi Chris. Thanks for your note and sorry I didn't get

the chance to say goodbye. But all the very best to you too and I hope things work out. Ed. PS Where should I forward your post to?

He'd forgotten that detail in his desperation to escape but never texted me back. Hey ho – he was gone and I had the house to myself. Perhaps that wouldn't be such a bad thing for a while. Either way, it was another sign that things were changing.

Cue the next surprise, the very next evening. I was cooking some pasta when Piers called. Would it be OK to drop round – now?

'Er, sure. What for?'

'I'll tell you when I see you. What's the address?'

I told him, he said he'd be there in about forty minutes, the call ended. Very odd. What was so urgent that it merited a mercy dash up the M1? After all, I'd be seeing him in the morning.

'Probably not,' said Piers, when he arrived. 'I'll either be late or actually not get there at all. So I want you to have these and get on with clearing the last of the overgrowth – OK?' He gave me three keys on a fob. 'And for God's sake don't lose them. Bernie's got that one, for the main gate, but that one's for the container with all our gear in it and there's no duplicate.'

'OK. And this one?'

'For the digger, the orange one. If I'm not back when you've finished the overgrowth you can start filling in the swimming pool.'

'Erm …'

'Ah, no, you're not insured, are you? Leave it to Luis then. And he knows what to do generally, so any questions, ask him – all right?'

'Not Rachel?'

'Uh, well, Rachel might not be there either, so—'

The doorbell rang. Piers almost jumped out of his skin. Outside, a familiar voice screamed his name.

'Pierce, you fuck! Open the door!'

Constanza thumped it, hard, rang the bell again, then gave the door an almighty kick. It shook on its hinges. Piers threw me a wild, astonished look and pulled me away from the door.

'You mustn't let her in!' he hissed.

The letter-flap rattled. 'Pierce, you fuck bastard! I know you're there!' Constanza was trying to look through but there was a bristle barrier.

'Piers, what's going on?' I whispered.

He stared at the door in wide-eyed terror. 'God knows. She's gone mad.'

'I can 'ear you!' Constanza screamed through the bristles. 'She with you – bastard?'

'OK, let her in,' said Piers, backing away towards the kitchen. 'But be careful – she might have a knife.' Piers saw my incredulity. 'She went for me before I came out.'

I shook my head – this was too bizarre – gathered my composure and opened the door.

Constanza was standing in the rain with no coat, just a long woollen cardigan buttoned over her bump. A little Renault was double-parked in the narrow street behind her, yellow warning lights flashing. The instant she saw me her expression of rage flipped to surprise, then confusion.

'Ed? Why – why you 'ere?'

'I live here.'

'I told you!' Piers called from the kitchen doorway. 'I said I was going to see Ed!'

Constanza glared at him over my shoulder, then at me. 'This where he fuck 'er, eh?' She barged past me, glared at

Piers, glanced maniacally around the room, then darted over to the stairs and sprinted up. Piers shouted after her.

'What are you doing, for God's ….? Con! And where's Bella?' I looked through the open front door. Bella was in a child seat in the back of the Renault, craning round, worried, trying to see where her mother had gone. I pointed. Piers's face darkened. 'Bloody hell!'

He dashed out to retrieve her, just as a car turned into the street and crawled up behind the Renault, lights blazing, engine idling. Piers signalled to the driver that he'd deal with the blockage as soon as he got the child in his arms into the house – and hurried in with her just as Constanza came back down the stairs.

'What the hell were you thinking?' he spluttered. 'You left her in the car!'

'Give 'er to me,' Constanza said with low menace, arms outstretched. 'And don't swear, you fuck bastard.'

A car horn barped outside, hard and impatient. Reluctantly, Piers passed the bewildered, sleepy Bella to her mother. 'Give me the keys,' he said. Constanza didn't move, staring hatred at him. The horn barped again – longer this time. Piers's anger rose. 'You're blocking the road, you stupid cow.'

Constanza was about to reply, then headed for the door. At the threshold she turned dramatically. 'And you never come near us, OK? Or I keel you.'

Piers rolled his eyes and yelled. 'It's my house!' But she was already gone. I crossed to the doorway and watched as she strapped Bella – now crying – back into the child seat.

'She must have followed me,' said Piers. 'All this way. Christ. Totally bloody bonkers.'

The waiting driver flashed his headlights and barped again, provoking the finger and a torrent of angry Catalan from Constanza. She threw a last, furious glance at Piers, then got into the car, slammed the door and roared off. We watched as the brake lights glowed hard red at the end of the street, then she turned sharp left and was gone.

I closed the front door and looked at Piers.

'Sorry about that,' he said, shamefaced. 'I told her I was coming to see you – about work – but she ...' He tailed off and stared at the floor, overcome by the encounter.

'Want a cup of tea, coffee, Scotch ...?'

His eyes snapped back to me. 'No, I'd better get home – before she changes the locks or ... Christ knows.' He sighed heavily and moved towards the door. 'But please look after those keys. And if Martin visits and I'm not there just say I'm ... I don't know, getting stuff – carpet, whatever. And he should call me.' Piers had put a notice on various recycling websites and had started to accumulate rolls of old carpet in our storage container.

'OK. So that would be you *and* Rachel "getting stuff"? Cos you did say she's not going to be there either.'

Piers looked at me uneasily. 'Mmm. I think you might safely infer that, yes.' He opened the door. 'Sorry again for the scene – and thanks awfully for holding the fort.' He nodded at the keys in my hand and strode off down the road towards his parked van.

Bloody hell, I thought, watching him walk away in the rain – got that wrong, didn't I? Not Luis and Rachel but Piers and Rachel. *Rachel.* When he's got a stunner like Constanza on tap? And she's expecting their second child. And he's a Buddhist, been chanting for seventeen years! Seventeen years of developing wisdom, courage and compassion – for this?

I shut the door and shook my head. One thing was clear at least. I really didn't understand anything. Or maybe this Buddhism lark was just a bunch of bollocks after all.

Chapter Seven

'**K**arma,' said Bernie simply.

It was next morning and we were sheltering in the atrium from the incessant wind and rain. Inside, the house was being steadily transformed, with studwork growing around the bare walls, waiting to be skimmed, and door frames in place around the openings leading off the atrium. Upstairs I could hear Bernie's crew hard at work, but I was the lone gardener and feeling pretty cheesed off. Piers always brought the other two in his van and I had no idea how Luis would get here by himself. A day beckoned of solo slog in the wet.

I felt let down, betrayed almost. I'd looked up to Piers, trusted him as a man of integrity – and now he'd behaved like a total dickhead. Having an affair was bad enough – but when his partner was *pregnant*? Sheesh.

'Karma?' I snorted. 'Not the first word that comes to my mind. More like ... bastard.'

Bernie licked the gum of the cigarette he was rolling and lit it. 'His dad was a serial shagger – did you know that?'

'I did, actually.' Piers had told me about his fornicating, boozing gambler of a father when we'd been digging the grounds of an estate not far from here. Apparently, he'd lost the family's vast fortune on the horses. 'But if you're saying that means screwing around's in his genes and he can't help it—'

'No.'

'Or that he's been conditioned by his old man's behaviour, even though he's always said he hated it—'

'Nope.' Bernie lit his roll-up and drew deeply on it.

'So what *are* you saying?' I was getting exasperated.

'It's all mixed up together: nature, nurture, life, the environment. It's inseparable – and all karma.'

This was too much for my little brain to process first thing in the morning. 'He's still responsible. You can't just say "karma" and wave away what he's done – which is pretty bloody rank in my book.'

'Who's waving it away?' Bernie blew out a lungful of smoke. 'It's a mess, could screw up everything, including the job here.'

'The main thing it'll screw up is Constanza,' I said. 'And Bella *and* the new baby, probably, when it arrives.' Bernie nodded with resigned regret. 'So why do it? And as for setting an example – ha!'

Bernie picked a strand of tobacco from his lip and relit the now brown and soggy cigarette. 'A cart overturned on the road ahead is a warning to the one behind.'

I groaned. 'A Buddhist quote for every occasion, eh?' I was getting more and more wound up by his lack of outrage. 'But it's all rubbish, isn't it, if after all this time you can't actually walk the talk.'

'Who can't?'

'Piers!' I was amazed he was being so dense.

'The point, my son, ain't what *he* does. It's what *you* do.' Bernie jabbed a finger into my chest. '"Follow the Law, not the person." Another quote you can suck on.'

'And my point,' I said, jabbing a finger into his chest, 'is how can I believe "the Law", how it's supposed to give you wisdom and courage and blah-di-bloody-blah, if someone who's been doing it for years and years can't keep his pants up when it matters? And Rachel – what's she thinking of? And all the other losers—' I bit my tongue. Bernie frowned.

'What – in the group?'

He was giving me such a hard stare I thought he might hit me. 'Not all of them,' I stammered. 'I mean, obviously you've come a long way—'

'Cheers. And you'd know cos you're such a fucking winner, eh?'

Ouch. On the button. 'No, you're … Look, I shouldn't have said that. I—'

'Too bloody right. Another quote: "Misfortune comes from one's mouth and ruins him." And take it from me, cos I know!'

Norris appeared, claw-hammer in hand. 'Bernie – this partition.'

'Yeah, just coming.' Norris disappeared back into the rear of the house. 'Look, I agree, Piers has been a royal twat, and he'll have to deal with it, cause and effect. But that's his problem. Yours is dealing with this in *your* life. How do you use it – positive or negative? It's the same with everything, Ed. The rest of that quote: "Fortune comes from one's mind and makes him worthy of respect." Anyway, right now a man's got to do what a man's got to do – which is work.' He pointed at the front door – for me – and went to join Norris.

I trudged round to the back of the house and looked down over the garden. We'd cleared away most of the overgrowth and the basic shape of lawn and borders was emerging. But what had seemed uplifting a few days ago now looked just bleak and windswept. What was the bloody point? All this hard work to produce a beautiful garden – for what? A rich philistine. A man who cared so little he'd ruin a fine building just to swim his laps uninterrupted.

But even as I was thinking these gloomy, pissed-off thoughts I became aware that nothing in the garden had changed – except me. My mood. My mind. When I changed again, so would the garden. My reality depended on my perception, and belief; and memories and hopes and expectations and assumptions. My emotions. They were all intertwined, interconnected, interdependent. That's what I'd realised when I'd come up here with my hangover. It was what my old mate Geoff had tried to drum into me, but I kept forgetting ...

From inside the house I heard the Poles laughing and shouting to each other. I envied them. We'd been like that – Piers and Rachel and Luis and me. Joking and teasing one another, even when the rain had been coming down in stair rods. But that camaraderie was now blown and I was going to miss it.

The Poles started singing – and I had another realisation. The clouds didn't part this time or the sun hit me with a golden spotlight. It was more the unfurling of a thought, like a flower revealing its heart. A feeling, always there but hidden – from myself – which had just this moment found its name.

I was lonely.

I craved comradeship, joint endeavour, the company of like minds working towards a common purpose. That's what I really enjoyed about this job. It's what I'd enjoyed when I'd first met and worked with Piers all those years ago. It's what I'd loved about my friendship with Geoff.

And I craved the companionship of one person in particular, someone I'd not found yet. Perhaps that's why, in the end, things hadn't worked out with any of the Fab Four: no common purpose. Correction – no *lasting* common purpose, because for a while with each of them there must have been something that had kept us on the same track.

I turned this thought over as I collected my tools from the container store and trudged down the slope to battle the last few ash saplings, sticking defiantly out of the ground.

Sharon: first love, growing up, exploring the world and each other together, till our paths simply diverged. Kimberley: young adults away from the harbour of home, navigating a course through the squalls of university and clinging to each other for safety. Angie: sex and fun, till we sensed we were just going round in circles, with no direction at all.

And Dora? Well, she had a very clear purpose: saving the world through Buddhism. She believed that if enough people could learn to live each day with wisdom, courage and compassion, society would gradually change and, bit by bit, the world be directed towards a better, more humane and sustainable future. Sounds great – but living with her was tough. I'd tried but, in the end, Dora's purpose wasn't mine.

But what was my purpose? Aye, there was the rub. Not 'to be or not to be' but what to be? Why to be? *Man's Search For Meaning*. I loved that book. Frankl's message is that 'Life' has no 'Meaning' – you have to create it yourself, for *your* life. If you don't, you don't truly live. You just exist.

I loved the book but took no notice of it. Because just existing is exactly what I'd been doing – and I was sick of it. Sick of living in my head. Sick of analysing everything and doing nothing. Sick of marking time, hoping something dramatic would happen to change everything. Sick of waiting for something that never arrived and never would, unless … what? I had no idea. Even if I won the lottery I wouldn't really know what to do with it. Buy a house, consume more stuff, more experiences – and then what? I wanted to *make* something, create something – with a partner. But what?

I scowled with frustration and looked at the crater I'd excavated around the sapling I was attacking. It was the only way to get it out: dig down till the taproot tapered to a pencil-sized thread, then give it a mighty whack with the machete.

No wonder none of those relationships had lasted, I thought, grunting hard as I dug and dug. How can two people build anything together if one of them hasn't the. Faintest. Idea. What. It. Is. That. He. Wants. To. Build.

WHACK. The sapling released its grip. And fell.

I didn't continue the conversation with Bernie at lunch-time because Piers turned up, with Luis. The Portuguese clearly didn't know what was going on and Piers didn't want to talk, beyond asking me if it'd be OK to collect Luis from the station for the next few days and bring him up to the house.

'Sure. But why?'

'I might be away.'

'Oh?'

'Mmm, Barcelona.' He turned away to signal that this was a conversation he didn't want to have. Too late. Bernie, joining us, overheard.

'Barcelona?' he boomed. 'What – done a bunk, has she?'

Piers looked at the ground, jiggled his van keys, then offered up a pained smile and climbed back into his van.

'What about Martin?' I asked.

'We're in touch,' said Piers, turning on the engine. 'But there's loads to keep you busy – I've given Luis all the gen. And anything major, just call.' And with that he reversed out of the gate and disappeared.

Bernie shook his head and trooped back into the house. Luis and I looked at one another, shrugged, and set off down the hill to buy a sandwich.

That afternoon passed uneventfully, as did the next day. My mood brightened with Luis for company. He practised his English conversation – and me my teaching skills – as we dug up the last of the ash saplings and started to cut and lay the old carpet over the expanse of cleared border. It looked bizarre – a patchwork of faded greens and reds, worn creams and the occasional swirl of seventies orange and brown – but oddly impressive. I even started to fantasise about entering it for the Chelsea Flower Show: 'The Garden as Room Outdoors'. But by the end of the second day we'd run out of carpet with the job half done, so I sent Piers a text asking where we could get some more.

'Expect delivery tomorrow a.m.,' came the reply.

'OK,' I texted back. 'Any progress your end?'

'Don't ask,' he answered. So I didn't.

Luis and I decided to call it a day. On the ride to the station he asked for the fourth time when Rachel would be coming back, and for the fourth time I tried to explain that she'd gone, permanently, but he shook his head.

'No. You have mobile – her mobile?'

'Sorry, I don't,' I said, which was true. And I didn't expect to see her again, unless she was destined to be Constanza's full-time replacement, a swap I couldn't get my head around. Luis brooded in a dark, Latin silence.

'Perhaps we can start filling in the pool tomorrow,' I suggested, trying to change the topic back to the job that united us. He looked at me blankly, his mind elsewhere. 'Digger – tomorrow?' I mimed the bucket scooping a large dollop of mud into the waiting hole, with sound effects.

His face lit up. 'Ah – *si*.'

Sex, food and operating heavy machinery – the quickest ways to a man's heart.

Luis was in his element next morning, churning up almost as much mud with the digger tracks as he was dumping into the hole with its bucket. Despite the rain coming down in sheets he'd filled half of it within thirty minutes and I was starting to wonder what we were going to do for the rest of the day. Then Bernie appeared at the back of the house, hollering and waving. Must be the carpet delivery, I thought, and hauled myself up the soft, slippery grass to join him.

'Not bad, eh?' I shouted against the wind, cheerfully nodding at Luis's handiwork.

'We got a situation,' said Bernie, a glint in his eye. Before I could ask what, he'd turned his back on me and was heading round towards the front of the house. I splashed after him.

Waiting by the gate were half a dozen men in hard hats and waterproofs. One of them – small and red-faced, with a swollen nose covered with a network of broken veins – carried a clipboard that was protected against the wet by a clear plastic covering. The knot of a tie peeped out of the small gap at the top of his waterproof, which could mean only one thing: tie plus clipboard equals Man in Charge. Especially as the other five were built like night-club bouncers.

As I sloshed up closer I saw that outside the gate a huge low-loader straddled most of the road, hazard lights flashing.

'Hello,' I said brightly. 'What's up?' Man in Charge thrust his clipboard into my hand.

'Repossession,' he said in a thick Scottish accent. 'Diggers, that and that.' He pointed in turn to the second digger, the containers-cum-offices and the cement silo. I blinked at the clipboard, shocked. Through the plastic covering, running with water, I could make out only two words, printed on the form in large, black letters: 'Insolvency Service'.

'Who's insolvent?' I squeaked. I feared the worst.

'Bettle Brothers.'

'Who?'

'Plant hire company.'

'Ah.' Phew. Not Martin then. I looked round for Bernie. He was in the porch to the house, mobile phone clamped to his ear – calling the boss, I hoped.

'There should be two diggers,' said Man in Charge, taking the clipboard from me. As if on cue Luis appeared, looking agitated.

'Hey, Ed – is broke! Digger!'

'No – broken. It's broken.'

'*Si*. I said – broke!'

I decided not to press the linguistic point and turned to Man in Charge. 'Sounds like one's just gone on the blink. Down the hill round the back.' He swore under his breath and turned away to confer with his heavies at the gate. Luis laboured through the mud sucking at his boots to join me.

'It stop!' he said, outraged, then jerked an enquiring thumb at the bouncers. '*Quem são eles?*'

I guessed his meaning. 'Bailiffs, I think.' Luis frowned. I tried again. 'They have come to take away the diggers.'

'No!' His eyes widened.

'Yes. And that and those.' I pointed to the cement silo and the containers.

'*Porquê?*' He was scandalised. First his best toy had broken down: now it was going to be carted off completely.

I shrugged. 'I hope Martin can say why.' A car horn beeped. I went out on to the road, expecting to see his shiny BMW, but was confronted by a battered, dirty white transit: the carpet delivery.

A busy day.

For the next twenty minutes Luis and I humped the misshapen rolls into the rear of the house – no point sticking them in the containers – while Man in Charge and his team tried to figure out how to get the dead digger back up the hill and on to the low-loader. Bernie had tried to persuade them to wait for Martin but Man in Charge insisted that they had the authority to proceed regardless, so they did.

In the end, after accepting that the digger absolutely would not start, they decided the only option was to put its tracks into neutral and drag it up the hill with the second digger.

The best laid plans ...

That wouldn't start either – the damp – and when it finally did cough into life and they rumbled it down to the half-filled hole in the ground, they discovered that it didn't have enough oomph to drag the dead digger anywhere. Its tracks wouldn't roll in the mud. Then the towing chain snapped. And then Martin arrived.

I'd expected him to be furious but he was remarkably sanguine – perhaps because he felt too tired for anger; he certainly looked it.

'Huh,' he said, watching them struggling in the garden from the soon-to-be-kitchen window at the rear of house. 'Perhaps now they'll bloody believe me.'

'About what?' I asked.

Martin explained that he'd been in long-running dispute with Bettle Brothers about the diggers, which had started breaking down soon after he'd hired them. Bettle Brothers had sent out a man to try to fix them, then promised to replace them but hadn't; so in frustration Martin had offered to get them fixed at his own expense if Bettle Brothers knocked the cost off the bill. They'd refused, so he threatened to hold the diggers hostage till he got a complete refund, parking one up against the locked gates each evening in case Bettle Brothers tried to liberate them in a midnight raid. So they'd sued him in the county court, but he'd countersued; and then the original house buyer had pulled out and he'd mothballed the site. Some time later he'd heard that Bettle Brothers had gone under.

'No bloody wonder with the crap they were sending out. Serve 'em bloody right.'

So that explained how Mart could afford to have the diggers on site all this time. The only surprise was that the Official Receiver had taken so long to send someone to recover the assets. He smiled thinly at the bailiffs slipping and sliding in the mud, struggling to get the dead digger moving now the towing chain had been reattached.

'It's like the Somme down there,' grunted Bernie. He'd been earwigging throughout Martin's explanation, alongside Luis, who'd understood barely a word.

'More like Harrods' bloody flooring department,' said Martin, clocking the collage of carpet laid over half the borders. 'What's all that about?'

I explained Piers's plan. Martin raised an eyebrow but seemed willing to give him the benefit of the doubt, as long as the buyer wouldn't see anything.

'Where is he anyway – Piers? And that girl – Rachel, was it?' Luis's ears pricked up at the mention of his object of desire.

'Sourcing more carpet,' I lied.

'Christ, how much you gonna need?' said Martin. 'The atrium's jammed with the stuff.' His phone rang. He checked the display and at once his demeanour darkened. He moved away to take the call. 'What's up?'

I turned to Bernie, who was contemplating the scene in the garden, stroking his beard. 'What did you make of all that?'

'Not much, as long as we get paid,' he said. 'But once people start playing silly buggers – Piers skipping off to Barcelona, Martin keeping us in the dark – well, you never know what's coming next, do you?'

Martin rejoined us. 'All right there?' said Bernie. 'Only you looked – you know – worried. And knackered.'

'Pah, just the normal crap,' said Martin. 'There is one thing, though.'

'Yeah?'

'There's been a slight glitch in the weekly transfer from the buyer's bank to mine, so your payment won't go through till Monday. That OK?'

Bernie folded his arms, his face assuming a 'here-we-go' expression. 'What glitch?'

'Some internal transfer thing. The guy's got several companies and he's restructuring, and the account from which our payments are made is being merged with another one and the money won't be available till Monday. Same with the payment to Piers, Ed – sorry.'

Bernie gazed at him, then sniffed. ''Fraid not, Mart.'

'Eh?' Martin looked surprised to be challenged.

'Won't do. These guys upstairs' – Bernie jerked his head towards the Poles laughing and singing overhead – 'live hand-to-mouth and I promised to pay them every Friday. Today.'

'It's only for the weekend, Bernie.'

Bernie shook his head. 'Nah, mate. A promise is a promise. So it'd be best if you found the cash for them and Norris – at least – before we knock off today.' His tone was calm but the hint of menace was unmistakable, perhaps because I couldn't help remembering his violent past.

I looked at Martin, who seemed to be having the same thought.

'Fair dos,' he said with a quick smile. 'Didn't realise how on the edge everyone was. How about you, Ed?'

'Monday's fine. Luis, can you wait for pay till Monday?' Luis frowned, trying to understand. I rubbed the thumb and fingers of my right hand together. 'Money – no today. Yes – Monday. OK?'

The penny dropped. He shrugged. 'Oh. OK.' But he didn't look thrilled.

'Good, thank you.' Martin sounded relieved. 'I'll sort that by close of play. Anything else?'

'We're going to need a new digger,' I said.

'Yes …' He seemed not to have thought of this. 'Can I leave that to you, Ed? Find it online, get it delivered asap?'

'You mean go home now?'

'Yeah. You'll be paid for the full week, don't worry. And meanwhile chummy here can be getting on with something else – laying more carpet perhaps?'

We all looked at Luis, who did a perfect impression of Manuel in *Fawlty Towers*. '*Que?*'

Finding another digger was easy enough; hiring it wasn't.

I tracked down three firms within a few miles' radius of the site but naturally they all wanted a deposit before parting with any machinery. I called Martin, who reluctantly gave me his company credit card details, but when I tried to close the deal with the first hire company I hit a snag: the delivery address.

'Hillview? That's near Watford, yeah?'

'Yuh, right by St Catherine's Academy.'

'This wouldn't be for MBU Properties?'

'That's the one.' Named after Martin's initials – Martin Brian Upton.

'Sorry, mate – no can do.'

'Oh? Why?'

'You Mr Upton?'

'No, an employee.'

'Well, I suggest you ask him then.'

And he hung up. Hmm. I tried the second firm and once again got as far as the company name before hitting the buffers.

'Oh,' said the girl on the other end of the line and asked me to hold. After a long silence she came back to tell me that sorry, they couldn't do business with us. Why? She didn't know – we were just 'on their list'.

'What – a blacklist?'

'I'm sorry, we can't help you.' She sounded flustered.

The third company solved the mystery. This time I asked upfront if they'd have a problem hiring out a digger to MBU Properties. The guy just laughed.

'Ha! Too right, sunshine.'

'OK,' I said. 'No skin off my nose – just doing my job. But could you say why?'

'You heard of Bettle Brothers?' he asked.

'Um …' I thought it best to play dumb.

'Well, they were friends of mine,' he continued. 'Friendly rivals. We all know each other in this business. Family firm, not very big. And your boss helped bankrupt them – wouldn't pay his bills. So you'll have to go a long way to find someone to hire you even a shovel. All right?'

He wasn't wrong. MBU Properties seemed to be on the blacklist of every plant hire company in south-east England. By lunchtime I'd been turned down eleven times. I called Martin again, explained the problem to his voicemail and asked if he wanted me to source a digger from further afield – at more expense.

Now what? I looked out of the window. The sky was black-grey, the wind howling and the rain almost horizontal. No way did I want to go back to Hillview in that.

I called Bernie and told him about the blacklist. He grunted but said he hadn't had any trouble himself because he ordered from his own suppliers with cash Martin advanced him.

'This isn't sounding good, though, is it?' A small knot of anxiety was starting to harden in my stomach.

Bernie snorted down the line. 'Ed, when you been in this game as long as I have nothing surprises you. The only thing that matters to me is: am I safe, are my guys safe, are we legal and are we gonna get paid? So it all comes down to if Martin turns up with our dosh at close of play.'

'The bailiffs still there?'

'Nah – just gone. Took one digger, coming back next week for the bust one and the rest of the stuff.'

I wondered about coming back for the afternoon but Bernie told me he'd felt sorry for Luis, struggling in the rain with a roll of sodden carpet, and had driven him to the station to go home. He'd even slipped him twenty quid to help him over the weekend. So if I had any sense I'd stay dry and make up the half-day when – or if – Martin came through with the money.

Sounded good to me. 'OK, see you on Monday. And I hope you get your cash.'

He didn't. He called at about five o'clock with the news that Martin had just been on the phone, incredibly apologetic, to say he couldn't pay them today. Something urgent had come up and he'd missed the bank, but he'd arranged a transfer to Bernie's account that would be credited tomorrow, Saturday.

'What did you say?'

'I told him if it wasn't he wouldn't see us again – and he'd be on another blacklist.'

'Why couldn't he just get your money from a cashpoint?'

'It's nearly four grand, mate.'

'So what do you reckon?' The knot in my stomach was starting to tighten again.

'Fuck knows. But my guys are pissed off and it's me on the hook for their wages. So it's very simple: no money, no work. And I'm going to stick in a load of Ds this weekend so whatever happens, something good comes out of this – if possible.'

Ds was shorthand for *daimoku*, another word for chanting. 'Did you suggest that Martin do some too?'

'Course. Not sure it went in though.'

I wanted to call Martin myself, there and then, but just as I was pressing the button I decided I'd better put in a few Ds first, too. Dora sometimes chanted for hours to prepare herself for big decisions or important events, which I'd always thought was pretty excessive. Now, though, I was starting to understand. It was like clearing the mind, clarifying what was important, how you felt and why. And overcoming the fear. Because often that's what's at the heart of these things. Fear of saying the wrong thing, making the wrong decision, screwing up in some way that will make things worse. Which was the last thing I wanted to do when I talked to Martin.

If things were indeed that bad. Because, as I chanted, I realised there was no real evidence they were. The diggers being repossessed and the blacklist were leftovers from past events, while the glitch with the money could be just that – a glitch, for exactly the reasons Martin had given. None of it was proof his affairs were on the slide.

As I chanted on I became aware that the knot in my

stomach had dissolved. I even felt cheerful again, as if I were back in control – of my emotions, if nothing else. It really was very odd, this chanting thing; that it could make me feel better and think more clearly, even though nothing objectively had changed at all. Just like when I was working in the garden: it was hell or heaven simply according to how I felt about it.

There was no reply from Martin's mobile when I called so I tried the landline. Fiona answered and sounded quite friendly. She'd get him to call as soon as he was out of the shower, but they didn't have much time as they were heading into London for the theatre. Huh – no way is he going to call me back, I thought. At which point he came on the line.

'Ed. Let me guess – Bernie's been on to you. Or is it the digger?'

'Hi, Mart. Well, both really. I was just wondering what's happening.'

He laughed. 'The world's falling apart, Ed. Snafu: you know, situation-normal-all-fucked-up. But apart from that everything's hunky-dory. Ask Fiona – she's seen this hundreds of times. Haven't you, Fi?'

I heard her faintly in the background. 'Lots, yes.'

'There you go,' said Martin. 'Par for the course. So just leave it to me, OK? You have a nice weekend, stop worrying and I'll see you on Monday – all right?'

'Bernie'll get his money tomorrow?'

'Yeah, yeah.'

'And the digger?'

'We'll sort it on Monday, Ed. Right now we're off to *Les Mis*, third time. Fi's favourite – isn't it, darling?' I heard her murmur in the background. Martin broke into song. 'Can you hear the people sing, singing the song of angry men ... See you Monday, matey. Bye!' He hung up.

Well. Either he was a bloody good actor or Bernie and I really were worrying about nothing.

Saturday morning brought something else to worry about: a letter from St Catherine's. It was signed by the chair of the governors and informed me that the Adamolis' insurance company was claiming from the school the cost of Valeria's ongoing medical treatment in Italy, plus the air ambulance home, plus compensation for her 'distress'. The school had referred the claim to their insurance company, which was querying it on the grounds of possible 'failure of duty of care' and wanted to interview me. Refusing to comply with this request 'could have serious consequences', so I might 'deem it prudent to take legal advice'.

Bloody hell. I'd forgotten about all this; or rather, I'd pushed it to the back of my mind and hoped it had simply gone away. Fat chance. Karma doesn't go away, does it? That's the whole point. You make the cause: at some point you must get the effect.

I was worrying about the potential ramifications of this 'interview' when my phone rang. Another piece of karma: the police, with news of the case against Big Boy and Smiler. They'd appeared at the local magistrates' court yesterday and – surprise, surprise – had pleaded guilty to the attack on me and the guy they'd followed off the bus.

'Well, that's a relief,' I said. One less thing to worry about. 'What did they get?'

'Community service,' said the copper. 'Both tagged, curfewed for six months, and they've got to pay you compensation – twenty-five quid each.'

'Is that all?'

The copper laughed. 'It's a twenty-to-one return on what they stole from you.'

'No, the community service. I mean, they battered the other bloke.'

The copper sympathised. 'Yeah, but first offence though, for both of them. Doesn't mean the first time they done it, of course, just the first time they got caught. And they're both juveniles, so ...'

'Oh. Right. Well, thanks. At least it means I don't have to testify.'

Plus it probably explained why Martin hadn't been called in for an ID parade; the boys must have put their hands up pretty quickly. The copper said my compensation would turn up in due course and asked if I'd consider getting involved in a restorative justice process, where I'd meet face-to-face with the offender and explain how I felt about what they did.

'Right. The point being ...?'

'A lot of these boys don't really understand what they've done, and being confronted with the victim can stop them doing it again sometimes – quite often, in fact. There's a trained person in there too, so you're not alone.'

That sounded interesting. I could give Big Boy and Smiler a verbal kicking if nothing else – and in safety. I told the copper to put my name down, he said the local youth offending team would be in touch if the lads agreed – it had to be voluntary on both sides for it to work, apparently – then he wished me well and left me to it.

So that was something to look forward to. In the meantime, though, what to do about this Valeria thing? It sounded pretty bloody scary.

But it was trumped by what came next.

It was past six, already dark, and I was listening to the news on the radio when my phone rang: Bernie, in a right lather. He'd been checking his bank account online every hour during the day but the money hadn't shown up. He'd also been trying to call Martin but kept getting his voice-mail. So did I have his landline number or, better still, his address?

'What – to go round there?' I was alarmed.

'Why not?'

'You going to beat it out of him?'

'Oh, do me a favour. I'm just going to be ... assertive.'

I didn't like the sound of that. 'If he hasn't got it, Bernie, he hasn't got it.'

'Well, we'll see, won't we? So you gonna give me his address or not?'

'Not.'

The last thing that would do us any good was an angry, possibly violent, exchange between Bernie and Martin on the latter's plush doorstep. There was a pause as Bernie processed my response.

'OK,' he said evenly, 'what about the landline?'

I gave him the number, wished him luck and he rang off. He called back two minutes later – no reply.

'Must be out,' I said. Bernie was silent. I could him hear him breathing heavily, thinking.

'Right – that does it. I'm pulling the plug.'

'What do you mean?'

'I'm going up there – now – and getting all my gear, tools, wood, board, everything, and pulling out.'

'Now?'

'Yeah. I got a feeling he's gonna pull a fast one, like with Bettle Brothers. Change the padlocks or something and shut us out.'

'He wouldn't do that.'

'Really? Why not?'

Good question. In fact, it's exactly what he'd done when his internet business went under back in 2000, leaving all his employees locked out of the office on the street, me included.

Bernie continued. 'Here's another quote for you, Ed. "Men on the brink of ruin are capable of anything." And I think that's where he is – on the brink. So if you got anything up there I suggest you do the same.'

'Well, there's only a few tools, a wheelbarrow …'

'All right, I'll bring them for you.'

'You can't – they're locked in our container, and I've got the key.' Luis and I had gone straight to the digger the previous morning and not used them.

There was nothing for it. I agreed to meet him at Hillview in half an hour to collect Piers's tools and help him load his stuff.

For the first time in a long while it hadn't rained that day, but the evening air was cold and wet and still. A film of fine droplets kept misting the windscreen as I drove, and by the time I climbed the hill to the site a heavy fog had settled, blurring the orange streetlights and forcing me to crawl along in second gear. As I pulled up outside Hillview a pair of headlights appeared through the murk ahead of me. Bernie. We parked nose to nose and got out, our breath condensing in the chill air.

'Ill met by moonlight, proud Titania.'

Bernie was not in the mood for levity. He scowled and pointed. 'That his car?'

Through the thick darkness I could just make out Martin's BMW parked hard against the gate.

'Looks like you were right,' I said. 'He's up to something.'

'Let's go and have a chat, eh?'

'Hang on.' I fetched a torch from my car and switched it on. The beam bounced off the fog, bathing Bernie in a glow of gentle white. 'Very soft focus,' I said.

'In,' he growled, pointing at the gate.

I squeezed past the BMW – the bonnet was warm – pushed open the hoarding and shone the torch at the house. It shimmered, ghostly in the fog, but the windows were dark. No sign of life – or Martin.

'Come on,' said Bernie. He went on ahead and I followed, picking out a path through the mud with the torch beam. At the threshold we paused. The front door hadn't been hung yet and a line of wet, muddy footprints led through the opening into the vestibule and beyond. Bernie stepped inside and called.

'Martin! It's Bernie! And Ed!' Silence. He turned to me. 'Give us the torch.'

I handed it over and he shone the beam along the line of footprints, which glistened across the concrete floor of the atrium to the stairs leading down to the basement. Bernie advanced, me behind, and called again.

'Martin! We want to talk about what's going on! So don't play silly buggers, all right – we just wanna talk!'

No reply. We reached the top of the stairs and Bernie shone the torch down into the blackness. The footprints were fainter but still visible. We looked at each other, puzzled.

I nodded at the stairs. 'After you.' Bernie frowned. 'You've got the torch.'

He sniffed, then started carefully down the curving concrete steps. I stuck close behind, straining to see I was placing my feet safely. Bernie called out a third time – like whistling in the dark, I thought.

'Martin, what the fuck you playing at? We know you're down here.' We stopped and listened. Still no response. 'Martin?'

We set off again. A dozen more steps and we were at the bottom. Bernie swept the torch around. Bare concrete walls – and a glint of light.

'What's that?'

'Where?'

I took the torch and shone it towards the centre of the space. A flash of glass. We went over and I picked up an empty brandy bottle.

'Armenian – his favourite.'

I showed it to Bernie, who frowned, uneasy. He took the torch back and swept the beam across the floor.

'Footprints have gone.'

He shone the beam back to the foot of the stairs, then to the right – and froze. I gasped.

Under the stairs, hanging from a short rope, was Martin.

Chapter Eight

Two hours later Bernie and I were sitting in the bleached white light of the A&E waiting area at Watford General.

Around us the detritus of a Saturday night was starting to accumulate: a lolling drunk with a gashed head; a young man, also drunk, with a hand bloody from a fight; a young woman who looked out of it on drugs, attended by an anxious friend; a plump, matronly black woman fussing over her wizened, white-haired father; a stocky, middle-aged guy in muddy football kit, hobbling around on a twisted ankle and complaining every few minutes that he'd been waiting since four o'clock and when the bloody hell was he going to be seen? And a young policewoman, keeping an eye on me and Bernie.

Beyond the dirty plastic swing doors opposite us, a team of medics was fighting to save Martin's life.

Bernie had been brilliant. A moment of shock, then he'd dashed over to Martin and grabbed him round the legs, heaving him up to take the weight off the rope. I'd been bloody useless, rooted with horror till Bernie's yell to get the rope from off Martin's neck had startled me awake, forced me forward – but I couldn't reach the knot. Bernie had screamed at me to get something to cut it, so I'd vaulted back up the stairs, leaving him in the dark bearing all that dead weight – and I had thought that Martin must be dead.

I'd hit 999 on my phone as I ran across the atrium and out into the fog, gabbling to the operator that we needed an ambulance at Hillview, fast, someone had tried to hang himself. Then I'd fallen in the mud before reaching the container. Shaking violently, I'd fumbled the key into the padlock, pulled open the heavy metal door, shone the torch into the blackness, grabbed the machete, stumbled back through the mud, into the house, across the atrium – all the while gasping out details, the address, my name, to the operator.

The signal had died as I descended back into the basement, back to Bernie – and the body.

I'd slashed the rope with the machete and we'd laid Martin down. Then Bernie had started pounding away at his chest, blowing air into his mouth, forcing me to take a turn – horrible, pointless, I thought. He's fucking dead, so why go on? But he was still warm, so there was hope. That's what Bernie had said.

And two minutes later – literally – a paramedic had turned up. We heard him shouting in the atrium and I'd rushed up with the torch to guide him down. He was on a motorbike, he'd explained, and was on his way home, less than a mile from where we were, when he'd got the call. An ambulance was coming too. He got to work on Martin at once, shocking him with a defibrillator and, amazingly, got his heart and breathing going again.

After that it was all a blur. The ambulance had turned up, and the police, and after stabilising his heartbeat they put Martin on a stretcher and lifted him up to the surface. Getting him through the gate was a problem – his BMW was in the way. So they'd had to fish through his pockets for his car keys. Then the young policewoman had moved it, they'd loaded him into the ambulance and sped off, blue light flashing silently till it disappeared into the fog.

The police took our details and wanted to know what we were doing there in the first place. They wouldn't let us take away our stuff and confiscated the site keys as this was a potential crime scene, they said. Bernie almost lost his rag at this – 'We saved his fucking life!' – but I put a hand on his arm and he shut up.

We'd been sitting here over an hour now. Hardly speaking. In shock, I suppose. I kept playing the loop of what had happened in that basement. Perhaps Bernie was too. And when it stopped for a moment all I could see was Martin's kids, dripping wet from the pool, snickering at us chanting, Amelia wriggling and giggling in his arms. And—

A baby-faced Chinese doctor – he looked barely twenty – pushed through the swing doors and glanced round the waiting area. His eyes fell on me and Bernie.

'Martin Upton?' His cultured English accent belied his looks. We hauled ourselves to our feet, stiff from the plastic seats, and the young policewoman came forward. 'You found him, yes?' We nodded. He glanced at the policewoman and hesitated, then moved away to a quiet corner. We all followed.

'He has a wife, family?'

'My colleague's trying to contact her,' said the young policewoman.

The doctor nodded. 'OK. Well, he's stable and we've sent him up to the ICU but that's all I can tell you for now as we really need to talk to the wife.'

'Any point us waiting?' said Bernie.

'Up to you,' said the doctor. 'But nothing's going to happen in the short term.'

At that moment Fiona burst into the waiting area, wild-eyed and desperate, the other copper who'd been at the scene close behind.

'Fiona.' I took a step towards her but she whirled round and screamed at me.

'What have you done? Where is he?'

I drew back, startled. The Chinese doctor came forward.

'Mrs Upton? I'm Dr Chu. I've been treating your husband. Shall we ...?' He gestured at a doorway leading into a small office – the bad news room, I guessed. Fiona stared at him, disorientated. 'I can explain the situation,' he continued. 'In private.' Fiona hesitated, then hurried into the office. Dr Chu followed and closed the door.

The PC who'd brought her – a thickset guy in his thirties – turned to me and Bernie. 'OK, gents. Best if we take statements while it's still fresh. All right?'

I thought it would be straightforward and quick, but I was wrong.

We drove to the cop shop, ten minutes away, and were taken into separate rooms to dictate our statements. But when they ran my name through the computer they turned up the mugging and the fact that Martin had been a witness; and despite my lengthy explanation the thickset copper seemed to find it difficult to accept that we'd known each other from years before and that Martin had then given me a job at Hillview.

'Bit of a coincidence, wasn't it?' he said. 'Him turning up like that.'

I agreed – it was. But life is strange sometimes.

'And then you turn up at the house tonight, to collect your tools, and you just happen to find Mr Upton attempting suicide – another coincidence.'

'Yes.' His eyes bored into mine, unblinking. I frowned,

starting to feel irritated. 'Are you saying that we're involved in this?'

'I'm not saying anything, sir. I'm just trying to understand. We come across a situation like this on a Saturday night, three people on a dark building site – it's not exactly normal.'

'Well, it's what happened. We found him, we called 999, the paramedics arrived, then you guys.' He held my gaze for a moment longer, then glanced down at the statement.

'And Mr Stevens – how long have you known him?'

I sighed. This was tedious. 'I told you. I met him about ten years ago and recently met him again through a Buddhist group we both attend.'

'And Mrs Upton – why did she shout at you like that, do you think? "What have you done?"'

I shrugged. 'Shock?' At that moment it was an easier answer than guessing at Fiona's tangled logic.

The thickset copper gave me another long, searching look, then sniffed and relaxed into routine police patter.

'Right. I'm going to read back your statement and if there's anything you want to change, just say. I'll make the correction and you initial it. And when you're satisfied it's your full statement, you sign and date it at the end. OK? Any questions?'

Yes, lots. But not for him.

Bernie was outside, smoking a roll-up, when I was finally buzzed through the security door to fresh air and freedom. We'd been there almost two hours. I joined him on the front step.

'Hi.' Bernie just grunted in reply. 'You all right?'

'No, I'm fucking not,' he said. 'All my gear is the wrong side of that fucking padlock and these bastards won't say when I can get it back. No gear, no work. I'm fucked.'

'Have you got some more work?'

'That's not the fucking point.'

I let him cool for a moment. 'They seem to think we might have something to do with it.'

'Yeah, well, fuck 'em. We saved him.'

'If he pulls through.'

Bernie glanced at me, then chucked away his roll-up, agitated. 'Look, I'm pushing off.'

'You don't fancy a drink? I got booze back at mine.'

'Mate, I could do with several. But I gotta drive. And I gotta get in some Ds first, cos this whole thing has …' He looked up and down the street, searching for the words to express how he felt. He didn't have to.

'I know,' I said. 'Me too.'

Bernie smiled grimly and slapped me on the arm. 'Look after yourself. And keep in touch. And if you hear anything, let me know – OK?'

'Sure.' He headed for his van. 'What about Piers? Shouldn't he know?'

'I sent him a text.'

'And?'

'Still waiting.' Bernie unlocked his van, climbed in and, with a nod, drove off.

As soon as I got home I opened a bottle of red. I should have done some chanting, like Bernie, but I didn't want to raise my life state. I wanted to numb it.

I worked my way through the bottle, slumped in front of *Match of the Day*, but the football was just colour and movement, dancing across the screen. I remembered that after my father died my mother would leave radios playing and lights on around the house, whether she was in the room or not. And when I chided her for wasting electricity she told me to mind my own business. It took me a while to realise that it was the sense of life she wanted – voices, warmth, energy. Which is what I wanted too, right now, watching football, because I felt empty and exhausted, desolate. And bewildered.

Last night Martin had been cheerful, carefree, out at the theatre with Fiona. This evening he'd tried to kill himself. Maybe succeeded. Six minutes without oxygen and there's virtually no hope – that's what the paramedic had said. And even if by some miracle he did survive there'd be major damage. The brain.

But how long had he been hanging there? The car bonnet was still warm, his body too. Then there was the brandy bottle. It looked as if he'd prepared everything, then got himself drunk enough to do the deed. Dutch courage. Or Armenian. Which means we must have found him not long after he ... a sudden image of Martin throwing himself into the black space of the basement flashed into my mind. Swinging, choking, gasping, eyes bulging, legs kicking, panic, no way back ...

I screwed up my eyes and shook my head, desperate to wipe away the picture, blank my mind. I couldn't. I opened them wide to stare at the TV, Rooney on the ball, to Carrick, Evra, Giggs, tackle, throw-in, Fletcher, Carrick, half-time.

What was he thinking? With kids, two lovely little kids. What was Fiona going to tell them? Christ, what a thing to lay on your loved ones. The ultimate act of anger, some people called it. But was it for Martin?

I remembered a guy I'd met at a dinner with Dora, a prison governor. He'd almost not come along because an inmate had topped himself that morning and he wasn't in the mood for dinner-party chit-chat. What struck me was him saying that this prisoner had only two weeks left on his sentence; in a fortnight he'd have been free. 'So why on earth did he kill himself?' I'd asked in my innocence.

Because it's not the length of the sentence, the governor had said, it's the depth of the despair. And outside prison this man had nothing. No one. No hope.

It's not the length of the sentence, it's the depth of the despair.

Poor Martin. Poor, suffering bastard. To do that. And poor Fiona. Poor Amelia. Poor Oliver. I wanted to call Fiona, tell her how sorry I was, how sad. But I didn't think she'd want to hear from me. Plus I was probably drunker than I thought.

I fetched a second bottle from the kitchen and poured another glass. I'd feel like shit in the morning but I didn't care. I had the whole of Sunday to recover. And Monday – no job now. And Tuesday, Wednesday, the rest of the week. The rest of my life, if I wanted. Not like Martin. Martin was dead. I knew it, in my gut. No way had we got there in time. No way. He was dead.

I did feel like shit in the morning – for most of the day in fact. But in a funny sort of way I didn't mind the nauseating, swirling hangover. As I drifted in and out of sleep my jumbled thoughts told me I was punishing myself for what Martin had done; that somehow I'd let him down or got him into something over his head or—

The doorbell rang. Or did I dream it?

It rang again – long, shrill, insistent. I groaned and pulled the duvet over my head. No one came calling on a Sunday afternoon apart from the Jehovah's Witnesses. Then my phone trilled. I reached out, retrieved it and focused blurry eyes on the display: 'Unknown number.' I fumbled for the answer button – and mystery solved. It was the police. Outside. Wanting to talk to me.

I opened the door in my dressing gown, unshaven, unkempt, head spinning and stomach churning. On the doorstep were two men, one short, close-cropped, about my age, with twinkling blue eyes and carrying a brown folder; the other younger, taller, leaner and meaner. At least, that was my instant sense of him, from his sharp cheekbones and unsmiling demeanour. Good cop, bad cop. They flashed their ID cards as the older man spoke.

'DC Horton – and this is DC Kelly. Mind if we come in?' I stepped aside to let them pass. 'Sorry to disturb,' he said cheerily as I closed the door. 'Late night?'

'Mmm.' I was wary of opening my mouth. Two plain-clothes coppers couldn't be good news. Plus I was afraid I might spew at any moment.

'We want to talk about Martin Upton.' DC Horton smiled. 'If you've got a moment?'

'Sure. How is he?'

DC Horton's smile disappeared. 'I'm afraid he died this lunchtime. Or to be more accurate, his life support was switched off, with his wife's permission. I'm sorry.'

A wave of sadness engulfed me. It's what I'd been expecting but emotionally I was still unprepared. I sat heavily on the edge of the sofa.

'You OK?' DC Horton looked concerned.

'Not really,' I said, massaging my eyes pricking with tears, then my cheeks and forehead with strong fingers. DC Horton continued.

'According to the medics he was brain-dead on arrival and basically the docs kept him going till his wife could, you know, bring herself to accept it.'

How fucking terrible. Poor Fiona. So that's what the baby-faced Chinese doctor had taken her into that room to explain. And she'd tossed and turned on the decision all night. Or maybe Amelia and Oliver had crawled into bed with her and they'd all fallen asleep weeping. Only for Fiona to wake early, pace around, drink black coffee, then set off to the hospital to decide the inevitable.

'Do you mind if I put some clothes on?' I said. 'Only take a couple of minutes.'

'Course,' said DC Horton.

DC Kelly was loitering on the landing as I came out of my bedroom a few minutes later – keeping an eye on me? Irritated, I went into the bathroom, splashed cold water over my face and brushed my teeth, preparing for battle, because that's what I was expecting. I joined DC Kelly back out on the landing and led the way downstairs. DC Horton was studying my bookshelves.

'Quite a reader,' he said. I ignored the comment and sat in the armchair. They sat side by side on the sofa, at right angles to me.

'Look,' I said, 'am I a suspect or something? Because if I am shouldn't we do everything at the police station with, you know, a solicitor?'

DC Horton studied me for a moment before answering. 'At this point, sir,' he said, 'the death's being treated as what we call "sudden and unexplained". So there are no suspects because we don't know what's happened.'

'He hanged himself. We found him hanging from a rope. What's unexplained – unless you think we put him there?'

'Suicide's a definite possibility. But we don't take any death at face value.'

'You haven't found a note then?' DC Horton shook his head. 'All right,' I said, bracing myself. 'How can I help?'

'We're trying to understand exactly what happened last night,' said DC Horton. 'What led up to it.' He took a bundle of papers from the brown folder. 'In your statement you said you thought Mr Upton had money problems.' He leafed through to the relevant page, found the sentence and read. '"I believe he did this because he was in debt and was going to lose everything." Could you tell us about that?' He smiled encouragement.

I told them everything, starting at ItsTheBusiness.com so they could see it all in context. With their questions it took more than an hour.

DC Kelly looked up from the notes he was taking. 'So the diggers being repossessed, the blacklist, the fact that he couldn't make the wages – you think it all built up and pushed him over the edge?'

I shrugged. 'Looks like it. Plus the fact it was all a secret from his wife. And God knows what else he's got hidden in the cupboard.'

'Oh?' DC Horton perked up.

'Martin played his cards close to his chest. I don't know if he was ever totally honest with anyone.'

'Not even you?' I shook my head. 'But you were his guru.'

'Eh?'

DC Horton frowned. 'Wasn't that the deal? He thought Buddhism would get him out of a jam, like the last time, and you were the teacher.'

I smiled sadly. 'I think Martin saw Buddhism as a sort of magic spell or something, and I had the secret.'

'And that's not how you see it?' DC Horton sounded curious.

'No,' I said. 'For me it's all about challenging how you think. How I think. My attitude to stuff, and behaviour. And if it's negative, changing it.'

'So Mr Upton thought the Buddhism had failed him then, did he? Because killing yourself's about as negative as it comes. If that's what he did.'

DC Kelly was nothing if not blunt. But perhaps he was right.

'I don't know,' I said. 'I tried to encourage him but ...' I was going to say 'I failed', but choked on the words as a spasm of regret gripped my chest. I coughed to hold back the tears.

'Interesting.' DC Horton looked out of the window, thoughtful. The dirty, slate-grey sky was turning black with the approach of evening. Silence. He seemed to come to a decision.

'Do you know a man called Colin McLellan?' He looked at me.

I thought. Did I? I shook my head.

'How about Gregorios or Greg Stylianou?'

'No.'

'Don Daley?'

I shook my head again. 'No. Who are they?'

The two men exchanged a glance. DC Kelly had been studying me hard as his colleague recited the names. He signalled his agreement with the slightest of nods.

'Stylianou was negotiating to buy Hillview,' said DC Horton. 'Greek. Colin McLellan was the middleman between him and Mr Upton.'

'Ah. Is he ginger – McLellan?'

DC Horton looked surprised. 'Yes, why? Have you met him?'

'No. But Martin mentioned a ginger bastard when he was trying to sell the place.'

'Right …' DC Horton seemed thrown off his stride. He recovered. 'And Don Daley is on the council, in Hertswood.'

I pulled a face. 'All news to me.'

'Mr Upton never mention them – any of them?'

'Nope.'

'You're sure?'

'Yes. Why?'

DC Horton wouldn't say. Not long afterwards they thanked me for my time and pushed off.

Something was up, obviously. But enough to drive

Martin to suicide – or even get him killed …? The latter seemed so ridiculously fanciful I dismissed it at once.
Bernie and I had found him and not for a second did we
think anyone else had been involved.

I picked up my phone to call Bernie but hesitated.
Maybe the police were tracking my calls, or would check
afterwards; you can't do anything these days without leaving some sort of digital footprint. And even though we
were both totally innocent a call might look suspicious – if
someone were watching … I looked out of the front window but saw no one – of course. So I just sent him a text
saying that Martin had died without coming round and
would he pass it on to Piers and the others in the group;
I didn't feel up to talking just now. A few minutes later he
sent a reply. 'Will do. V sad – but not a surprise. Call whenever you can. Bx'

By now it was fully dark; the streetlights had clicked
on, casting a glow of false warmth along the road. Time to
pop out for a bottle of red. My hangover hadn't completely
faded but I knew that before long I'd be ready for a glass
or two. Or more. Hair of the dog. Despite the sickness,
the thumping head, the wasted day in bed, I had a strong
urge to do it all again; to seek unconsciousness, if only for
a while. And deep down, I knew that something in me was
slipping. I could feel it.

I went upstairs to my bedroom. The bed was a crumpled
mess. Checking in the mirror I saw that my face wasn't
much better. My chin was rough with stubble, my eyes were
black pits deep in their sockets, my hair was exploding at
all angles, as if I'd stuck a finger into the plug socket. What
must the cops have made of me?

My eye fell on my cue card: *Enjoy life. Win.*

Ha. Some joke.

I turned my back on it, found my trainers by the bed

and sat down to put them on. But the card kept nagging away, just out of my eyeline. I sighed, reached for it and stared at the words.

Enjoy life. Win.

What did it mean – really? I'd written it down and I still hadn't a clue. Except that getting wasted surely couldn't be part of it. Well, maybe now and then, in a happy way, if there was something to celebrate. But not like this. Not this grim, focused, deliberate ... choice.

Another realisation. That was it: choice. I choose. Positive or negative. Dark or light. Challenge or – what? No challenge. Submission. Defeat. Despair ... Death.

This was the choice Martin must have faced. Fight or flight. Joy or despair. Life or death. And he'd chosen death. Except he must have believed he had no choice, that there was only one way ... pointing to the exit. That's what negativity does for you: cuts the options, closes things down, especially your mind.

I looked at the card again: *Enjoy life. Win.*

What if I flipped it, turned each word to its opposite?

Suffer. Death. Lose.

Martin's fate, to a T. Submit to the negative and that was the ultimate destination. And if not literal death, then metaphorical death – of hope, enthusiasm, creativity. All of which meant that to enjoy life and win you had to challenge. *I* had to challenge. There was no alternative. No escape. So no red wine – not tonight, anyway.

I put down the card and started to chant. I didn't want to – I wanted to get drunk – but I felt I must. And very soon I felt something stirring within me, as if a rusty generator were slowly turning and gradually, painfully, gathering speed, creating energy and focus. And then I was lost in my thoughts.

OK, I reasoned, to enjoy life and win you had to challenge.

No challenge, no joy. Or perhaps to challenge *was* to enjoy life and win – cause and effect bound together? Except lots of people faced severe challenges just to survive. The joy wasn't automatic. So you had to challenge from a high enough life state. Which meant that the fundamental challenge must be to raise your life state. My life state.

It always came back to that. Just what Dora used to tell me. And Geoff. And Piers, when I first knew him. So I guessed his life state must have slipped with Rachel. Maybe. I'd have to talk to him when he got back from Barcelona …

Right now, though, as I chanted I was getting a strong urge to call Fiona. She must be feeling terrible. Did she have anyone to talk to – friends, family? Even if she did, I had to say something to her myself, if only how sorry I was. After all, I'd found her husband. I'd cut him down. Or should that be … let him down?

And all at once I understood why I'd got so blindingly drunk, and wanted to again. There was something I didn't want to face, or feel.

Guilt.

Yes, he'd fended me off, but I could have tried harder to support him, encourage him to challenge his demons. If I had, maybe he'd still be alive. And what about Fiona? I'd kept his secret from her. And if his finances were at the root of his suicide she'd have another very nasty shock coming – no?

I had to steel myself to call her; it was only a few hours since she'd made the decision to turn off the machine and I expected her emotions to be raw. But when she answered she didn't sound hostile or suspicious, just exhausted. And relieved I'd taken the initiative – she wanted to talk about Martin too. But not on the phone.

'I could come round,' I heard myself saying.

She hesitated, then, 'Thank you. That's kind.'

Kind? No. I owed it to her. If Martin had taken her out to the theatre only the night before he hanged himself – and hadn't even left a note – she deserved some sort of explanation. I had to tell her what I knew. Everything.

She opened the door barefoot, in jeans and a blue mohair sweater, her hair gathered in a simple ponytail. But her face was ghostly pale, with no make-up or colour. Apart from her eyes. Dark shadows had formed under them, deepening their green intensity.

She led me into the white, bright kitchen. Their au pair – the sturdy young woman I'd seen through the window playing in the pool with the kids – was filling a dog bowl with food as Dave looked on, tail gently wagging.

'Have you met Vanda?' said Fiona.

'No.' Slept in her bed but never met. 'Hi.'

'Hello.' A mittel-European accent I couldn't place.

'Ed was a friend of Martin's,' Fiona explained. Vanda nodded – an uninterested kind of a nod – and took the dog bowl to the corner. Dave padded after her and immediately buried his face in the food as she put it down. 'Could you do the children's baths now?' asked Fiona.

'Of course.' Vanda bustled out, relieved to escape the emotional turmoil she sensed my arrival heralded.

'Where's she from?'

'Romania,' said Fiona, going to the fridge. 'And wants to go back. At least she says she does. I think she just wants another job.' She took out a bottle of white wine.

'Because of what's happened?'

'No. Because – ah, what's it matter? Will you join me?' She waggled the bottle.

'Thanks, no – I'm driving.' And I've just got rid of a mighty hangover. And don't trust myself not to get off my face again and do or say something foolish.

'You sure?'

'Something soft will be fine. Whatever.' Fiona raised an eyebrow but pulled a bottle of tonic water from the fridge. She picked up a corkscrew and a couple of glasses and we moved to the kitchen table.

'So how are you?'

She thought for a moment, then poured the tonic water. 'Dunno. Shocked, numb …'

'The kids?'

'Gutted. They worshipped him.' She passed me my drink.

'What did you tell them?'

She glanced round, then got up and closed the kitchen door. She came back to the table and answered in a murmur.

'That he had an accident. At work.' I watched her as she started to open the wine.

'And friends, family? Yours, his …?'

'His parents are both dead. He has a sister in Durham. She doesn't know yet. My family I don't see and don't want to.'

'Oh?'

She ignored me. 'Friends? Sod 'em – they're all snobs. Round here anyway. And the ones back home – well …'

'So there's not much support?' She scoffed and pulled the cork with a loud 'pop'. I took a deep breath – it was time to open a few cupboard doors. 'I had a visit from the police this afternoon,' I said. 'That's how I found out he'd …'

'There was no point going on,' she said. 'He was dead.'

'No. I'm really sorry.'

The finality hung for a moment in the silence. Fiona stared at her glass.

'I was Christmas shopping when he … Christmas shopping! For the— ' She swallowed hard, fighting tears. 'In town. And the kids were at the cinema, with Vanda.' She drained her glass in one and refilled it. 'They were here too

– the police. Searched his office, took his laptop, locked everything when they left, put tape across the door: "Police. Do not enter". In my house, my own home!'

Yikes. That didn't sound good. 'Did they say why?'

Fiona shook her head. 'No. Did they say anything to you?'

I took another deep breath – and told her everything I knew. The look of alarm grew on her face until she stopped me to ask the $64,000 question.

'You mean, I could lose the house?'

'That's my understanding, from what Martin said. Obviously, I don't know what his finances were like when he, you know, but …' Fiona's face, already pale, turned white. I thought she might faint. 'Martin didn't want to tell you because – well, he didn't want to worry you.'

She took a gulp of wine and refilled her glass again, this time with a shaking hand.

'And you went along with it?' she said bitterly. 'All boys together.'

'I'm sorry. But I didn't think it was for me to—'

'Go on,' she snapped. 'What else?'

'Well, that's about all I know,' I said. 'Though the police asked about three guys whose names I didn't recognise: McLellan, a Greek called Stylianou, and Don Daley, a local councillor. So …' I paused. Fiona was staring at me hard. 'Have you heard of them?'

'Not till the police asked me. But I googled them. Did you?'

'Not yet.' In my hungover state it hadn't occurred to me. She poured another glass of wine. I noticed the bottle was nearly empty.

'There's nothing on McLellan. Stylianou is some Greek shipping tycoon, fingers in lots of pies. And Daley – well, he's chair of the planning committee for Hertswood.' She looked at me, quivering between a bitter smile and tears. 'Starting to smell a bit shite, hmm?' She gulped more wine, clutching the glass like a lifebelt in a storm.

I felt like joining her now. 'Chair of the planning committee' had warning lights flashing all over it. Had Martin been slipping him backhanders to grease the wheels of local government? I wouldn't put it past him. And it would explain why the police had locked up his study.

Before I could say anything the kitchen door swung open to reveal Amelia, in pyjamas and dressing gown, fresh from her bath. She hesitated, taking in the scene.

'Hello,' I said. Amelia came slowly into the room and climbed on to Fiona's lap. She buried her face in the soft wool of her mother's sweater and murmured something.

'I'm sad, too, poppet,' said Fiona, cuddling her. Amelia murmured again. Fiona stroked her head. 'No, no school tomorrow.'

Amelia lifted her head and glanced at me, then pulled Fiona's head down to whisper in her ear. Fiona frowned, glanced at me, then sat Amelia up straight to look her in the eye. Amelia returned the stare, a picture of innocence.

'All right,' said Fiona after a moment. 'If he wants to.'

'What?' I was intrigued.

Amelia shot me a glance and went coy. She whispered again to Fiona, who was having none of it.

'You ask him.'

Amelia slowly pulled something from her dressing gown pocket and held it up shyly – her string of chanting beads.

'Is that OK?' Fiona was clearly torn between disapproval and not wanting to block something that might help Amelia with the loss of her father.

'Sure, no problem.' I was as surprised as she was. Amelia slid off Fiona's lap, happy.

'But just a few minutes, because Ed has to go – don't you?'

'That's right.' I smiled at Amelia but Fiona and I both knew I was being dismissed. Amelia took my hand and, glancing at her mother, led me from the room.

'Will Oliver want to join us?' I asked as we headed for the gym.

'No. He thinks it's stupid,' said Amelia. I wanted to ask her about Martin, if he'd been practising, but now was not the right time – if it ever would be.

We reached the gym. I took the key from the hook on the wall, unlocked the door and in we went. Amelia reached up for the light switch, then pulled the bench carefully into place, sat down and looked round for me to join her. As I did she pulled a gongyo book from her pocket. Another surprise.

'Have you been learning it?'

She nodded proudly. 'From the CD Daddy got.'

'I'll have to share your book then,' I said, 'I don't know it by heart yet.'

'Of course you can,' she said seriously, and moved closer so I could see the text. 'Haven't you got any beads?'

'It doesn't matter. I don't need them. Ready?'

She nodded and we started reciting the text. I was astonished at how she kept up – but after less than a minute she stopped. I turned to investigate and saw her staring hard at the page.

'Am I going too fast?'

She shook her head.

'Is there a problem?' She nodded firmly, twice. 'What?'

She burst into sobs.

Ah – stupid. Of course there's a problem. Her dad died a few hours ago. But what to say? I had no idea. I put an arm around her juddering shoulders, shushing her, welling up myself.

'Do you want to stop?' She shook her head. 'OK. Shall I do some chanting and you just join in when you're ready?' She nodded, splashing tears on to her book.

I took my arm away, sucked in a deep breath and started to chant in a low voice. It seemed to do the trick. The sobbing slowed, then stopped. Amelia put her hands together and chanted four times, then jumped up.

'I'm going now. Bye.'

Just like that.

'Bye.'

I twisted round to watch her go – and saw Fiona in the doorway, leaning against the frame. Amelia darted behind her, then poked her head round Fiona's hip, gave me a wave and disappeared.

'Be up in a moment!' Fiona called after her, speech slurred. The alcohol was kicking in. Amelia didn't reply, already gone. Fiona turned her stare on to me. Her deep green eyes were glazing over.

'I'll be off then.'

She ushered me unsteadily to the front door but as I stepped out into the damp night I felt a strong sense of unfinished business.

'Look,' I said, 'things could get pretty difficult over the next … So if there's anything you need help with – big, small, in-between – then please just ask, OK? Anything. I mean it.'

Fiona's lip curled in a scornful, twisted smile. She shut the door with a gentle click.

Well then. *In vino veritas.*

I drove home, drank a bottle of red and collapsed into bed.

Chapter Nine

I woke with a jolt.

Where was I? I felt sick, and scared. A bad dream?

04:04 was glowing white through the blackness. Then I remembered: red wine, Martin dead, CPR. Horrible. I took a deep breath, then let out a long, long sigh.

Four in the morning. In Japan, *ushitora*: the hours of the ox and tiger, of perfect balance, like the turning of the tide. Dead time, when your life force is at its lowest. That's what Dora used to say. Where was she right now? In the Caribbean? In bed? Alone?

08:13.

Good – another four hours of sleep. Turn over for some more; no, better get up. It was Monday, a work day. Then I remembered: I didn't have any work.

I swung my feet out of the bed, sat on the edge ... and no spinning head, nausea – hooray. Another bottle poured down my neck and nothing this morning but fatigue and an ache behind the eyes. First win of the day.

I tottered downstairs, made black coffee and chomped on some toast while the *Today* programme flitted through the news agenda for the week ahead. Government cuts, political spats about who was to blame for the greatest crash since 1929, the weather.

I was only half listening. What about my week ahead? No work, so no money; my savings would pay the mortgage to the end of January but only if I didn't eat, or use the electricity, or drive anywhere. Or drink red wine.

I had to get another lodger – I'd been slack on that front. Better put a card in the corner-shop window, an ad on the local rag's website. And Piers should be back today. Perhaps he'd have something lined up. I'd give him a call, mid-morning. What was the time now?

08:47.

Bam. I felt as if I'd been hit by the zapper the paramedic had used on Martin.

Luis! He wasn't in the loop. He'd be waiting for me at the station – and I was half an hour late. More than. Shit.

I galloped up the stairs, dragged on some clothes, gulped down the rest of my coffee and dashed out. Yes, I was probably over the limit again but this was an emergency.

The ring road. Traffic. Road rage. Why was I doing this? I didn't owe Luis anything. But there was something trusting about him. Childlike, vulnerable. For some reason I couldn't bear to see that abused. Not after the whole Rachel debacle and the job shifting under his feet. And his lack of English, which made everything doubly confusing for him.

He wasn't there when I screeched into the station forecourt, almost an hour late. Had he gone home already – or set off to Hillview on foot? Hmm. He hadn't been paid, he needed his money … No-brainer, really. And it was only a half-hour walk.

I saw him as I crested the hill – along with Man in Charge and his gang of bailiffs, milling around in the road outside the site. There were two low-loaders this time and, a little further on, a mobile crane, all with hazard lights blinking, eager to remove the containers, finish the job. No Poles, though, or Norris. Bernie must have warned them off.

I parked some way back and advanced on the scrum of men and machines, hands deep in my jacket pockets, collar turned up against the biting wind. Faces pinched from the cold turned towards me. Man in Charge took the phone from his ear and scowled. He looked deeply pissed off and itching for someone to blame. Luis's face lit up as he saw me. I nodded to him as I went up to Man in Charge.

'Morning,' I said, trying to sound businesslike.

Man in Charge got straight to the point. 'D'ye know what the hell's going on?' He pointed to a ribbon of blue and white plastic tape stretched across the site gate: *Police – Do Not Cross*. 'I bin calling but no one knows bugger all.' His Scottish accent seemed to broaden as his frustration rose.

'Shifts have probably changed,' I said.

'Eh?' His scowl deepened. I glanced around. All eyes were on me. Time for the bombshell.

'Martin Upton – the boss, the developer … He hanged himself in the basement here on Saturday night.'

Mouths fell open. Eyebrows climbed. There were gasps, hissed expletives, shaking heads. And on Luis's face a look of confusion, consternation.

I told the tale briefly, in bullet-points almost. As I did these burly bailiffs became a group of six-year-olds again, gathered around teacher to listen to a story. There were more whistles, head shaking, stunned expletives when I finished – and a deep, angry exhalation from Man in Charge.

'Well, that's that then. Waste of bloody time.' He turned to his men. 'OK, lads – back on the bus.' They drifted away to their mini-van, the drivers of the low-loaders and the crane to their cabs.

'Your first one?' I asked innocently.

Man in Charge scowled. 'Eh?'

'Suicide. With all these repossessions ...?'

Man in Charge opened his mouth to deliver a stinging riposte, then clamped it shut and stalked off, leaving me and Luis alone by the gate.

'Is no good, no good.' He was almost in tears.

'I know, man.' He looked so miserable I put my arm round his shoulder to comfort him. 'Come on, I'll give you a lift back to the station.'

We made the trip in silence, broken only by Luis's shuddering sighs, which came every couple of minutes with a slow, bewildered shake of the head. We arrived at the station forecourt and sat for a couple of minutes, the engine idling. He should contact Piers about his money, I said, and maybe we'd see each other at one of his Buddhist meetings, or on another job. But I was only being polite – I didn't expect our paths to cross again – and stuck my hand out to say goodbye. He looked at it pensively, as if it were some alien object, then shook it.

'Is strange,' he said. 'England.'

He got out of the car and disappeared into the station.

Now what? And not just now, this instant, but all the nows to come, my life from this point on? Geoff's line came back to me: 'The future is a vacuum waiting to be filled with reality.' Yes, and mine was being shaped by forces beyond my control. I *had* to make money to pay the mortgage. I *had* to deal with this bloody Valeria insurance business. And possibly I still *had* to convince the police that Martin's death was nothing to do with me – how bizarre was that? But it was all reactive, stuff I *had* to do just to survive. Nothing proactive, nothing creative.

Except, maybe, once she'd cooled down, Fiona might let me help her and the kids. Exactly how I had no idea. But that at least would feel positive – and creative, as in creating a bit of good in the world. Poison into medicine.

A car horn blared: I was blocking the drop-off zone at the entrance to the station. I put the car in gear and headed home.

When I got there I chanted. I didn't want to, I felt tired and depressed. But there was that bloody card staring at me: *Enjoy life. Win.* Huh. What a joke. But the alternative was even less funny: Suffer. Death. Lose.

I had to challenge – myself, my thinking, this horrible, creeping ache that was filling my chest. Chant, challenge, change …

I forced myself to sit down, put my hands together and started.

At once I saw the bailiffs that morning in the road outside Hillview, stamping their feet against the cold; then, seamlessly, the scene dissolved to the day ItsTheBusiness. com went bust ten years ago – we'd milled around on the pavement then, too.

Karma. If you keep on doing what you've always done, you'll keep on getting what you've always got. Martin had taken a flier on both businesses, kept them going by juggling the finances, spinning the plates of income and expenditure, credit and debt, till the market turned and nothing he did could stop the plates from falling to earth. Gravity conquers all – eventually. And the bigger the bust, the greater the price. The dot.com crash of 2000 had cost him his company; the crash of 2008 had cost him his life.

I saw him again, hanging inert in the torch's beam, his face blue and bloated, the rope cutting into a swollen neck … I shuddered. Awful. Horrible. And then I was back on the road up the hill to St Catherine's, Smiler and Big Boy were running off past the BMW and 'Ed?' – Martin's amazed expression at realising it was me. Then a jumble of images: hacking at the undergrowth at Hillview, wandering around the shell of the house, then chanting with Martin and Amelia and Oliver in his gym. Fiona barging in on us, all blonde hair and black tracksuit, me thinking, there you are, and—

I stopped. What was that – there you are? *There you are*? What the hell did that mean? I didn't think that – did I …?

I started to chant again, and the truffle hound went straight to the moment, to the treasure. Me seeing Fiona for the first time, my feeling that she was somehow familiar and, yes, the instant thought: there you are. *There you are.* A moment of recognition, as if she'd just popped out for a while and come back in. *There you are.* No excitement, no bells and whistles, just … *There you are.* A fact. But in the very same instant buried, like I'd buried my coward's reaction to Big Boy. That had been from shame, whereas this …? What was I trying to hide from myself, and why?

There you are. I was bewildered, uncomfortable. But I had to find out.

More chanting, the truffle hound snuffling through the leaf litter. This surely couldn't be one of those eternal partners things, could it, where you're destined to meet the same person in lifetime after lifetime, repeating the same, endlessly doomed love affair? No, it couldn't – because that was just a load of romantic Buddhist bollocks. Plus I was tired and vulnerable and emotionally washed-out from Martin's suicide. And probably still pissed, technically; I doubted if the alcohol level in my blood ever dropped to zero these days.

But I hadn't been feeling any of those things when I'd first seen her.

There you are.

So was this just a way of signalling that I was secretly attracted to her? Show me, truffle hound.

Well, yes, she was attractive – physically. But scary. She'd scowled the first time our eyes had met, so obviously there wasn't a *There you are* from her side. Or maybe, if I was secretly attracted, I'd buried it because she was off-limits, forbidden – the friend's wife. Except he was now dead, so … Bloody hell! Surely that wasn't *why* he was dead – so that the strange, mysterious machinery of karma, of destiny, could work through its relentless gears and throw me and Fiona together … again?

No. That was nuts. Completely and utterly bonkers – all of it. I really did need a good sleep, or maybe a long walk and lots of fresh air. I was letting a febrile imagination run away with me.

My phone rang and broke the fantasy – thank God. It was Bernie.

'How you doing, sunshine?' It was good to hear his voice.

'Oh, you know – getting there. You?'

'I'm all right – apart from the Bill not saying when I'll get me tools back. I've just had Starsky and fucking Hutch here for the past hour and a half.'

'Horton and Kelly?'

'That's the ones, yeah. I think I just about convinced them we're not murderers, but who knows? Thick as pigshit, most coppers.' A pause. 'How's Martin's missus, and the kids?'

'Rollercoaster. Shock, anger, tears …'

Bernie sighed deeply. 'Yeah. Poor little …' He sighed again.

'You heard from Piers?'

'Back at lunchtime, wants a meet. You up for it?'

We gathered at Piers's place that afternoon. It felt cold, and not just because the central heating had been off for a few days. Constanza and Bella were still in Barcelona and their absence cast a chill over everything. As we sat around the table in his basement kitchen, hands wrapped around steaming mugs of coffee, my eye kept straying to a primary school picture stuck to the fridge: Bella's eager handprints in vivid blue, red, yellow and green; signs of a life not here, a family fractured.

Piers was subdued, haggard. Coming on top of his domestic troubles, Martin's suicide and the collapse of the job at Hillview were blows he was struggling to absorb. And he felt ashamed, he said, that he hadn't contacted me the moment he got Bernie's text. I told him not to worry about it but I could see he wasn't listening; he seemed to have a real downer on himself.

Bernie and I related our tale yet again, and the three of us dissected the events of the weekend from every possible angle. Yes, we'd all sensed the risk of getting involved with Martin – in fact, he might have approached Piers and Bernie precisely because they didn't know anything about him – but we'd gone ahead anyway; so we had no one to blame but ourselves for any losses we'd suffer. And Piers and Bernie both insisted they'd pay their teams in full for the work done – a deal's a deal, even if it left them out of pocket. So that much we could all accept: the part we'd played. But Martin's suicide and possible criminality – well, that was a lot harder, especially for Piers.

'While she was Christmas shopping …' He shook his head, incredulous.

'Yeah,' said Bernie. 'And the kids at the pictures.'

'Awful.' Piers swallowed hard, upset. 'How are they taking it?'

I described my visit to Fiona, including Amelia's surprise request to do some chanting together.

'How old is she?' asked Piers wistfully.

'Six. She taught herself gongyo from a CD he'd bought.'

'Blimey. That's some six-year-old,' said Bernie, rolling a cigarette.

'Probably practised in a former life,' Piers murmured, staring out of the french windows at a child's blue and yellow plastic slide, sitting in the middle of the minuscule courtyard.

'Do you actually believe that?' I asked. Piers looked at me. 'You know, the whole reincarnation bit?'

He shrugged. 'Life's got to come from somewhere.'

'D'you mind if I . . . ?' Bernie waved the finished cigarette.

Piers hesitated. 'Oh, sod it. Go on. Constanza won't have smoking in the house but she's not here, is she?' He unfolded his lanky frame and fetched a saucer for an ashtray. Bernie lit up, took a deep drag and exhaled with evident relish.

'Ta.'

'What about the eternal partners thing?' I asked as Piers sat back down at the table. 'You know, that karma means you end up with the same person again and again?'

'Christ, I hope not,' said Bernie. 'And the wife's with me on that one.'

Piers smiled – the first time he'd cracked his face since we'd arrived. He saw me waiting for an answer.

'I really don't think I'm much of an expert on relationships, Ed – sorry.'

No help with the Fiona issue there then. 'OK,' I said, 'another karma question. How can you practise Buddhism and still commit suicide, because "One day of life is more valuable than the treasures of the universe," right? That's what Buddhism teaches?' Piers nodded. 'Right. So suicide is the ultimate disrespect for your own life, isn't it? Plus, if you believe in the eternity of life it's no escape anyway. You're just making a massive negative cause that's going to come back and bite you next time round.'

'But was Martin actually practising?' said Piers.

'Probably not,' I said. 'But even just knowing the theory—'

'Theory!' Bernie blew out a long plume of smoke. 'Talking the talk and *walking* the talk are totally different things, mate.'

'Yes, obviously.' I couldn't help glancing up at Bella's hand paintings. Piers winced, guessing my thoughts. 'I'm sorry,' I said. 'I didn't mean to imply . . .'

'No, it's a fair point,' he said. 'I'm supposed to be a . . . a shining example of wisdom and . . .' He sighed. 'And I've screwed up humongously, haven't I? Stunning partner, lovely little girl, baby on the way – don't even contact a friend in need . . .' I waved it away but he nodded glumly. 'It's true.'

Silence. Bernie and I waited. Piers stared at his coffee mug, turned it round once, twice on the table, took a deep breath, hesitated – then began.

'The thing is . . . the plain, unvarnished truth . . .' He sighed again, then looked me straight in the eye. 'Constanza is an absolute bloody nightmare. It's like living with a . . . an exotic volcano that just explodes the whole time. I've never known someone so angry. I was seriously thinking of, you know, ending it after about a year, but then she got pregnant with Bella and just the merest hint of a suggestion that she might *possibly* like to think about, you know, whether she *really* wanted to keep it – or maybe not – produced this . . . this . . . Krakatoa.'

He mimed the eruption with his hands, then flopped them on to the table, spent.

'I told myself a baby might calm her down, bring us together, you know, as a family. Which it did – for a while. Building the nest, preparing. But after Bella was born . . .' He shook his head, remembering. 'Constanza has this thing about hot-housing, you see, but I think Bella should, you know, be a *child* – just play and grow and learn at her own pace. So there's been … conflict. To say the least.'

'Why have another one then?' Bernie sat there, arms folded across his chest.

Piers smiled ruefully. 'Accident.'

Bernie grunted. 'What trouble our willies do get us into, eh? Took me years to tame mine.'

'What's the secret?' I asked.

'Chastity belt,' said Bernie. 'For me. Wife's got the key.' He turned back to Piers. 'Rachel?'

Piers got up again and crossed to the french windows to stare out at the untidy dahlias in the tiny beds that bordered the courtyard. 'Constanza always wondered why our garden looked so bloody awful, if I was a professional. "Pierce, our garden is sheet! Why? You want Bella to grow up in sheet?" Non-stop.'

It was a good imitation, but sad.

'Rachel?' Bernie was a dog with a bone.

Piers thought for a moment. 'Rachel was fun. On the same wavelength. We got on.' He turned his back on the courtyard. 'And one day, after work, we were in the pub – it was a beautiful summer evening, we'd been slaving away all day – and she was chatting to this chap who was working with us at the time. Morgan, young Welsh chap. Anyway, she laughed at something he said and the sun caught her in a – I don't know, it sounds so … bloody cheesy. Anyway, at that moment she just sort of … shone. And a thought popped into my head: "I love this woman." From nowhere. Total shock. And it was so forbidden I pushed it aside at once. Can't have thoughts like that – not with a wife and child at home.'

Bloody hell – coincidence or what? I'd done exactly the same with my forbidden thought. *There you are …*

'This was before the happy accident,' said Piers. 'And

when I say "wife" we're not actually married. Good as – but that's another issue between us.' He stared out of the window. A light rain had started to fall.

'So how did it develop?' I tried to sound relaxed but could feel my neck muscles tensing. The cart overturned on the road ahead ...

Piers glanced at me and sighed again. 'Well, it came up when I was chanting, of course, and each time I pushed it away. And then, once, I didn't. I thought, have a look at it. Try to be honest. That's what I do when I chant.'

'And ...?'

'And I liked what I saw. Which led, eventually, to ...' He faded off into another bleak, middle-distance stare. If he was remembering sins of the flesh they didn't seem to give him much joy.

'No warning bells, sirens, keep-off-the-fucking-grass?' Bernie sounded matter-of-fact, already rolling another cigarette. Piers came back to the table.

'Well, yes – of course. But I ignored them. No – *chose* to ignore them.' He sat down heavily, as if tired of the whole thing.

'But what about your "Buddha nature"?' I asked, trying not to sound sarcastic. 'I thought you're supposed to learn stuff after all these years – wisdom.'

Piers nodded. 'Mmm, you are. You should become master of your mind, rather than let your mind master you.'

'Buddhist quote,' said Bernie helpfully.

'But how does *that* work?' I said. 'I mean, how can you control the thing that's in control?'

'No, not easy, is it?' said Piers. He reflected for a moment. 'When I thought about Rachel, even when I chanted about her, I was ... feeding a fantasy. I should have been challenging it but I didn't want to. I wanted to escape – from this.' He waved an arm at the kitchen. 'My life here. My reality.

Rather than deal with it, or myself.' He glanced again at the plastic slide in the garden. 'It's a powerful urge, escape.'

There was a moment of silence. Bernie broke it.

'So that's it – *finito*, you split up?'

Piers shrugged. 'Don't know. Hope not.'

'Rachel?'

'Gone.'

Bernie shook his head. 'Well. No fool like an old fool, eh?'

Piers smiled. 'You're such a comfort, Bernie.'

Bernie suggested we do some chanting together before I left – for Martin.

'Because far as I'm concerned,' he said, 'if he was practising or not ain't the point. Or if he was a Buddhist, Hindu, Jew, Muslim, atheist, whatever. He was in my life. *Is* in my life. Always will be. Yours too. cos the fact that you and me found him means there's some sort of karmic connection. So when we chant it reaches him, helps him.'

'How?' I really struggled with this sort of stuff.

'The oneness of life and death,' said Bernie. 'The oneness of self and the environment, and mind and body. We're all connected, all part of the great big cuddly universe – always.' I grimaced with the effort to understand. He smiled. 'Just chant. You'll see. It'll come.'

So we chanted – but it didn't come. In fact, try as I might I couldn't focus on Martin at all. Kneeling behind Piers, I found myself staring at the back of his head and wondering about the forbidden thought that had popped into it; a thought he'd fed, and which had grown and grown to the point where he'd acted. And look at the consequences. But Piers had related his story just a few hours after I'd remembered my forbidden thought – and if there's no such thing as coincidence ...

There was no getting round it – this was a sign from the universe. *Leave Fiona alone.*

Good. I felt better, as if something had been settled. So *now* I could focus on Martin and what Bernie had said about us still being connected to him. But I struggled. If Martin really hadn't done himself any favours by committing suicide I truly hoped our chanting would do him some good. To be honest, though, I was more inclined towards the Jewish approach. You mourn the dead but look after the living. Which brought me back to Fiona and Amelia and Oliver. Help them as a unit, a family, in a friendly way. No ulterior motives …

It was dark when I got home. The house was cold and uninviting. And I was restless. The thought of sitting in front of the telly, working my way through another bottle, watching nothing … I turned on the heating and went straight back out, into the centre of town, to the high street, looking for life, warmth, people.

A few minutes' walking and I'd reached the ring road, the moat that separated the shopping area from the town's residential areas. Down into the underpass, the orange of the streetlamps changing to the neon of the concrete tunnel, then up into the busyness of shops and pubs, cafés and restaurants, the covered market and the mall. Christmas was coming – only a few weeks now – and a series of large, twinkling snowflakes were being strung by a gang of workmen along the high street over the road. In better days they would have been illuminated – thousands of little light bulbs in festive colours twinkling good cheer on to the Christmas shoppers below. But since the crash the local retailers had been forced to make economies, so these snowflakes were made of shiny, fake-metallic plastic strips – red, blue, green, silver and gold – which shimmered in the light of the stores and streetlamps. Glitter on the cheap.

Times were tough. You could see that just walking down the street. Every fifth shop was dark or boarded up. If you pressed your nose against the plate glass you could see empty shelves and display cabinets, or simply a vacant space where cakes and bread and hot sausage rolls had once been sold, or videos rented, or – ironic for this time of year – where greetings cards for every conceivable occasion had been pored over by the good citizens of Watford. In desperation, some shops had already launched pre-Christmas sales.

I crossed the road and pushed through the doors into the mall. At once I could sense that there was something wrong. The atmosphere was hushed, echoing almost. Normally it bustled, busy with the flow of people in and out, eyeing stuff, trying stuff, buying stuff. But now it was almost deserted. Yes, it was a Monday and the opening hours had only just been extended in the run-up to Christmas, but where was everybody? The angel of retail death had obviously passed through here, too. The strike rate was not as high as out on the street but every so often, sandwiched between brightly lit boutiques of ladies fashion and tinsel-decked stores of up-to-the-minute electronic gadgetry, the sad shutters of an empty shop told the tale of another casualty.

One space, though, had been revived, for a while at least. Last Edition was a cut-price clearance outlet for remaindered books – and I couldn't resist.

Inside, the shelves of the previous shop were still in place, but now lined with volumes of every shape, size and colour. Trestle tables covered in green cloth ran along the walls and down the centre of the store, stacked high with a jumble of hardbacks and paperbacks. Handwritten cardboard signs Blu-tacked to the wall announced the goods:

'History', 'Crime Fiction', 'Women', 'Fishing', 'New Age', 'Gardens', 'Pot Luck' (the largest section) and, next to the door, 'Bargain Bucket' over a large, black bin. Apart from that, and a bearded, balding chap in a purple jumper on the till, there was no discernible order. It was every biblio-phile for himself. Browsing heaven.

Where to start? I wandered along the tables to the History section: piles of picture books about Nazis, ancient Egypt, the Chinese emperors ... and Watford. On the cover was a montage of period photographs, in the centre of which a smiling Queen Mother shook hands with a bewigged local official in a ceremonial gown. I was intrigued. I picked it up – the book was heavy – and started to turn the 372 large-format pages.

It was a revelation. As a true-born Londoner I'd always been rather snobbish about Watford; to me it was just a grim satellite town at the end of the Metropolitan Line. But here was a rich history, a tale in miniature of the country of which it was a part, from the coming of the railway (and the camera) to the final decade of the twentieth century.

A photo showed the town turning out to celebrate the wedding of the Prince of Wales in 1863, rows of people standing stock-still in their black and white Sunday best for the commemorative photograph. Another image was of hundreds of sheep, penned in the high street on a market day in the spring of 1885. In another, His Majesty King Edward VII and entourage were sweeping through the town in a fleet of motor cars in 1906. There were images showing the construction of the railway line from London, and the local breweries and printing works for which the town would become renowned. Smiling volunteers marching off to the trenches in 1914 and mob-capped girls and women working in the 'filling' – munitions – factories. The huge peace celebration in Cassiobury Park in 1918. A

1930s news report described fighting with razors and lead piping between locals and 'Welshmen' searching for work during the slump. More uniforms in 1939 as the country geared up for war again. Children with gas masks climbing into trains at Watford Junction to escape the bombing to come – then burned-out houses, marching troops, Sea Cadets, the Home Guard ...

On I went, turning the pages through the 1940s and 1950s. Then, in the 1960s, the character of the town seemed to change. Suddenly there were more cars. Traffic jams appeared, piecemeal construction gave way to 'development', concrete, ring roads – and something was lost. The town seemed to become segmented, the centre cut off, smoothed out into something bland and uniform. National brands started to take over the high street. Rivers of traffic flowed through and around islands of corralled pedestrians. The car was king. Shopping was queen. Credit was God.

Throughout the book the lives of the ordinary people of the town seemed to have been picked up and carried along by forces completely beyond their control. Railways, wars, booms and busts, 'development' – their future was a vacuum waiting to be filled with a reality ... made by someone else.

Like my life, now.

'You going to buy that – now you've read it?'

The bearded chap in the purple jumper had appeared at my elbow. I checked my watch: I'd been immersed in the book for almost half an hour. I smiled apologetically and looked at the price. Five quid – a bargain. And all I had on me.

I followed him to the till. He rang up the sale, dropped my purchase into a recycled plastic bag and I turned to leave. As I did my eye fell on a familiar blue and white cover in the bargain bucket. Not ... Yes, bloody hell – my book! My heart leapt; it was like seeing an old friend. But down on his luck, hanging out with the vagrants. And this heartless bastard was trying to flog it for a quid! I rescued it from the bin – then froze.

Sauntering past the plate-glass window were Big Boy and Smiler.

My stomach turned over. Adrenalin surged up my spine. I could feel a tingling in my scalp. My eyes followed them, my body rigid with shock. Please, God, don't look into the shop, I thought. Please keep walking ... They did – and passed out of sight.

'That'll be a pound please.' The bearded chap in the purple jumper was waiting to ring the till.

'Er, can you hang on to it for me?' I said. 'I've just got to get some more cash.'

I didn't wait for him to answer but stepped into the doorway and peeped out. Big Boy and Smiler were ambling along, joshing each other, taking no interest in anything or anyone around them. It was too early for their curfew, I guessed, but what were they doing here – Christmas shopping, or Christmas shoppers? Were they out on the rob? Only one way to find out. Heart pounding, hanging well back, tracking along the far side of the concourse, I set out after them.

What would they do if they saw me? Turn on me? Run? Nothing? Would they even recognise me? One thing was for sure: I didn't want to find out.

They stopped outside a jewellery store. Surely they weren't planning to rob that? They pointed at something in the window and I remembered that Big Boy wore a diamond ear-stud. Smiler gave Big Boy a punch on the arm, they laughed raucously, then moved on. I followed. They stepped on to an escalator and were carried upwards. And

just as they crested the top Big Boy turned, looked down ...
And our eyes met. Instant recognition. He pulled Smiler's
jacket, pointed – and they were gone.

Shit.

I turned and walked fast in the opposite direction. As I
did my phone rang. They didn't have the number, did they?
Don't be stupid. How could they? I'd left it in the car when
they'd mugged me.

Hand trembling, I dug it out of my pocket and checked
the display: 'Martin (Home)'. Freaky. I pressed the button.

'Hello?'

'Ed?' A female voice, foreign.

'Yes.'

'Is Vanda – Fiona's au pair?'

'Oh yes. Hi.' Looking over my shoulder, but no sight of
Big Boy or Smiler. I hurried towards the exit.

'I'm sorry I call but I don't know what to do.'

She sounded scared. I looked round again – still no sign.

'What's the problem?'

'Is Fiona. I think she gone mad.'

Chapter Ten

Vanda yanked open the front door before I could ring the bell. She looked anxious, edgy.

'Hi.'

I tried to sound cheerful and relaxed, even though I'd run home – terrified that Big Boy and Smiler might be coming after me – jumped into my car and driven straight here. Vanda glanced nervously over her shoulder, pulled me inside and closed the door.

'Thank you so much. I did not want the police,' she whispered.

'No problem,' I murmured back. 'Where ...?'

Vanda nodded to a door off the hallway: the sitting room. 'It has been no noise for a while. But before – terrible. Scrims, creshing ...'

I tiptoed to the door and listened. Silence. I tiptoed back.

'How are the kids?'

'Tense. In my room.'

Tense? I glanced up the stairs, then back at the sitting room door.

'Has she been drinking?' Vanda nodded her disapproval. 'How much?'

'A lot.'

I squared my shoulders, readying myself. 'OK. If it gets

– you know – rough, and I shout out, you'll have to call the police, I'm afraid. All right?' Vanda nodded again, relieved that someone else was taking charge. 'But you did the right thing calling me first.' The flicker of a smile passed over her face.

'Right.' I approached the sitting room door, took a deep breath, hesitated, then twisted the doorknob, pushed and—

'Get the fock out! How many times I got to—' Fiona saw me and stopped, taken aback. What was I doing here?

The room looked as if a small bomb had gone off. The screen of the huge, wall-mounted plasma TV was scattered like shiny confetti across the carpet, along with the smashed glass fronts of two cabinets and their contents of Waterford crystal. A large cut-glass vase had been hurled against the wall, exploding a dramatic burst of water across the hand-painted wallpaper. Below it, shards of glass twinkled in a tangle of greenery and deep red roses. Between the cream sofas, a spider's web of lines radiated from the centre of the glass coffee table; a heavy blow had fractured but not broken it. The plump leather cushions of the sofas had been slashed, white foam padding spilling out from deep gashes like the blubber of a harpooned whale. Even the uplighters around the walls had been smashed, as had the chandelier overhead – glass tear-drops were strewn to the four corners of the room …

… in one of which, between the lamp on a sideboard and the sliding picture windows, stood Fiona. With a golf club – an iron.

Vanda was right: she did look as if she'd gone mad. Or been caught in the bomb blast. On her head was a bird's nest of blonde hair, sticking out at all angles and falling into her eyes. Black smears of mascara across her cheeks suggested angry tears. Her nose was red and running with snot. She seemed utterly lost.

'What d'you want?' Her words were slurred, thickening her accent.

'Just ... thought I'd drop by, see how you were.'

'Liar,' she mumbled. 'A focking liar. You're all focking liars!' She swayed unsteadily, blinking hard, trying to focus. Then, with sudden violence, she swung the club backhanded against the window. It bounced off – thank God.

'Whoa, whoa! Hey, Fiona! What's going on? What's happened? What's—' I took a step towards her but she grabbed something from the sideboard – a carving knife. She pointed it at my face, the curved blade catching the light from the one working lamp in the room.

'Don't come focking near me,' she hissed. 'I know what you want, what you all want – focking men!'

I stared at her, shocked, dismayed – then noticed something on the carpet. Blood. Streaks of it. Footprints.

'Christ, Fiona – your feet.'

She frowned, caught unawares. 'Wha—'

'You've been walking on the glass – in bare feet.' I pointed. She looked down at them, puzzled. 'Doesn't it hurt?' She thought, then shook her head, wide-eyed with surprise. 'We should get the splinters out, get some plasters on. Could get infected otherwise.'

She stared at her feet, up at me, glassy-eyed, then back down at her feet, disorientated.

'We should stop the bleeding, anyway.'

She considered this for a moment. 'K.'

'OK. If you sit down I'll get some water – warm water, to clean up the blood. And plasters – in the bathroom?' I wanted to sound matter-of-fact, practical, to take the heat out of the moment.

Fiona grunted. 'Na cabinet.'

'You want some help getting to the chair? Don't want to

cut your feet any more, do you?' She scanned the minefield of broken glass between her and the armchair, back and forth, the realisation sinking through her befuddled brain that there was no way across. 'If you just put those things down we'll get on with it.' She hesitated, then laid the carving knife and golf club on the sideboard. She straightened to face me, trying not to sway.

'Ready?'

She nodded. I crunched across the carpet and for an awkward moment we stood eye-to-eye, close. How to do this – fireman's lift, piggy-back? Could I even lift her? Only one way to find out. I bent down, slipped an arm behind her knees, the other around her waist, and in a single swift movement lifted her off the ground.

'Oh.' She seemed surprised, but put her arm around my shoulders.

'OK?'

'Uh-huh.'

I staggered the few crunching steps to the armchair and plonked her down as lightly as I could.

'There we are.'

'Q ...' She collapsed into the chair before I could brush off any splinters of glass.

'Right. I'll get the water.' As I turned to go my eye fell on the carving-knife and golf club. I crunched back to the sideboard and picked them up. 'Still want these?' She thought, then shook her head. All the rage seemed to have drained from her. 'OK. Don't go anywhere.' I smiled, opened the door – and caught Vanda eavesdropping.

She jumped back at the sight of the carving knife and golf club but had heard everything. I asked her to fetch the first-aid kit from the bathroom, then headed for the kitchen. Dave looked up from his basket but didn't stir as I half-filled the washing-up bowl with warm water, then returned with it to the hallway. Vanda was waiting with a red plastic box – the first-aid kit.

'Thanks.'

As she tucked it under my arm a movement caught my eye. Amelia and Oliver were spying on us from the first-floor landing, through the banisters. 'Hello,' I said cheerfully, as if attending to their mother with a washing-up bowl of water and a first-aid kit were the most normal thing in the world. 'Mummy's just cut her foot, but it's nothing to worry about, OK?'

They exchanged a look, clearly not buying it. Vanda clapped her hands. 'Come on – bed now. I'm coming up there.' Reluctantly, they peeled themselves away and disappeared from view. Vanda turned to me. 'You will sleep here, yes? Because if you go and in the night ...' She glanced anxiously at the sitting room door.

I hadn't thought of this. 'Let's get her sorted and then we'll see, OK?' Vanda seemed willing to accept this – just. She pushed open the sitting room door and pulled it shut behind me.

Fiona had passed out in the armchair. I was tempted to leave her, but the thought of her waking up at some point and stumbling around with glass in her feet made me wince. I put the bowl down by the chair and gently shook her.

'Fiona?'

No reaction. I checked there was no glass lurking in the carpet, then knelt down and rolled up the bottoms of her jeans. Her ankles were slim, her manicured toenails painted plum red.

I pulled the bowl closer and lowered her feet into the water. Again, no reaction. Then she yawned dreamily, smiling, in foot-bath heaven. I swished the water around and gently rubbed to clean off the dried blood. Fiona let out a low moan of pleasure, opened her eyes – and looked at me with blank incomprehension.

'What's …?'

I cleared my throat. 'You cut your feet. Just washing off the blood. Won't take long.'

A slow smile crossed her face as she closed her eyes again. 'No, no – you take as long as you like.'

I swished and rubbed some more, then carefully raised each foot out of the water to inspect the wounds. Most of the blood had come from a large splinter of glass that I could probably get out with my fingers. I glanced up. Fiona was asleep again, breathing deeply. With luck she wouldn't feel a thing. I gripped the splinter and tugged.

'Eeow!' She jerked awake, kicking water everywhere – and me in the nose. 'Jesus! Fock – what! Christ!'

'Sorry,' I said, my eyes watering and nose throbbing from her kick. 'That was the big one. The others should be no problem.'

Fiona glared at me. 'Other what?'

She really was out of it. 'Splinters in your feet – glass.'

She looked at them, shocked, then seemed to remember and settled back in the armchair. She watched me uneasily as I found the tweezers and, with a combination of sight and touch, gingerly removed the other bits of glass. Gradually she relaxed and by the time I'd finished was almost back in the land of nod.

'There – done.' She opened her eyes and stared groggily at her feet, as if trying to work out what they were for. 'Just have to dry them off, slap on a few plasters and you can hobble away into the night. I'll get a towel.' I hauled myself up and crunched over to the door.

'Are you 'lightened?' I stopped and turned. What was that? She dragged her gaze from her wet feet up to my face. 'Only I got a question – if you're 'lightened.'

Ah – *enlightened*. 'Well, I'm not sure what that means but go on.'

'This little fly today was buzzin' round. All day.' She twirled a finger in the air above her head, then dropped her hand with a thump on to the armrest.

'Yes …?'

'Was that Martin? Comin' back to say hello?'

Eh? What to say? 'I … I doubt it. No.'

'Oh.' She thought for a moment, head waggling. 'Or there was this robin – sweet, lovely little robin – by the window. All day. Hoppin', hoppin', hoppin'. Wouldn't go away.'

She looked at me enquiringly, hopeful, trying to focus. I chose my words carefully.

'Well, even if Martin did decide to come back as a robin, it wouldn't be that one, would it? Because that one would have hatched before he died. D'you see?'

'Oh. Hmm.' She thought, then nodded seriously, seeming to accept this.

'I'll get the towel,' I said, turning the door handle.

'Wasn't the money,' she mumbled. I looked round; what was she on about now? 'Was me. No sex. Didn't love him …' She pulled her face into a crooked smile, jerked a sad shrug and closed her eyes.

Dear God, what a mess. Complicated, confused, vulnerable. As I left the room she started to snore, a soft buzz on every intake of breath.

Vanda accosted me on the landing as I was coming out of the bathroom with a towel.

'It's all right,' I murmured. 'She's asleep. Kids OK?'

'In bed, yes. They were scared. Me also. She said she would kill me.' She took a deep breath to calm the emotion that recalling the threat stirred in her.

'It was the drink talking. I'm sure she didn't mean it.'

Vanda drew herself up, offended. 'You do not know. You are not there.'

Fair enough. 'Has anything like this happened before?'

'Not after I have been here. But she and Martin …' She shook her head.

'Fought?' She nodded. 'Physically?'

She shook her head. 'With silence – for days.'

I sighed, remembering the ice age that had descended towards the end of my time with Dora: the death of humour, of physical contact, of the easy intimacy that marks a good relationship. And the sex, of course.

'You will sleep here – just in case?' Vanda looked anxious.

'OK, sure.'

She smiled for the first time that evening.

Fiona snored peacefully through what came next – me drying off her feet and sticking plasters on her cuts, Vanda gathering up shards of glass and vacuuming around us with the Dyson. When we'd finished we left Fiona covered in a blanket in the armchair and decided to lock all the sharp knives in the gym, along with Martin's golf clubs, all the booze and his multi-socket car spanner set – she could do a lot of damage with one of those.

I was about to lock the gym when the sight of the bench opposite the blank wall reminded me that I hadn't done my evening chanting, so while Vanda went to check on the kids I quickly pulled the bench into place and sat down.

The first thing that came into my mind wasn't the situation here; it was Big Boy and Smiler, my shock at seeing them, the fear that they might know where I lived. But they couldn't. I'd looked over my shoulder every few yards on my way back home, checking they hadn't followed me.

Going through that underpass was a moment, though.

Real fear. As I chanted I saw myself running down into it ...

Smiler suddenly appears at the other end – smiling, sauntering, casual. How the hell did he get there? I judder to a halt, turn to run back but Big Boy has materialised behind me – and he's not smiling. He never smiles.

This is it: the showdown. They want to kill me, to take revenge for helping to convict them. Thank God for the martial arts training I've been taking, the hours building up my muscles, the spiritual exercises to still my mind – for this, the moment of truth. I crouch, grounded, ready for whatever they—

Hang on. What *is* this? Oh dear. Another post-traumatic fantasy loop. Put it down, Ed. Focus on reality, not some mental video game where you get to beat up the bad guys, over and over ... For all you know they might have been running as fast as possible in the opposite direction, terrified of breaching the terms of their sentence.

But to think I still had all that gut-wrenching fear hiding away inside me, unknown, unseen. Another invisible landmine just waiting for the right foot to fall ... then Detonation. Visceral. Overwhelming.

The persistence of things. Karma.

I wondered what landmine Fiona had stepped on this evening. Was all that blind destruction a way of trying *not* to look at her role in Martin's death? Or maybe an expression of her fear that his business failure was made worse by having no sympathy at home?

Poor bugger. No haven, no tenderness, no escape. He must have felt totally alone. But who knows? It was hard enough trying to fathom my own motivation, let alone someone else's. And he hadn't left a note.

I checked my watch – thirty minutes. That was enough chanting for now. But how to pass the hours till bedtime?

My eyes strayed to the bottles we'd stashed. I wandered over, picked one and checked the label: Château de Gueyze, 2004, Appellation Buzet Contrôlée. Perfect – another Buzet evening. I really should have worked in advertising, I thought, as I locked the door.

I drank it in the kitchen over the next couple of hours, listening to the radio. I did look for another TV and found one in the master bedroom, but it felt too intimate to watch it in there, so I climbed up to Martin's office. The police tape had been ripped off the door, leaving scars in the paintwork. Was it no longer out of bounds? I tried the handle and the door swung open. I flicked on the light.

All Martin's building samples had been piled neatly in the centre of the room. His desk was bare and every drawer had been emptied; ditto the filing cabinet.

I went down a flight and knocked on Vanda's door. After a moment she opened it but she didn't know if the police had been back; Fiona had asked her to take the kids to Hamleys that afternoon, to buy toys. Over her shoulder I could see them asleep in her bed, like the babes in the wood.

'Oh – and you're in there tonight,' she said, pointing across the landing to the spare room. 'It's where Martin slept.'

'Ah.' So that's why I'd been put in her room when I'd stayed over. Vanda sensed my lack of enthusiasm.

'Don't worry,' she said. 'I changed the sheets. For luck.'

Black. Darkness. My old friend.

I checked my phone: 04:18. *Ushitora* – again. This could become a habit. I'd have to add insomnia to my list of things to worry about.

I was in Martin's bed. Perhaps that's why I felt so low – he'd somehow imbued the mattress with his desolation.

He'd slept here for his last night of life. If he'd slept. He always looked knackered when I saw him. But why wouldn't he? Carrying around all that weight on his shoulders; never able to take a breath deep enough to clear the heaviness in his chest, or his heart. It's not the length of the sentence, it's the depth of the despair...

I sighed – I had to sleep. So think about something else. Women. Angie. Dora...

I dreamed.

I was scrambling through a bombed house, over rubble-splintered joists. There was a fire somewhere, and torn wallpaper, but clear sky above.

Someone was after me – the Nazis. They wanted to kill me. I climbed up. It was difficult, treacherous.

Then a door opened in the wall opposite – across the void. A bomb had blown the floor away. Amelia was there. 'Come on,' she said. 'Come on, you can do it!' She reached out her hand.

Daylight.

Weak, grey morning seeped around the edge of the heavy winter curtains. Quiet throughout the house, and outside too. I checked my phone: 07:11.

I sat up on the edge of the bed, gingerly, and ... no dizziness or nausea. Excellent. *Mis en bouteille à la propriété* – that was how you avoided a hangover. Or by not drinking, of course, but where was the fun in that? I stood up – still OK – crossed to the window and peeped through the curtains.

Fiona was at the bottom of the garden, standing on the edge of the swimming pool. Staring in.

Bloody hell.

I was about to rush down and save her when – hang on,

a steaming mug was in her hand. And the pool cover was on. Not an obvious suicide scenario. I calmed down.

So what was she doing? It was cold and damp, the grass was soaking, and she was standing there in just the jeans and mohair jumper she had worn the night before, plus the fluffy slippers Vanda had left by the armchair. I started pulling on my clothes. Couldn't let her get sick now. She had young children to look after.

She did a double-take, startled when she saw me striding down the lawn towards her.

'Jesus. Where did you spring from?'

'The spare room. I stayed over.' She looked blank. 'I was here last night.' Still no comprehension. 'You don't remember?'

'What?'

'You didn't see the sitting room?'

'When?'

'When you woke up.'

'I woke up in bed.'

'Wearing that?' She looked down at her clothes, as if seeing them for the first time. 'And how are your feet?' The question took her aback.

'Sore – why?'

'You cut them – walking on broken glass.' She stared at me, starting to look worried. 'Come on.'

I crooked my finger and led her back to the house, past the tail-wagging Dave in the kitchen, to the sitting room. Fiona stepped inside – and her mouth fell open. She glanced back at me, her green eyes full of horror, imploring me to say that the smashed TV and cabinets, the shattered lights, the ripped furniture weren't her work. But I nodded.

''Fraid so. With Martin's 7 iron. And a carving knife.'

She groaned and sat down hard on the arm of one of the sofas, appalled. 'Jesus.'

'How much did you have to drink?'

'Don't know. Can't remember. Or this – any of it.' She sounded almost scared.

'We found an empty half-bottle of vodka, and a couple of empty wine bottles,' I said. She nodded slowly, trying to take everything in. 'Haven't you got a hangover?'

'Don't get them. I'm lucky. Or unlucky, maybe.'

I knew what she meant. I suspected it was only my apocalyptic morning-after-the-night-befores that had saved me from the slippery slope into alcoholism – although some would doubtless say I was already halfway down it.

'You're probably still drunk,' I said. 'I know I would be.'

She sniffed. 'Well, I'm not you. And I'm fine.' Her fingers traced the filigree of fractures in the coffee table.

'Vanda cleared up. And I patched your feet.'

She glanced down at her fluffy slippers, kicked one off and inspected the plasterwork. 'Thanks.' She put the slipper back on, embarrassed, sheepish.

'D'you mind if I ask … why?' I gestured to the wreckage. Fiona studied my face, as if deciding whether she could trust me. 'I'm cheaper than a shrink.'

She didn't appreciate the joke. 'You saying I'm mad?'

'Not at all. It's just that – well, you might feel better talking about it, that's all.'

Fiona considered, then sighed. 'All right; as long as you don't tell anyone.'

'I am a clam,' I said, crossing my heart.

'OK. But first, a shower.'

When she next joined me in the kitchen she was clean and clear-eyed, almost sparkling, as if she'd been through some kind of human valet car wash. Watching her make tea and toast, and feed Dave, her blonde hair swinging back and forth in a damp ponytail, I found it hard to believe that this was the drunken wreck from only a few hours earlier. She was certainly a tough cookie – physically, at least.

She brought the tea and toast to the table, sat down – and began.

Yesterday had proved the old saying about trouble coming in threes. First, she'd arranged an urgent meeting with the bank manager, who'd laid out the full extent of the bad news – as far as he could see it.

'There's accounts all over the place: Spain, Ireland, Cyprus, Iceland ... *Iceland* for God's sake!' Her eyes widened at the very thought. 'Basically, anywhere he could get cheap euros during the boom. And he's been moving his money from this one to that one, paying off here, borrowing there. He's even remortgaged this place at least twice – without me knowing. So I've no idea who we're paying even, or if we're in arrears or what, cos the police cleaned out his office, took everything – thanks very much!'

'Because?'

She laughed bitterly. 'I'll come to that. But the bottom line, according to the bank – and the accountant, who got shot of him months ago, cos he wouldn't pay that bill either – the bottom line is that selling this place won't come close to covering what's owed. Not within a mile.' She shook her head, staggered at the scale of Martin's gamble.

'And it's all in his name?'

'Everything. And you know what really pisses me off?' Her green eyes flashed with anger. 'He had almost three grand, in cash, sitting in one of his accounts here, in Radlett. And did he transfer it to me? No, he goes and ... Without a thought for me or the kids, when just five minutes online and that money could have come to us, helped us – a bit. Now it's just going to go to the bank and every other bastard he owes money to. And we're screwed. No

money for gas, the electric. *Food*. And as for a lawyer ...'
She took a slug of tea, incensed.

'So you trashed the sitting room?'

She twisted her mouth into a bitter smile. 'Not sure why
I did that, exactly. But sounds about right, eh? Not mine, is
it? Never was. Or Martin's. It's all borrowed, the bank's – all
of it.' She scanned the top-of-the-range kitchen units and
cupboards, the shot-marble work surfaces. 'A borrowed
life. And now they want it back.'

For some reason I felt the need to defend Martin, perhaps because I doubted that anyone else would. But also
because, even if Fiona hadn't loved him, from what I'd seen
he'd doted on his family – well, the kids. Which made what
he'd done all the harder to understand.

'The thing is,' I said carefully, 'when people kill themselves it's – what's the phrase? "The balance of the mind
was disturbed." He obviously wasn't thinking straight.'

Fiona scoffed. 'He was thinking straight enough to send
me into town, and the kids to the pictures, to get a bottle of
brandy and rope and a torch and drive up there in the fog
and ...' She shook her head angrily. 'No, he just didn't care
about us. I mean, how could he, on any level, and do this?'

Then came the second of the three troubles. She'd
returned from the bank to find DCs Horton and Kelly
parked in the drive. They'd sat her down and, as compas-
sionately as they could, passed on the conclusion of the
post-mortem: that Martin's injuries were consistent with
hanging and they weren't looking for anyone else in rela-
tion to his death.

'You know, a tiny part of me was clinging to the hope
that he didn't ... you know, that that maybe someone else
... oh, I don't know. But he did.' She stared into her tea, on
the point of tears. 'To me. To the kids ... Christ.'

'You swore.'

Fiona whirled round. Oliver was in the doorway, in dressing gown and pyjamas, his brows knitted with suspicion. How long had he been there? Fiona jumped up and shuffled painfully across to him.

'I'm sorry, darling,' she said, smothering him in a hug. 'And for last night. Did I scare you?' Oliver nodded glumly, his bottom lip jutting out. 'Well, it wasn't really me – it was my evil twin sister, Fo-eena.'

'Fo-eena?'

'Yes, I'm Fiona and she's Fo-eena. She comes to visit sometimes – not very often, cos she's not very nice, is she?' Oliver shook his head. 'No. But it's OK – she's gone now. And I've told her one hundred per cent not to come back here ever again. All right?' Oliver nodded, unsure. 'You want some breakfast?'

'Coco Pops?'

'Sure,' said Fiona brightly. 'Sit down and I'll get them for you.'

I gave him a friendly smile as he sat at the far end of the table, but he blanked me. He took a small console from his dressing gown pocket and started playing a game as Fiona busied herself with his breakfast order.

'I can do you bacon and eggs if you like. Or scrambled, on toast? Cos Coco Pops aren't much of a start just by themselves, are they?'

Oliver shook his head. Perhaps, like me, he sensed she was trying to distract him from what he might have heard.

'What are you playing?' I asked. He shrugged, eyes locked on the beeping, chirruping screen. Fiona put a cereal bowl and spoon in front of him.

'Come on, no games while you're eating.' He put down the console and stared at the bowl. Fiona looked anxious. 'What's the matter?'

'I want it in my bowl. Harry Potter.'

Fiona stifled an irritated sigh, whipped away the offending tableware, transferred the contents to his special bowl and plonked it back in front of him.

'There,' she said, forcing a smile. Oliver picked up the spoon and started to munch. 'Vanda normally does breakfast,' she explained to me. 'But she must be having a lie-in this morning. And why not, if she's had a hard night?' She ruffled Oliver's hair, squeezing out another strained smile. He looked up from his cereal.

'Can I eat in front of the telly?'

Fiona's bonhomie vanished. I stepped in. 'There's a problem with the TV down here. Unless he can watch it in your room?'

Fiona's smile bounced back. 'Oh. Yes, OK – just this once. But spill any of that on the carpet and I'll ki—' She stopped herself. 'I'll be seriously cross. Come on.' She picked up his bowl, took his hand and led him out of the kitchen, on tiptoes to spare her cut soles.

She returned a couple of minutes later, looking worried. 'D'you think he heard? Christ knows how I'm going to explain the sitting room.'

'Well, you could keep it locked till it's fixed or—'

'How'm I going to get it fixed? I haven't got any money – remember? And I can't lock it cos I don't know where the key is.' She started to refill the kettle, biting her lip to stop it trembling.

'That reminds me,' I said. I took a key from my pocket and put it on the table. 'We locked all the booze in the gym last night, and the knives. Just in case.' She studied the key, her tears retreating. 'And for the sitting room – do you have the police tape, from the study door? I wasn't snooping,' I said quickly. 'I was looking for a TV myself, last night, and saw it'd gone.'

Fiona thought for a moment, then slid the waste bin

from the sink unit, rooted around and pulled out a tangled ball of blue and white tape. We exchanged a look. She dropped it back into the bin.

'The police have finished here, then?'

'Ha!' Fiona slammed the bin back into the unit. Cue trouble number three.

During their visit, DCs Horton and Kelly had told her why they were investigating Martin: he'd been accused by Councillor Daley of offering him £5,000 to reverse on appeal the planning committee's decision to reject the Hillview pool extension. Horton and Kelly had made an appointment with Martin later this week to talk about 'various business matters', but obviously that wasn't going to happen now. So they'd locked his office to safeguard any evidence of wrongdoing, and yesterday cleared it out.

It was my turn to be incensed. 'You mean they knew all that and still tried to suggest that Bernie and I were involved? Classic!'

'Yeah, well, that's the police, isn't it? Got their own agenda,' said Fiona. I barked a scornful laugh. 'The inquest opens tomorrow, by the way,' she continued, 'but it's just, you know, formal. They adjourn it while the police are still investigating. Though they've released the body. Which is another thing I've got to sort out.'

'God, talk about screwing up.' Fiona nodded, her lip starting to tremble again. I reached out and squeezed her hand. 'But you shouldn't blame yourself. Martin brought everything on himself – that's obvious.'

Fiona drew back and pulled her hand away. 'Who says I blame myself?'

'Well, last night ...' I stopped at her anxious expression. She obviously had no memory of her confession.

'What? What did I say?'

'Nothing. It was just drunken—'

'What did I say?' Her tone was hard, fearful.

'Just that things between you and Martin weren't, you know ... great.' I didn't want to embarrass her. 'But that's hardly surprising if he was under all that pressure.'

She stared at my face, trying to gauge if I was holding anything back. Then her eyes slid to the doorway and at once her expression brightened.

'Hello, darling.'

Amelia had just wandered in, tousled from sleep, clutching a blue stuffed rabbit. She meandered over for a good morning kiss and hug.

'Did you sleep well, poppet?' Amelia nodded, rubbing her eyes. 'Would you like some breakfast – boiled egg and soldiers?' Amelia nodded again. 'All right, sit down, I'll make it. Like some juice?'

Amelia nodded a third time and sat at the table. Unlike her brother, she gave me a wide smile. I pointed to her rabbit.

'What's his name?'

'Rabbit.' Obviously. She turned to Fiona. 'Mummy, where's Vanda?'

'Still in bed I should think, darling.'

Amelia shook her head. 'No. And her toothbrush isn't there.'

Not just her toothbrush. We discovered that all her clothes were gone too, plus her three large suitcases and rucksack. The kids had woken up in their own beds, so at some point in the night she must have carried them back to their rooms, then packed all her things and quietly slipped out to a waiting cab. Or maybe she'd called a friend. We'd never know because, like Martin, she didn't leave a note.

At first Fiona was spitting with rage; losing another person close to them, without warning, was the last thing her children needed. I was pretty pissed off myself – Vanda had used me as cover to make her escape. But once Fiona had calmed down she saw a silver lining: one less mouth to feed. On no money.

I didn't see them for the next few days; more than a week, in fact. I repeated my offer of help – I was worried about them – but Fiona insisted that she'd manage and I didn't want to force the issue. The shock, the grief, the sudden change of fortune: Martin's death was an emotional earthquake they each had to process in their own way. She did promise to let me know about the funeral, though, once she'd worked out how to pay for it. Perhaps Martin's sister might help.

And I still had my own stuff to deal with, of course. Top of the list was getting a new lodger, but every time I sat down to write the advert something stopped me. After the third attempt I realised that I just couldn't face sharing my space with someone I didn't know; not now, at this precise moment. And chanting about it I realised that Martin's death had shaken me, too, more profoundly than I'd thought. Which was strange because we weren't close; in fact, for years I'd never even thought about him. And yet at a key moment he'd turned up again in my life, yanking me out of a rut and into a different reality, one to which I was still trying to adjust. Mega-money and mega-debt. Criminality. His family. His wife. *There you are.* And there you'll stay. Though I will help if I can.

Martin had also revived my connection to Buddhism, although that didn't feel so strange second time around. If anything, it was the one reference point I kept returning to. And speaking of returning, I went back to Last Edition a couple of days after finding my book there – keeping an eye open for Big Boy and Smiler – but it had gone. The chap in the purple jumper said a young Asian woman had spotted it and as he didn't think I'd be coming back he'd sold it to her. Which cheered up me up – that someone actually still wanted to read it.

And then life took another twist.

I got a text from Piers announcing that, despite speculation to the contrary, he would indeed be holding the regular monthly discussion meeting at his place. Topic – the eternity of life. No prizes for guessing what had prompted that.

I duly turned up to be greeted by the usual crew – Piers and Bernie, Jenny, Darren and Aidan – and Luis, who I was sure had dragged himself along in the vain, lovelorn hope that Rachel would be there. She wasn't, and neither was Constanza or Bella. But there was a surprise guest, some-one I really didn't expect to see, ever.

Dora.

Chapter Eleven

She was looking good – a little curvier maybe, a few flecks of grey in her close-cropped curls; but she radiated health. Her skin was smooth and glowing, and her dark brown eyes shone with curiosity. The Caribbean sun clearly liked her.

She was here to complete the sale of her flat, she said. She'd been renting it out since moving to Barbados to look after her ailing mother; but she'd recently got a great new job and couldn't see herself returning to the UK, so selling up was the logical thing to do. I wanted to hear more but Piers interrupted. The meeting was starting.

It was odd being in that room with her. We'd been so intimate once, known each other inside out. Yet the period since we'd split was a mystery to us both – a sea we'd crossed, leaving our old selves on the distant shore. At one point, as the discussion flowed back and forth, Dora caught me studying her and flashed a quick, knowing smile. And a little later I caught her studying me and grinned back – touché. She smiled and looked away, a silent dialogue running between us.

We began the meeting by talking about the eternity of life but the discussion quickly turned to Martin's suicide, then shifted on to depression. Everyone seemed to have a tale to tell, of themselves or someone close.

Darren wondered if Martin had gone through what he'd suffered during his employment dispute, because at one point he'd contemplated suicide. But his experience was topped by Aidan's, which had been triggered by something that seemed totally trivial: failing his driving test.

'It's that feeling of being a useless person that Darren's just described. I'd been terrible at school and my dad used to say I was a complete waste of space. Shout at me. Hit me, in fact. And I suppose when I grew up I used to do drink and drugs to try to hide from those thoughts. But not passing my test, for the third time – that just confirmed it was all true, you know? I *was* a waste of space, a total failure. So I just did more booze and more cocaine, cos at the time I was actually making a lot of money.'

I was puzzled. 'And you still thought you were useless?'

'Totally – it came too easily. I was a model. I didn't have to actually *do* anything, apart from going to the gym. It was just the way I looked. So people paying me loadsa money just confirmed what I thought about myself: a fake. Pretty on the outside, nothing on the inside. The more I made, the more I despised myself. And the more I worried about what would happen once people saw through me, saw how empty I really was. Depression's like that – it twists everything upside-down. It screws up the nice stuff and anything not nice is what you deserve anyway.'

There were nods of recognition around the room, even from Luis, who seemed somehow to be keeping up with the story.

'Anyhow, I went into this nosedive and had to turn down work, and bit by bit thinking and communicating became harder and harder and just … knackering. I mean, just deciding what to do first in the day, what next, what to wear, what to eat … And I had this sort of low-level headache the whole time – you know, in the background. Except sometimes it was really intense, like someone kicking your head in. Being with people was agony. Having to talk, choose words, explain how I felt ... And people being positive, giving advice, trying to help ...'

He shook his head, still pained at the memory.

'Plus I felt ashamed at how I was, so I hid it, like Martin must have, and eventually I stopped going out and practically became a hermit. Which doesn't help, of course, cos then you're trapped with just yourself and your thoughts going round and round, like a washing-machine – except it's a washing-machine that makes everything dirty. And in the end I didn't know who I was any more, and I was so shattered I really didn't care if I lived or died. I just wanted some rest – you know, take a break. Sleep – the Big Sleep. So the next step, logically, is to do it yourself.'

He stopped and glanced round the circle of eyes focused in on him. Jenny broke the silence.

'But you didn't?'

Aidan gave a strange smile. 'Well, I chanted about it, actually. That was about the only thing I could do, in fact. But I couldn't decide the best way. Like, I'd walk down the street and look at the trees and think, that's a good hanging tree. But then, no, they'd cut me down before I could finish it. So I decided it had to be something quick, with no chance of being stopped or changing my mind. The Tube.'

I grimaced and saw Jenny wince. The image was horrible. Aidan pressed on.

'But I decided to do a goodbye gongyo first. I suppose part of me wanted to test if it would change my mind, cos I'd heard stories of Buddhists doing this and saying a final thank you in their minds to all the people who'd helped them during their lives, and the gratitude that came up stopping them going through with it. Or them realising all the hurt they'd do to their family and friends and stuff. But as I chanted I just thought they'd all be well shot of me, good riddance to bad rubbish. Especially my dad – get that fat lump of uselessness out of his life.

'So I finished, and locked up, and headed off to the Tube – Kilburn. It was about three o'clock and I thought it'd be quiet, not too many people around. I climbed the stairs and went to the end of the platform, the far end, where there was nobody, and waited in the sunshine for the train. I didn't think what it would do to the driver, or anybody else who saw it. I just wanted … oblivion.

'Then I heard the rails start to, you know, sing – like they do when there's a train coming. And my mind went blank. I wasn't scared, or nervous, just focused on the timing, getting it right. I looked up – the train was about thirty yards away, coming fast – and I caught the driver's eye. I saw this look of shock, like he suddenly realised what I was going to do. But it was too late. The train was – what – two seconds away? And I was just going to fall when these arms came round my chest and grabbed me, and pulled me back. Piers.'

All eyes swivelled as one to Piers, who was following the story with a frown of concentration.

'He marched me down to the doctor's, once he'd dragged out of me what was happening,' said Aidan. 'And the upshot: I live to fight another day. Cheers.'

He gave Piers a thumbs-up – and promptly welled up. Which set us all off.

'You never told us about this,' said Jenny.

'Private,' said Piers. 'And another coincidence.'

There was silence. I looked at Aidan, wiping his eyes on his sleeve. That took some balls, I thought – admitting you'd tried to kill yourself. But who'd have thought it? Mr

Handsome, Mr Perfect Bod. The guy who has to fight off the ladies with a stick ...

Dora cleared her throat. 'When Piers told me the topic for tonight I was going to give an experience about my mum, who died in March.'

'Oh, I'm sorry,' I murmured. 'I didn't know.'

Dora waved a forgiving hand. 'Why would you? But it still sort of fits with depression, I think.'

Piers gestured for her to speak. Dora smiled.

'So – my parents were from Barbados and came over in 1960 for work. My dad worked for British Rail and my mum was a cleaner. So I was born here and grew up as a Londoner. Anyway, fast-forward many years, my dad dies and about ten – no, twelve – years ago my mum decides to go back to Barbados to retire, because they always kept a little house there, near the beach.

'So there she is, in this little house, all fine and dandy, till about four years ago she starts to develop dementia, to the point where my auntie's calling me every day almost, saying she's forgetting this, forgetting that, even forgetting to eat, or eating stuff raw – like raw fish – because she's forgotten to cook it. And there's no one to look after her, because my auntie's in her eighties and in a wheelchair, and my two brothers and me live over here. And we don't want to just dump her in a home. So, after a lot of chanting, I decide to rent out my flat, up sticks and do the daughterly thing, i.e. go out and look after her. I'm single, no kids, got a bit saved up and can just about live off what I'm getting from the flat. Plus there's sun!'

She laughed, flashing a bright smile around the room – and was suddenly the sexy, vibrant Dora I'd fallen for ten years earlier.

'And for a while it was great, like being on holiday. Mum was OK – forgetful, but more in an absent-minded sort of way than, you know, wandering through the traffic in her dressing gown. And she could just about remember who I was, which was a good start, and we got on well – mother and daughter – and joked about her forgetting things. She was sweet, really.

'But gradually she got worse – and so did I. I started to have a drink in the evenings as a kind of reward for getting through the day. Then it became two or three, or more. And as that increased my chanting decreased. I thought I'd be this pioneering Buddhist, showing – you know – strength in adversity, proof of the practice, but actually I was just sinking. And couldn't see it.

'Basically, I was lonely. Being with Mum all the time was like a kind of prison. There's a small Buddhist group on the island, but whenever I went out – just for the evening, even if there was a friend with her – I felt guilty. Or worried. Stupid really, but ... Anyway, it took me a long time to admit to myself that I was depressed. And whether that was making me drink or the drinking was making me depressed – what was cause and what was effect – I couldn't say. Probably both. But realising that the alcohol wasn't helping took a long time, too.'

I listened with incredulity. Dora was the strongest person I'd ever met – and the most committed Buddhist. The number of times she'd lectured me about challenging my weaknesses – and here she was admitting to being imperfect. But the weird thing was it made her more attractive, not less. More – well – human. I could feel a faint flutter in my chest.

'Part of the problem was sleeping. Here, I used to go to bed and fall asleep like that.' She clicked her fingers. 'Seven hours later wake up, yawn, jump out of bed and bang – into the day. But out there I was going to bed later and later, usually half-drunk, and never sleeping through. I'd wake up, like clockwork, around four in the morning, which I now think was invented as a special kind of torture, when all your fundamental darkness creeps out and tells you what a terrible person you are and how there's no point going on because some kind of personal apocalypse is coming.'

We laughed but I was even more amazed. It could have been me talking – the drinking, the loneliness, the early morning desolation. But a thought occurred to me: had Dora been so tough on my weaknesses because, beneath everything, she'd been scared of admitting that she shared them? I looked at Piers and remembered something he'd said years ago: that he'd hated in his dad what he'd been most reluctant to see in himself. His roving eye, for instance.

Dora continued. 'Anyway, one day Mum decided she wanted fried plantain – at two in the morning. Then forgot what she was doing and the pan caught fire. But – incredible protection – her friend next door was up, saw the flames through the window and rushed over. But what was really mortifying was I slept through the whole thing, till the neighbour burst in screaming and gave me a right earful. I'd had four large – and I mean *large* – rum and cokes.

'So that was a real wake-up call – literally. I stopped drinking – bang, the next day – and haven't had a drop since. And racked up my chanting, which made me realise I needed a job, even part-time, just to keep me – you know – sane. So I got one and most of the money actually went on paying someone to look after Mum while I was at work, but boy was it worth it! And basically, that's how it was till she died in March, in her sleep.

'But I realised something one evening as I was walking home along the beach. The tide was out and some tourists were picking their way across a big bunch of rocks sticking out of the sand, looking into the pools. And it occurred to me that on my way to work the tide had been in and people were swimming and snorkelling at that same spot. The rocks were still there but they were under the water. And I saw that the negativity in my life was like those rocks. It's always there, and when my life state's low the rocks appear and I get stranded on them. But when my life state's high it covers the rocks and I can swim about. Being with my mum I'd let the tide go out. But I could also make the tide come back in with my practice, and change how I was living. Which is what I did. And I started swimming again.'

I wanted to hear more about Dora's experience after the group discussion had ended and people were hanging around, chatting over tea and coffee, but she had to rush off to speak to someone about her flat. So I gave her my number and she promised to call to fix a lunch date.

It's funny how things can change. The last time we'd been in the same room together we could barely look at one another. But now, with no demands or expectations, we'd been relaxed and friendly and curious about what was going on in each other's life. How ironic – and sad – if the closer we got to others the less freedom we gave them to be themselves. Maybe I'd bring it up during our lunch – if it wasn't too intimate. After all, it would be the first time in five years we'd be alone together. But we used to have great talks, me and Dora, about everything. In the early days, at least; before the tide started to go out, the rocks appeared – and our relationship ran on to them.

I was turning this over during my chanting the following morning when my phone rang: Fiona. Perhaps she had news about the funeral. I pressed the answer button – and was plunged headlong into another crisis.

'Ed, the bailiffs are here!' There was panic in her voice.

'Wha – why?'

'They're repossessing the house!'

'What! How? They can't do that.'

'They're doing it!'

'But there's a whole legal process they've got to—'

'They've done it – with Martin! He just ignored it! They want us out, they're going to change the locks!'

'Bloody hell. Are they in the house?'

'No – outside.'

'OK, don't let them in. I'll be right there.'

Talk about drama. As I sped over I tried to work out what might have happened. Martin juggles money around to protect the funding for Hillview and gambles on not paying his mortgage. He falls further and further behind till the lender loses patience and starts proceedings for repossession. Which Martin hides from Fiona, of course, because he's got a light at the end of the tunnel: selling Hillview to Stylianou. Once the house is finished and the rest of the money is handed over he'll be home and free ...

But then – disaster. The council turns down planning permission for the swimming pool extension. The sale's about to unravel. In desperation Martin offers the commit-tee chairman a bung but Daley goes to the police. Who try to interview Martin. Who buys time by making an appointment to see them this week – but then receives a repossession notice from the court. For today. He knows the game's up, he can't keep the plates spinning any longer, it's all going to come crashing down. There's only one way out ...

Unless he did it for the life insurance. Now, there's a thought. But did he have any? Would it pay out on suicide? And if it did, would the money go to Fiona or just get swal-lowed up by the big black hole of his debt?

I sighed. Nothing would become clear until the police released the papers they'd taken. And right now I had to deal with the emergency in front of me. A gaggle of bailiffs seemed to be shouting at the front door, with two bored PCs looking on from the property boundary.

As I pulled up behind a blue transit with 'ABC Emergency Locks' printed in large letters on the side, one of the bailiffs turned to clock me: my old friend, Man in Charge. His bibulous features creased into a scowl as I approached.

'What d'ye want?' he growled in broad Scots.

'Mrs Upton, who lives here,' I said, smiling, 'is the widow of Martin Upton, who you might remember was the developer of Hillview who, er' – I dropped my voice – 'died the other weekend.' I couldn't be sure that Oliver and Amelia weren't listening on the other side of the front door.

'So?'

'Well, as you might have realised by now, she knew nothing about this repossession until you lot turned up.'

Man in Charge held his clipboard up to my face. 'This is a warrant of possession, an order of the court. A legal document that I'm empowered by the court, the law of the land, to enforce.'

'I understand that,' I said, trying to sound reasonable. 'But it was her husband who was dealing with it – or rather, not dealing with it – and this has come as a total shock to her. And her two children, of six and eight. They haven't packed, they haven't made any arrangements; they're still in trauma from Mr Upton's death. Are you seriously telling me you're going to put them on the street?'

Man in Charge tutted. 'If I had a quid for every sob story I heard ...'

'It's not a sob story – it's true.' He shrugged. 'So you are going to throw them out – on to the street?' I could feel my blood rising.

Man in Charge thrust his face forward. He was getting irritated too. 'I have a court order. An *order*, from the court, that I *have* to carry out. Because that's what an *order* means.'

'But—'

'It's the end of the line – *sir*. Now, if you'll excuse me.' He nodded to one of his goons, who I saw with alarm was carrying what the police call an enforcer – a small but very solid battering ram used to smash doorlocks.

'Whoa! You can't do that, just break in!'

'You should know your law, sir. I can – and will.'

I turned in desperation to the coppers watching from the pavement. 'They can't do that, can they – just break in?' They nodded. 'But it's a breach of the peace, surely?' They shook their heads.

'Happy?' Man in Charge looked so smug I was tempted to put my fist in his face – at which moment a car horn sounded.

We looked round to see a Range Rover accelerating between speed bumps, brake hard to bounce over the last one, then judder to a halt across the entrance to the drive. A young woman in a figure-hugging grey suit jumped out, grabbed an attaché case and clattered on high heels across the block-paved drive towards us.

'Sorry I'm late,' she said, flustered. 'Thanks for waiting.'

'Who are you?'

'Sally Damien – Ivy, James and Kenway, Solicitors. For the lenders.' She whipped out a business card and gave it to me. 'And you are …?'

'Friend of the family – who know nothing about this. All the papers went to the husband, Martin Upton, who' – I lowered my voice again and pulled her away from Man in Charge – 'committed suicide a few days ago. He hid everything from his wife and kids, who are now going to be thrown into the street!'

'Oh.' Ms Damien looked shaken. 'Is that true?'

'If you call off the pack, we can go inside and you can find out for yourself.'

She glanced at the front door, unsure. 'I don't think it's going to make any difference. The lenders are being liquidated.' She saw my puzzled expression. 'Wound up. They're under a legal obligation to call in their non-performing loans, like this one.'

'Who are *they*?'

'Kaupthing – in Iceland.'

I groaned; trust Martin to have ended up with one of the dodgiest banks around.

'OK,' I said, 'but let's at least do things humanely, hmm? Give them a chance to pack up and leave with dignity. There are two little kids in there.'

Ms Damien hesitated. 'I'll have to call my office. And the receivers. They might grant an extension on compassionate grounds, but obviously I can't promise anything. Unless there's a chance of the arrears being cleared?' I gave a hollow laugh. 'Well, then …'

'All right, thanks. And perhaps you could have a word with the guy in charge?'

Ms Damien smiled. As she sashayed across to the bailiffs I strode over to the front door, rang the bell and knocked.

'Fiona – it's Ed.'

There was a moment of silence, then the rattle of the chain, the click of the catch and the clunk of the mortice turning. The door swung open, I stepped inside and Fiona slammed it behind me, locking and chaining it with shaking hands.

'I wouldn't bother,' I said. 'They'll only break it down.' I pushed away Dave's enthusiastic, groin-greeting head. No sense of crisis, that dog – unlike Fiona, who paced back and forth across the hall, running manic fingers through her hair.

'It's a nightmare. I can't believe he'd ... It's just –' She slumped on to the stairs, overwhelmed, hands pressed to her temples.

'Yeah, it's pretty bad. But we might have a breathing space.' Fiona looked up, desperate for some hope. 'Their lawyer's outside and seeing if she can get you an extension so that—'

'An extension! This is our home!'

'Fiona, it's no good shouting at me. I'm trying to help – OK?'

She slumped again, deflated. 'Sorry. I'm just . . .' She covered her face. Her shoulders started to heave. A sob broke from between her fingers. I crossed the hall and instinctively stroked her head. It was the first time I'd seen her cry.

'It's OK. Don't worry. You're under a lot of pressure.' She snapped up straight and sucked in a deep breath.

'No – that's pathetic, crying.' She wiped the sleeve of her jumper across her sniffling nose and dabbed her eyes with the cuffs.

I looked up the stairs. 'Where are the kids?'

'School. They've got to rehearse the nativity play. Ha!'

The doorbell rang. I peered through the spyhole. The distended, fish-eyed features of Sally Damien loomed back.

'Lawyer,' I said. Fiona darted into the downstairs loo to splash water on her face while I unlocked the Fort Knox defences and held off Dave as Ms Damien slipped in. I closed the door behind her as Fiona emerged from the loo. The two women stared at each other.

'I've, er, spoken to the office,' Ms Damien said after an uncomfortable moment, 'and they've agreed that as long as the order's enforced by the close of business today that should be OK. Sorry it can't be longer but we're at the end of a very long road and patience has finally—'

Fiona cut her off. 'So that's what – out by six?'

'At the latest, yes.' Ms Damien sounded ill at ease. 'But if you act fast you might be able to get a warrant suspending repossession. I shouldn't really be telling you this because I'm on the other side, obviously. But anyway, that's up to you. I'm sorry I can't do any more.'

Fiona didn't respond, just peered through the spyhole, then opened the door for her to leave. Man in Charge, his gang and the locksmith were already going, watched by the police, who were about to follow.

'Thanks,' I said. 'It's appreciated. Is all the stuff in the house repossessed as well or …'

'No. That can be removed by arrangement, but we do have to change the locks.' Another awkward moment. 'Well – good luck.'

She stepped outside and headed for the Range Rover. I closed the door again and turned to see Fiona sitting back on the stairs, petting Dave.

'What do you want to do?'

'Die.' She caught my panicked expression. 'Don't worry – one suicide's enough. And I'd never do that to my children.' She looked Dave in the eye. 'Knew what was coming, didn't he? The coward.' She stood up. 'Cup of tea?'

'I meant,' I said, following her into the warmth of the kitchen, 'do you want to try to get a warrant for suspension or whatever it's called? I could help, I'm not doing anything …'

'Thanks, but it's no good.' She snapped on the kettle, then leaned back against the units, arms folded, suddenly calm. 'It's all over. My solicitor doesn't want to know. Martin owes him thousands. He didn't even want to take my call when I last tried. So just getting a lawyer's going to be … Then even if we do there's no guarantee we'll get a hearing in time. And I've got to pick up the kids at half three so …' She forced a smile and turned to make the tea.

'But where are you going to go?'

She shook her head and stared out of the window at the garden.

'I know the council are legally obliged to—'

'There is *no way* me and my kids are going to sit in some stinking council B&B, even for a night. No way.'

'So – what?'

She shook her head again. There was a silence, apart from the noise of the kettle coming to the boil. I felt I had to encourage her, if I could.

'Well, at least your feet have healed,' I said. 'You're not limping anyway.'

She nodded, her back still turned to me. Then her shoulders started to heave again as she fought another attack of tears. I wanted to give her a hug but restrained myself. I couldn't stop the words coming out though.

'Well, you can always … stay at mine if you're really desperate.' Her shoulders stopped shaking. 'Just for a bit – you know, till you've got things sorted.' She turned to look at me. 'Because there's only two bedrooms, so you could have one and the kids could share the other – it's a double bed. And there's a sofa bed downstairs which I could …' I hesitated, disconcerted by her searching gaze. It was exactly the look she'd given me during that dinner here with Martin – the stare that said she really didn't know what to make of me. 'I mean, it's nothing like as grand as this, but any port in a storm, eh?'

I could feel my skin prickling, the heat rising. Oh God. One of my blushes was starting. Bloody hell. Up until that one with Martin and Chris this part of my sad, dysfunctional life had disappeared. And here it was – back again in lurid Technicolor.

Fiona's expression changed – from forensic stare, to puzzlement, to concern, then amusement.

'No strings attached?'

'Absolutely not.' I probably said it with too much emphasis. 'In fact, it was the thought that you might think that, that's – you know …' I pointed at my face, down which sweat was now trickling.

Fiona grinned and threw me a tea-towel. I wiped my face, then escaped into the utility room and unlocked the side door. Damp air hit me like a cool flannel. Bliss.

'OK?' Fiona was struggling to keep a straight face as I returned to the kitchen.

'Thank you. And I want to make it absolutely clear that I'm going to be downstairs on the sofa bed throughout, whether it's one night or more – which is entirely up to you. But if you're worried I'm quite happy to move out, let you and the kids—'

'Don't be silly.'

'No, I mean it. I don't want you to feel on edge. I just want to help because, well – I can.'

'What about him?' She nodded at Dave, who was sitting staring up at her, tail patiently thumping the tiled floor. Damn. I'd forgotten about him.

'Sure,' I said with a nonchalant shrug. 'He can share the sofa bed.'

She said she wanted to think about it, which gave me the chance to drive home, do a quick tour of the house and realise that it was completely unsuitable for another three people and a dog; especially the dog. Where to put him? The kitchen was far too small, the only space in the main room for his basket was under the table, and my back 'garden' was a concrete pen barely four metres square. In fact, 15 Bladon Street in its entirety was a shoebox.

So I was beginning to have serious doubts about my offer when Fiona called to accept it, with thanks. They'd be there only a few nights, she promised – a week at most – while she sorted out something more permanent. But she really didn't want to take the kids out of school; it wasn't long till the holidays and having somewhere local would be a real benefit. Besides, the fees were paid till the end of term – one debt Martin didn't leave.

I asked how she'd explain the situation to Amelia and Oliver but she batted the question away, along with my offer of help with the move; just expect to see them some time before six o'clock. She wanted to be out and away before the kids saw the bailiffs.

I spent the rest of the day getting ready for their arrival. The beds needed clean sheets, which meant a trip to the launderette; then a whizz round the house with the hoover, cleaning the bath, a supermarket raid. But what did they eat – because kids could be fussy, right? I couldn't get through to Fiona for guidance so was forced to drift in a dither up and down the aisles.

I was looking through the ready-meals when my phone rang: an 'unknown number' that turned out to be a bloke with a Geordie accent called Greg Turner, from Herts Mediation Group. He wanted to talk about Carl Macer and restorative justice.

'Who?'

'Carl Macer. He was convicted of robbing you in the street back in August.'

'Ah. OK.' I realised that in all this time I'd never known – had never asked – what Big Boy or Smiler's real names were.

'You should have had a letter from the court with the verdict, details of the sentence, compensation …?'

'Er, no. I got a call from the police and some leaflets, but not a letter.'

'Oh. Well, don't know what happened there. But Carl has

indicated he's willing to take part in an RJ programme and I've been asked to facilitate by the youth offending team, who've said you're happy to take part too. Is that right?'

'Erm, I didn't go to court,' I said, 'so which one is he – the big one or the little one?'

'The big one.'

'Right...' If it had been Smiler, sure. But Big Boy? He was a nasty piece of work. 'What about his mate?'

'His brother, actually, younger brother – Kevan. Doesn't want to be involved yet. It's voluntary, on all sides.'

'And the other victim?'

'Not interested.'

'Hmm. So what can you tell me about him – Carl Macer?'

'Right now, nothing.'

'Oh?'

'No, sorry, we can only pass on what the participants are willing to share, and before the meeting and some trust has been established, usually that's not much.'

'Oh. So what does he know about me?'

'Just your name.'

'Good.'

Turner sensed my hesitation. 'I appreciate you might have various concerns and questions, so before you make any decision I could come to visit you to talk things through, or if you prefer you could come to my office—'

'Yes, I'll come to you,' I said quickly. I wanted to keep all of this as far from 15 Bladon Street as possible.

We made a time and date, I got his office details and the call ended. Almost at once my phone rang again: 'unknown number'. Turner must have forgotten to say something, I thought, but this time it was Dora. How about lunch tomorrow? I hesitated, for a moment overwhelmed by the rapidity with which things were coming at me. Fiona and her kids' imminent arrival, the prospect of sitting down opposite Big Boy – correction: Carl Macer – and now lunch with my ex-partner. Life seemed to be speeding up.

'But if that's a problem we can find another time,' Dora said.

'No, that's good.'

We agreed on a restaurant and, emboldened, I made an executive decision on supper – pizza. Kids love pizza. Can't go wrong with that.

The doorbell rang at 5.36. Fiona ushered in Oliver and Amelia, who both looked shell-shocked. Each carried a small bag of their prized possessions, like the wartime evacuees I'd seen in that local history book, and Amelia clutched Rabbit tight to her chest.

'Hello,' I said cheerily. 'There's juice and biscuits through there. I'll just help your mum with the bags.' They wandered into the kitchen, dazed, as Fiona and I went out to the car, a little Skoda. Dave was grinning at us from the back seat, raring to go. Unlike the children.

'What did you tell them?'

'Men are coming to work on the house and we have to move out for a bit.'

'Did they buy it?'

She shrugged and clicked open the boot. Somehow she'd managed to cram in eight large bags, all full of clothes and shoes.

'What happened to the BMW?' I asked. 'Did you sell it?'

'Huh. No, it was leased through Martin's company. I took it back. This one's going back too, tomorrow.'

We ferried the bags into the house and piled them in the centre of the living room, where Amelia and Oliver sat on the sofa timidly sipping their juice cartons. Fiona made one last trip for Dave, I closed the front door and turned to the four of them with a big, nervous smile.

'Well, hello again – and welcome.'

Amelia and Oliver sat mute. Fiona gave them a nudge and they muttered a hello.

'So, when you've finished your drink and biscuit I'll show you your room, OK?' They exchanged a glance and Oliver raised his hand. 'You don't have to put your hand up, Oliver,' I said. He pulled it down with a frown. 'But what's your question?'

'Why are we here?'

'Ah – a philosopher.' I laughed, glancing at Fiona for help.

'I explained all that – remember?' she said, with false brightness. 'Men are coming to do work on the house and we have to move out for a bit.'

Oliver wasn't satisfied. 'But why have we come *here*?'

'Because Ed has very kindly offered to help us while the work's being done – OK?' Fiona flashed a brittle smile.

'Will we be home for Christmas?' Amelia's face was the picture of trusting innocence.

'Not sure yet, Puddle,' said Fiona, 'but we'll have a lovely Christmas wherever we are. Now, let's see your room, shall we?' Amelia and Oliver exchanged another look, unconvinced.

'This way,' I said. 'And perhaps put Dave outside while we do the tour?'

It would be an understatement to say that Amelia and Oliver were not impressed by their new accommodation. They looked on in silent shock as I showed them the wardrobe – assembled from a flat-pack with my own fair hands – and slid out the deep storage drawers from under the bed.

'You mean we have to share?' Oliver was starting to realise the full horror of their situation.

'You've shared before,' said Fiona from the doorway.

'When?' said Oliver.

'On holiday,' snapped Fiona, struggling to control Dave. 'He wouldn't go outside,' she explained to me. 'He took one look and just dug in his heels.'

'Cos he hates it,' said Oliver. He plonked himself down on the end of the bed and crossed his arms, angry.

Amelia was at the window, looking up and down the street – a row of dowdy terraced cottages, two lines of parked cars. If she craned her neck she might just be able to glimpse the tree on the corner. She turned away and sat on the bed, her mouth trembling with the effort not to cry. Fiona looked torn between the urge to comfort them both and the fear that this would open the floodgates of recrimination.

'You're next door,' I said, coming to her rescue.

She was stoical about her – my – room. It was slightly bigger than the kids' and held a large oak chest of drawers in addition to the wardrobe. I'd cleared space in both for her, which she accepted with a breezy 'That's fine.' But the house suddenly seemed very, very small. Because it was.

Supper seemed to confirm the disaster that had engulfed the family. The children picked at the fancy deep-pan pizza I'd bought – Fiona explained, embarrassed, that they ate only thin-crust margheritas – and most of what was on their plates ended up inside Dave; which was just as well, as I'd forgotten to buy dog food. I then took him to the local cemetery – the only vaguely green space within easy distance – for a post-prandial dump while Fiona cooked some way-past-its-sell-by-date pasta she'd found in the cupboard for her still hungry offspring.

'Don't worry,' she assured me when Dave and I returned forty minutes later. 'It's only temporary.'

I'd wanted to give her and the kids some time alone to

adjust to their new circumstances, and she confessed that Oliver had thrown a tantrum and Amelia had wailed for her daddy as soon as I'd left the house. They'd been pacified – for now – with the luxury ice cream I'd bought for this first night, plus the promise that if they were good and didn't complain Father Christmas would bring them each an extra special present.

'What?'

Fiona shrugged. 'I'll think of something.'

I didn't like the sound of that. 'Aren't you just digging a bigger hole for yourself further down the line?'

'Olly was threatening to run away and that's a big enough hole right there – OK?'

'OK, fine.' No point pushing it – she was clearly under stress.

'Don't worry,' she repeated. 'They're kids. They'll adjust to anything.'

Oliver and Amelia kept to their room for the rest of the evening, but passing the door en route to the bathroom I caught an exchange as Fiona was settling them down for the night.

'Is he your boyfriend?' asked Amelia. I stopped in my tracks.

Fiona laughed. 'No, of course not. He's a friend of Daddy's who's just helping us.'

'I hate him,' said Oliver.

'Don't say that! How can you hate him, Olly? He's been nothing but kind.' Fiona's question was met with silence. 'I want you to be nice to him, Olly – d'you hear?' More silence. 'Oliver?' He grunted. 'Right. Well, no talking now. Sleep. School tomorrow.'

I turned and fled downstairs before she turned out their light. *Hate?* I was shaken. What had I done to have earned that?

Fiona came down a few moments later but made it clear she wasn't in the mood to talk. I asked her about her plans for tomorrow but she was vague, said she was exhausted – it had been a day of turmoil – and disappeared to her room for an early night, leaving me and Dave to stare at one another. Not that I minded. There was a lot to think and chant about – starting with Oliver.

'Sounds like you're way out of your depth there,' said Dora, through a mouthful of chicken kiev.

We were in a dim and almost empty Italian bistro not far from her flat. Fading prints of Tuscan hills hung from the walls, and candles in Chianti bottles dripped wax on to the tables. It was raining outside – inevitably – and I'd spent the first half-hour bringing her up to speed on how Martin had come into my life again, with all that had followed since. Dora had listened carefully, asking the odd question, but this was the first opinion she'd ventured.

'Probably,' I said, bridling. She knew me well enough to catch the tone.

'No – what you're doing's really thoughtful, obviously.' She smiled and wiped the corners of her mouth with her napkin. 'It's just that old saying about when you reach into the pit to pull someone out, you've got to be careful they don't drag you in.'

'Well, I won't be pulling for long, so no need to worry.' Dora's dark eyes searched my face – a look that always made me feel nervous. 'What?'

'What's she like, this Fiona?'

I shrugged. 'Irish.'

She laughed. 'And what's that?'

'What do you want to know?'

'Describe her. Like – is she attractive?'

'Ish. Not that it's relevant.'

'No?'

'To be honest,' I said, 'I'm more concerned about the kids. I mean, to have your father hang himself ...'

'Even if one of them hates you?'

I shrugged again. 'He's angry and looking for someone to blame for everything. I'm convenient.' Dora nodded as if this made sense to her. 'But what about you? I want to hear all about this move – selling up, this great new job you've got.' And I wanted to stop talking about Fiona. It made me uneasy.

Dora smiled broadly. 'Well ...' She sawed at her chicken and started talking.

Her part-time job had been in the staff department of a large hotel on the island, where she'd been spotted as someone with obvious managerial experience. The company had invited her to apply for a senior HR post, with responsibility across their entire Caribbean chain, but after a gruelling series of interviews she didn't get it. Instead, they offered her the newly created position of Head of Corporate Social Responsibility.

'Which means looking after how the company relates to the environment, our impact on the local communities where we operate, responsible tourism, conflict management – everything, basically.'

'Coo.' I was genuinely impressed.

'Yes. Some turnaround.'

'Good thing you stopped drinking. You're going to be busy.' She laughed and I confessed how surprised I'd been that someone as strong as her could slip like that.

'Well, it sort of crept up on me,' she said, playing with her spoon on the tablecloth as we waited for coffee. 'And like I said, I was lonely.'

'I thought you'd have a line of admirers beating at your door.'

'What – with my aged mum going gaga in the next room?' She smiled.

'So – has there been anyone since we …?' A delicate subject.

She shook her head. 'You?'

'No.'

'Because?'

'You spoiled me for all women, Dora. After you, everyone just seems so – ow!' She'd rapped my knuckles with her spoon. 'Anyway, you'll be too busy to be lonely now, won't you? Or you'll meet some fabulous multimillionaire, zipping round the Caribbean from one luxury hotel to the next.'

She smiled as I rubbed my knuckles. 'Maybe. But I am chanting for Mr Right, cos being alone's no fun, is it? And I'm getting a pretty clear picture of what I want.'

'Uh-huh. And what's that?'

'Well, a face keeps coming into my mind when I chant.'

'Oh?'

'Mmm. Yours.'

Chapter Twelve

Duh. I was so shocked by Dora's declaration that I just laughed. But she was completely serious. She'd been surprised too, she confessed, and hard as she tried to push it away, whenever she chanted my face kept bouncing back into frame. So she thought she'd check me out on this visit, and when she heard I was on the Buddhist wagon again she'd taken it as a sign that she might indeed be on the right track.

'Because when you stopped practising, it was like someone turning down the dimmer switch,' she said, 'and that lovely person I'd been with started to slide back into the dark – which was sad. But perhaps the dimmer's being turned up again …'

I should have been flattered, but this was so left-field I simply didn't know how to react. Dora, bless her, saw my confusion and left me to think about it.

'No rush. It's a big thing. But if you want to try again, I'm happy to give it a go – a step at a time.'

We parted with a hug and a lingering press of cheeks that hinted at the possibility of being – again – more than just friends. I drove home in a daze.

Barbados! Bloody hell. Compared to Watford it seemed like paradise. It *was* paradise! From rain to sunshine, black and white to colour, unemployment to – what?

'That's for you to decide,' Dora had said. 'There's tourism – you could start a business, maybe? Or write another book – you could do that anywhere. Or teach? But we'd be pretty well off, what with the money from my flat and what you'd get from renting out your house, and we could live at my mum's while we see how things turn out. And if we decide to make a go of it, you can sell your place and we could get somewhere really nice. Especially as I'll be making a good salary, and with whatever you bring in …'

'Got it all worked out, haven't you?'

She'd smiled and I could tell she was blushing, but was pleased to have put her cards on the table.

Sheesh – talk about good fortune! By the time I reached Bladon Street I was feeling more cheerful than I could remember for years; since before we'd split up, in fact. Getting together again would be like a fairy tale. Boy meets Girl. Boy loses Girl. Boy wins Girl back again. *If* it worked …

But there'd been good signs at lunch. We'd been relaxed, friendly, the bantering humour had started to reappear, she'd said some nice things about me. And Barbados! I couldn't believe it.

The patter of rain had become a monsoon by the time I reached home. I got drenched dashing between the car and the front door, but it didn't matter. As I turned the key in the lock the sun was shining in my heart.

'Don't you speak to me like that, you frigid cow!'

Fiona was pacing in and out of the kitchen, furious, her mobile clamped to her ear, as Dave watched fretfully from his basket under the dining table.

'Yeah, you do that – and thanks for nothing!'

She ended the call with a jab of her finger and turned to me.

'Martin's sister – the cow! She's gonna pay for the funeral, but not down here. Oh no. Up in Durham, where *she* lives. So *we've* got to travel – the three of us, no car, no money. And it's going to be *all* expense spared, you know what I mean? Bottom of the range – why give cash to the undertakers? So no reception and won't even put us up ... Christ!'

'Well, don't worry,' I said. 'I'll drive you. If the car holds out.' After that lunch I was feeling generous.

'Oh.' Fiona was taken aback. 'You don't have to.'

'How else am I going to get there? Unless I'm not welcome ...?'

'No, course you are. You found him.' I had a sudden image of Martin's eyes bulging in the torch beam. 'I mean, you were his friend,' she said quickly. The shock must have shown on my face. 'You tried to help him.'

My laptop was on the table. I sat down, nudging Dave out of the way with my foot, opened Google Maps and typed in 'Durham'.

'Four hours – five with stops. Should just about be able to do it in a day, there and back.'

'Right ...' Her outrage had collapsed, like a hot-air balloon crumpling after a flight, and she seemed at a loss, as if kindness were something unexpected, unusual. 'I mean, if I still had the car, the Skoda ... but it had to go back this morning, you know?'

'It's no problem – really.'

'Well – thanks.' A pause as she gathered her wits. 'Would you like a cup of tea?'

'Please.'

She flashed a sheepish smile and disappeared into the kitchen. 'Am I insured on your car? Only we could share the driving ...'

'Not sure,' I said, googling Barbados. Rows of images

sprang on to the screen: palm trees, white beaches, tur-
quoise sea. I scrolled down. More beaches, sea, bikinis ...

'Barbados?' Fiona placed my mug of tea next to the
computer.

How to play this? Sharing good news with someone
who'd just suffered a terrible blow – two terrible blows –
seemed a tad insensitive. And anyway it felt too intimate.
'Idle fancy,' I said. 'When the weather's like this I, you know,
daydream.' As if prompted, a gust of wind dashed the rain
against the window.

'Me too.' She smiled. 'Only mine's South America.
Machu Picchu. And the Iguazu Falls – you know, on the
border of Brazil and Argentina and Paraguay. I've always
wanted to—'

I groaned.

'What?'

'Email.' The subject line had appeared in a pop-up:
'Valeria Adamoli.' I'd forgotten her – again. I opened it.

Mr Barry Raymonds of Havant Loss Adjusters, apologising for the long silence and now the short notice, but a
slot had appeared in his diary and as he was in the Watford
area would it be convenient to conduct the interview about
Ms Adamoli's injury tomorrow morning?

'Bad news?' Fiona looked concerned. When I'd told her
the story she was indignant. 'Bastard insurance companies.
Always try to wriggle out of paying. How much?'

'The school didn't say exactly.'

Fiona tutted. 'Bastards.'

'Well, I've got the police on my side. Open and shut case,
I'd have thought, insurance-wise.'

But I wasn't as confident as I sounded. I knew that I'd
gambled on getting back in time for the Italians and I feared
that Mr Barry Raymonds of Havant Loss Adjusters would
probe away till he found some tiny chink in my story that

proved my reckless irresponsibility – or at least gave the insurers enough excuse not to pay up.

For now, though, Fiona was reassured. 'Well, I'm on your side,' she said with a cheerful smile. 'And I've a favour to ask.'

'What?'

'Well, seeing as I'm carless, would you mind helping me pick up the kids from school?'

Radlett Manor Preparatory School was another St Catherine's Academy and, like hundreds of its type scattered through the English countryside, hidden down a long, winding lane flanked by thick hedgerows. A discreet gateway opened on to an avenue of oak and horse chestnut trees that swept through acres of lawn up to a grand, turreted Victorian house of red, ivy-covered brick. As we rattled up in the Civic scores of little fair-haired, blue-eyed boys and girls, in Lincoln-green blazers piped with purple, were pouring out of the front door. They were running and skipping across the forecourt towards the phalanx of large cars, where gaggles of yummy mummies stood around chatting.

'Very, um ... white – isn't it?'

'You get what you pay for,' said Fiona drily.

'Local primary's going to come as a shock then.'

Fiona threw me a cool glance, then pointed. 'Over there.' I pulled into a space between a Merc and a shiny black Land Rover. 'I'll see if I can find them. They're not the quickest out.'

She left me and Dave in the car and headed for the house, just as Amelia appeared on the steps, with Oliver close behind. As she went to meet them I became aware of a movement among a small knot of mothers. The arrival of the Civic had been hard to miss but it was Fiona's emergence that sent a visible frisson through the group. They nudged and murmured to each other, and nodded in her direction, till one bold soul detached herself and called out.

I watched the mime show unfold before me: Fiona stopping and turning; the yummy mummy tripping towards her, offering a few consoling words, a sympathetic hand on her arm; Fiona's look of alarm, her quick, frightened glance at Amelia and Oliver running up, her flustered response to the woman and agitated attempt to hurry the children towards the car; their happy, bright faces collapsing as she snapped at them ... and they saw me waiting.

I started the engine as they climbed in.

'Problem?'

'No,' said Fiona tersely. 'Let's go.'

'Where's our car?' In the mirror I could see Oliver examining the Civic's interior with distaste.

'In the garage, being fixed.' Fiona's tone was hard, her eyes locked straight ahead, and her message clear: no more questions. We drove home in heavy silence.

It wasn't till the kids had gone upstairs to change that she hissed to me the reason for her sudden change of mood.

'It's in the local paper! Everything! The suicide, eviction ...' She dropped on to a chair at the table.

'God – that's terrible.'

'I told the headmaster and their teachers but now it's out there all the kids'll be on it.' She started to cry. 'I can't let them go back. It'll be torture.'

'You'll have to tell them.' She shook her head, scared. 'What – so you're going to keep them off school for the rest of term? And locked up here, in case they bump into someone they know?'

She knew I was right but just looked away. There was the sound of a door being wrenched open, a brief scuffle, a cry from Amelia. Fiona hurriedly wiped her eyes.

'What's going on up there? What did I say about fighting?'

'Oliver's being horrible to me!'

'I'm not – you liar!'

As Fiona dragged herself up the stairs to mediate I googled Martin's name and there it was: 'Local business-man found hanged'. A bleary-eyed photo of him grinning at a charity dinner topped a column of text.

I was incensed. Not that the local rag would be so callous as to publish the story without thinking of the hurt it could do to the family. That was standard. But I recognised echoes of my own statement; which meant the source must have been a police officer.

Fiona read the page in silent anguish when she came down a few minutes later.

'It's going to be online for ever,' I said. 'And when the inquest—'

'Yes, all right.' She snapped the laptop shut. 'Oliver knows something's up. Moving out, losing the car, Vanda going ... He's not stupid.'

'Did he see what you'd done to the sitting room?'

'I found the key and locked it, pulled the curtains. But that's not normal either, is it?' She sighed, conceding the inevitable. 'I'll tell them at bedtime. And they can come in with me tonight if they want. We can all cry together – again.'

Which is pretty much what happened. Fiona made burgers and chips for supper – the kids' favourite – then they did their homework, Amelia at the table and Oliver upstairs, while I took Dave for his evening walk. When I got back we all watched a Harry Potter DVD, after which Fiona shooed them up for a bath, teeth and bed.

'Good luck,' I murmured. She smiled faintly, steeled herself and climbed the stairs after them.

Just me and Dave again, staring at each other. I pointed to his basket and, good dog, he climbed into it. Of all of us, he was adapting the best – apart from his refusal to go into the backyard.

I strained to listen. Nothing.

Might as well do my evening practice. With us all living on top of one another I had to grab the opportunity when I could, plus I wanted to chant for Fiona and the kids. After all, if it could help Martin – and he was dead – it must be able to reach the upstairs bedroom. Anyway, it felt the right thing to do.

I chanted quietly for a while, then stopped to listen again. Still silence.

I wondered what Fiona's revelation would do to those young lives – scar them for ever? Or would there be room for change and growth, for some kind of positive outcome despite the pain?

It had to be the latter. People weren't automatically condemned by what had happened in their past, however horrible it might have been. Look at Viktor Frankl. He'd emerged from Auschwitz not just with no bitterness, but with a deeper humanity. Or Nelson Mandela: twenty-seven years in prison and, again, no bitterness, just magnanimity and wisdom. And loads of others throughout history. But why could some people do this while others couldn't? What made the difference?

I checked my watch. Half an hour had passed and there was still silence – apart from Dave's gentle snoring under the table.

I padded up the stairs and along the landing to where a soft light shone from under the kids' door. I listened, then eased it open and peeped through the crack.

Fiona was lying on top of the duvet, with Amelia and Oliver pressed in to her on either side, like a lioness with her cubs. They were all breathing deeply, fast asleep.

I crept in and clicked off the bedside light. Let them get some peace while they could.

There was no clue next morning that they'd suffered any trauma. Amelia seemed more subdued than normal and Oliver again refused to make eye contact; he'd clearly decided to deal with the problem of my existence by simply ignoring it. My enquiring look to Fiona was brushed aside with a muttered, 'Not now.'

It wasn't till the drive back from school that we were able to talk. She'd left me in the car with Dave again while she went to see the headmaster, and emerged, grim-faced, twenty minutes later. Looking straight ahead to avoid the other mothers, she hurried back to the car and we drove off.

'OK?'

She grunted and turned away to study the hedgerows rushing past. I left it for a minute, then tried again.

'How was last night?'

Silence.

'I found you all asleep, turned the light off.'

More silence. When she answered it was in a flat monotone, still looking out of the window.

'I said I had something difficult to tell them but I thought they should know. They were old enough, grown up enough.' She took a deep breath, steadying her voice. 'Their daddy hadn't died in an accident. He'd made a very bad mistake in his work and lost all our money. And he'd felt so awful about it ... Well, you can't sugar that pill, can you?' She finally looked round at me.

'Guess not.'

She took another deep breath. 'He'd felt so terrible, and so mixed up, that he decided the best thing for everyone was to ... go to the house he was building and put a rope around his neck and jump so the rope squeezed his neck and he couldn't breathe. And I hadn't told them this before because I was so upset and sad myself. But now I thought they should know.'

'Wow. That's pretty ... graphic.'

'Better from me than someone else.'

True enough. 'How did they react?'

'Amelia started to cry and said, did that mean ...?' She caught her breath. 'Did that mean Daddy didn't love us? And I said, no, he loved us very much. He just thought this was the best thing. But I'm not sure, to be honest.' She wiped her eyes. I could feel myself starting to fill up too. I coughed.

'Oliver?'

'Very quiet. Didn't ask a thing about Martin. Just wanted to know if we were going to live here for ever – at your place.'

'And?'

'I said no but he wanted to know how we were going to buy a house if we didn't have any money. I said I'd get a job, but he just ... Oh, I don't know.'

She turned to look out of her window again. The hedgerows had given way to houses and a small parade of shops. Commuters were scurrying to the station, heads down and bundled up against the morning damp.

'How were they this morning, about going to school and everything?'

Fiona shrugged. 'Well, you saw them. The head said he'll call if there's any trouble.'

'Let's hope there isn't.'

As soon as we got home Fiona went back to bed – she hadn't slept well, she said. But I wondered if it weren't more than just a broken night. In a few short days she'd lost her husband, her house, her wealth – all the fixed points in her

237

life except her children, whose futures were now up in the air. As was her own. In her shoes I don't know how I'd have got out of bed each morning.

A little later the doorbell rang. Dave went nuts – our first visitor to his new house – and I struggled to hold him as I opened the door.

'Barry Raymonds, Havant Loss Adjusters.'

The speaker was Al Pacino – with a Brummy accent. About sixty, short and thin, his tanned, deeply lined features were topped by an incongruous wedge of thick, jet-black hair – a wig, I quickly realised. He wore a dark grey suit, with a pale blue shirt, pink silk tie and gold cufflinks. And a Rolex.

It soon became clear that Mr Raymonds was driven by one thing only: a relentless, forensic curiosity. He took me through my encounter with Smiler and Big Boy in such minute detail that trying to lie to him about an insurance claim would have been useless. Not that I was, of course.

'So, just to clarify,' he said, looking up from his notes, 'when you decided to follow the boys on the 258 bus, did you know where it was going?'

'Um …'

'Or how long they might be on it?'

Good question. His mission was to show that I'd failed in my duty of care towards my students and setting off on the low-speed bus chase was the nub of it.

'Well, I knew it went to Harrow, which wasn't a million miles away, but not exactly where. And I was keeping an eye on the clock throughout.'

'Ah. So what time did they get on the bus then?'

Oof – walked into that one. 'Um, well, when I say I was keeping an eye on the clock I mean I was aware I couldn't spend, you know, the whole afternoon chasing them. I had to be back, obviously, for Valeria and the others. And I expected the police to appear and take over at any moment because, as I said, I was talking to them the whole time on the phone. But I can't be precise – sorry.'

'So you didn't think to check your watch to see you had time for this ... adventure?'

I looked away from his ice-blue eyes, pretending to search my memory. I *had* checked my watch – it had been about half one – but best to fudge it.

'Well, I wouldn't call it an adventure. More an act of public service.' Raymonds acknowledged the correction with a nod and took a note. 'But let me see. Swimming, then going to the baker's, the attack, Martin turning up ... Must have been ten past, a quarter past one?'

Raymonds dipped his tanned, liver-spotted hand into his shiny black briefcase.

'Perhaps this might help,' he said, producing a well-thumbed manual. 'Transport for London timetable.' He leafed through the pages and ran a bony, well-manicured finger down one of the columns. 'Let's see. From the High Street there's a 258 at ... 13.22 and 13.37. Which one would it have been, do you think?'

It would have been the 13.37. But that meant admitting I'd rushed off less than an hour before the return of the Italians. Reckless as charged ...

'The 13.22, I guess. Or maybe the one before even. But as I say, I couldn't swear to it.'

'Uh-huh. So it *might* have been the 13.37?'

'Um ...'

'Take your time.' His leathery face creased into an encouraging smile but his eyes held me in a cool, unblinking gaze. I thought – and shrugged. 'Well, never mind,' he said. 'The police log their calls. I'll see if I can get hold of a copy.'

Ah.

'Or perhaps a conversation with your friend might help – the driver. If you want to clear things up before then. Martin …?'

'Upton.'

He made a note of the name. 'Might it be possible for me to talk to him, do you think?'

'Er, no – sadly. He's dead.'

Raymonds looked up sharply, his smile gone. I relayed the whole tragic tale, then leaned back and waited for his reaction.

'So Mrs Upton is staying here, and the kiddies?'

'Till she can sort something out. She's upstairs sleeping, in fact.' I nodded towards the bedrooms. 'She told the children last night – you know, about the suicide – and I think they all slept pretty badly.' Raymonds glanced up the stairs, thoughtful. 'Though the children went to school, which is pretty brave, I think, considering.'

'Can be tough little mites, can't they?' Raymonds seemed moved.

'Certainly can.' A thought occurred to me. 'If he had life insurance, would it pay out, do you think?'

Raymonds continued to gaze up the stairs. 'Most policies have an exemption clause for suicide within the first year or two,' he murmured, 'but outside that …'

'Right. Though the money would go towards his debts, I suppose?'

'Normally.'

'And abnormally?'

His attention switched back to me. 'Depends on his accountant, how clever he was.'

Probably too clever by half, knowing Martin. But there was a scintilla of hope. Maybe.

We heard a door open upstairs and a moment later Fiona

appeared, rumpled and groggy from her sleep. Raymonds jumped to his feet and, hand on heart, made a shallow bow.

'Mrs Upton.'

Fiona looked nonplussed at the unexpected gallantry. I introduced him and her expression changed in an instant.

'You mean the bastard who's trying to skip out of that policy?'

For a second Raymonds froze with surprise, then he slipped effortlessly into a well-rehearsed routine. 'Mrs Upton,' he said with a helpless sigh, 'if it was in my power I'd pay out on every claim – truly. But where the company wants to be doubly sure they use me as an independent – and I stress, *independent* – adviser. My task is to assess—'

'Fuck off,' said Fiona. 'Your task is to save them money, in this case by sticking the bill on Ed – when he was out there trying to catch a couple of muggers. When he was a victim! And you're going to make him pay?'

'Mrs Upton, I can assure—'

'No! It's not fair! ' Fiona was getting into her stride. 'I mean, how much we talking about – exactly?' Raymonds hesitated. 'He should at least know what he's looking at, don't you think?'

Raymonds' eyes flickered uneasily between us. Then he coughed and consulted a sheet of paper in his file. 'The sum is currently standing at . . . £18,554.16.'

'What!' I was incredulous. Fiona was outraged.

'For a broken arm!'

'That became infected,' explained Raymonds. 'I understand Miss Adamoli is still receiving treatment.'

I groaned. This was turning into a Grade One, Total and Utter Disaster. But Fiona wasn't having it.

'So why's Ed got to pay for it? He didn't make her dance on the desk! They're trying it on!' She turned to me. 'Have you got eighteen grand?'

I had barely the strength to utter a weak 'Ha!'

Fiona turned back to Raymonds. 'So what happens if you do your job properly then? Where's he supposed to get the money?'

I didn't wait for his answer. 'I'd have to sell up.'

'Well, that's ridiculous! You haven't done anything!' Fiona was practically spitting. 'Why should you lose your home?'

'How should I know?' I snapped. 'Why should you lose yours? Because.' I saw her face crumple and immediately regretted my response. 'I'm sorry. I just—'

'No, you're right,' she said. 'Life's not fair. Not with bastards like this around.'

Raymonds smiled thinly and put his papers back into his case. 'I won't take up any more of your time,' he said. 'I think I've got enough and I do have to be in Bedford in forty minutes.' He checked his Rolex, clicked the case shut and crossed to the door. 'Thank you for cooperating, especially considering the, er ... circumstances. You'll hear something in due course.' And with a polite nod to us both, he was gone.

I glowered at Fiona. She bridled. 'What?'

'How to win friends and influence people?'

'Ah, do me a favour. You can't make friends with insurance companies! They just want money. We don't matter, folk like you and me. We're just their victims.'

I didn't bother arguing because a large part of me agreed with her. The other part was thinking about Barbados.

It was during my evening chant that I began to see things differently. Yes, the insurers might screw me over in due course, but they hadn't yet. And I wasn't 'just a victim'. This whole situation had come about through my running after Big Boy and Smiler without any thought of the consequences. And despite receiving that warning letter from the chair of governors I hadn't taken any legal advice or, well, actually *done* anything about it either. To my shame I hadn't even thought about Valeria since her return to Italy, much less attempted to find out how she was. Out of sight, out of mind. I'd assumed that flying her home in an air ambulance was simply the absurd over-reaction of indulgent parents. It never occurred to me that it might have been necessary. That she might not make a full and speedy recovery. And that, ultimately, I might be held *responsible*.

As I chanted, a sentence Dora used to quote came back to me, like a boomerang whizzing unseen from out of the sky: 'Though invisible to the eye, the error piles up until it sends one plummeting to hell.' Which didn't mean a place full of devils with pitchforks, but that you suffer through causes you've made yourself.

So what was my invisible error then? The answer came almost at once: impulsiveness, neglect, irresponsibility. And as I chanted I could see that they were linked by something more basic – I just didn't *care* enough. About the school, about the students, about Valeria once she'd disappeared from my life. It was hard but I had to face it: I was selfish and self-absorbed. And that, fundamentally, was why I was in this situation – punished not by some angry, finger-wagging god, but by my own actions, which included what I *hadn't* done as much as what I had. The sins of omission. As ye sow, so shall ye reap. Karma.

But there was hope. Make different causes and I'd get different effects. If I *didn't* keep on doing what I'd always done, I *wouldn't* keep on getting what I'd always got …

I tried to explain this in a roundabout way to Fiona later that evening. She'd settled Oliver and Amelia – relieved that their day at school had passed without incident – I'd opened the inevitable bottle, and we'd sat at the table for the full and frank discussion that our predicaments demanded. I didn't mention karma by name – I could tell she viewed 'the whole Buddhist thing' with suspicion – but she was having none of it anyway. I was being ridiculously hard on myself, Valeria should take responsibility for *her* actions, and Raymonds and the insurance company were trying to bully me. I had to fight them.

'How? If they dump me with the bill I'm stuffed. I mean, I can't afford to take them to court or anything.'

'Well, I don't know, just …' She huffed, exasperated and bent down to pet Dave under the table. 'Why don't you just go and bite them all, Dave, hmm?' He gazed up at her with eager, uncomprehending eyes.

'And if you don't, Dave, I will.' A lame joke, but she laughed. The Merlot was unwinding her – and me. And before long we were telling each other the story of our lives. Not everything. Fiona showed no interest in Buddhism, or the fact that I'd written a book, but she was curious about my relationships, especially with Dora.

'So how long were you together?'

'Five years.'

'She was the big love then?'

'Well, the longest. And the most significant, I suppose. But it wasn't a wild, passionate thing. More sort of … grown-up. A partnership.'

She laughed ruefully. 'Sounds like a marriage – or how a marriage should be. So why'd it go wrong?'

I hesitated. Dora's comment about my dimmer switch came to mind but I didn't want to go into all that.

'I stopped trying,' I said simply.

'Because?'

I shrugged. 'Laziness? Stupidity?'

Fiona smiled. 'You still in touch?'

'Well, actually, until a few days ago, not at all.'

'Oh?'

'Yes. She turned up out of the blue at a meeting I went to – you know, the Buddhists. Total surprise.'

'And?' Fiona was eager for detail.

'And ... it was OK.' I sipped my wine. There was a pause.

'OK?'

'Yes.'

'You live with someone for five years, you don't see her for another five – or even talk – and when you do it's just *OK*?'

'Like I said, we're very grown up.'

And I left it at that. But why? Why not tell her about Barbados and Dora's offer? I met her puzzled gaze with a sip of wine and tried to push away the three words that seem to press for attention whenever we were together.

There you are.

'So how about you and Martin?' I asked, uncorking a second bottle. 'I never got quite to the bottom of how you two hooked up.'

Another rueful smile into her glass, a sigh – and then her story.

She was the third of five children, from a little village near Limerick. Her father owned a dairy farm and had made a fortune during the Celtic Tiger years by selling off parts of the land for development to feed the booming property market. She'd been good at art and crafts at school and went on to Dublin to study interior design – the first of her family ever to go to college.

But disaster struck. One drunken evening during her second term she'd decided it was time to lose her virginity – and got pregnant. She was horrified and her strict Catholic parents were livid. An abortion was out of the question – and illegal in Ireland at the time – so they made a plan to send her away to an uncle in Canada to avoid the disgrace. She was to have the baby there, put it up for adoption, then return to Ireland for a life on the straight and narrow. No more fancy-schmancy, morally corrupting art nonsense.

But Fiona had other ideas. After a flaming row she'd packed her bags and fled across the water to Manchester, where she'd got a job as a waitress, rented a room and had a termination. A week later she was working as a model – an agent had spotted her one evening in the restaurant. It was a world away from the catwalks of London or Paris, or *Vogue* cover shoots – her agency specialised in trade shows, hospitality and the growing market of online cata- logues – but it paid the rent and a bit more.

'Anyway, after a couple of years of that I was ready for a change and met this flash Londoner – Martin. He was making loads of money, property developments all over the place, and he let me help do a few of them up. I was going to go back to college, finish my course ... But then Olly came along and this time that was that – marriage, motherhood. And then Amelia.'

'They're great kids.'

'God, don't get me wrong – I don't regret having them at all.'

'But Martin ...?'

She dipped a finger into her wine-glass and ran it round the rim, producing a low hum. 'Martin had his own demons. He was desperate to prove himself. You know his dad went bankrupt?'

'I didn't, no.' Interesting.

She dipped her finger in the wine again, ran it once around the glass rim, then sucked it clean. 'Anyway, he just wasn't straight with me. I think he was having affairs, actually. I couldn't prove it but ... I don't know – call it feminine intuition. And he never let me bother my pretty little head about the business, of course. After Amelia it all just …' She mimed a downhill slope with her hand and topped up her glass. There was a brief silence.

'And you're not close to any of your siblings?'

Her smile had a trace of bitterness. 'My sister, the eldest, is a nun – Mary. As far as she's concerned I'm off to hell, if I'm not there already. My big brother, Rob, is going to inherit the farm and wouldn't say boo to a goose – and certainly not my dad. And my little brothers have emigrated, to Canada and Australia. Might as well be on another planet.' She stared into her glass, then shrugged and drained it. 'Anyway, that's all past.' She yawned. 'And I'm for my bed. Can't drink till the wee hours like I used to at college.'

I checked my watch. 'Ten to eleven? Hardly the wee hours.'

'Wait till you're a parent.' She smiled, patted my cheek, and wobbled a little unsteadily towards the staircase; we'd almost finished the second bottle.

'Sleep well.'

She raised a hand and waggled her fingers without turning round, then climbed the stairs out of sight.

I had that dream again. Fiona standing in the dark by my bed. Except this time she spoke.

'I'm cold.'

'Eh?'

'I need warming up.'

My God. It wasn't a dream. She was actually standing there in her silk robe, shivering. I pulled myself up on one elbow, woozy with sleep and alcohol.

'Fiona?'

She knelt by the sofa bed so our faces were level. 'It's silly, you being down here when it's so cold. Why don't you come up?'

I couldn't believe what I was hearing. 'This isn't a dream, is it? Because when I stayed at your place the first time—'

She laughed softly. 'That wasn't a dream either. I just changed my mind.'

'Wha—'

'I was pissed off with Martin, cos of that bikini crap and everything. Was going to teach him a lesson. But then I thought it's not fair on you, so I didn't.'

'Right …' I didn't know what to make of this.

'But that's all changed now, so …'

'You sure?'

She answered me with a soft, warm kiss. 'Come on.'

I slipped out of the sofa bed, covered my nakedness with my dressing gown – a pointless nod to decorum in the circumstances – and took Fiona's hand. Blimey. What a result. I couldn't believe it.

But a strange sensation started to come over me as she led me up the stairs – an unease that grew with each of the fourteen steps. By the time we reached the landing I was actually shaking. Fiona must have felt it.

'You OK?' she whispered.

'Cold.'

She put her finger to her lips and led me into the bedroom. The streetlamp outside cast a soft orange glow through the curtains on to the bed as Fiona slipped off her robe and jumped in under the duvet, pulling it up to her chin and grinning like a naked, naughty teenager.

'What about the kids?' I murmured, nodding at the wall that separated us.

'Ah, they'll be fine – don't worry. Unless you're a screamer?' She giggled and patted the space beside her.

'Hang on,' I whispered. 'Just got to pay a visit.'

I hurried into the bathroom and flipped on the light, my heart pounding – but not from excitement. My sex life was non-existent, an attractive younger woman was actually waiting for me in bed – and I was in a total funk.

There you are.

What the hell did it mean – really? That Fiona was 'the one'? That we were destined to be together? That the universe had somehow shuffled the pieces around so that, despite every unlikely thing – husband, children, totally different paths through life – we would be reunited? And what about Dora, about jumping into the sack with another woman while supposedly considering a reboot of our relationship?

There you are.

I gripped the basin and searched my face in the mirror. I had to know. Because this moment, what I was about to do with Fiona, felt as if it could decide everything.

There was only one thing for it. It seemed nuts, but as I looked in the mirror I asked myself – out loud, softly – 'Should I sleep with Fiona?' And then I chanted three times under my breath. The answer was instantaneous.

'No!'

I was shocked. Where had *that* come from? It was in my head, of course, but a shriek almost. And one hundred per cent certain.

Bloody hell. What *was* this? I chanted again in my head and this time Bernie's voice answered. 'What trouble our willies do get us into, eh?' And all at once I understood.

I couldn't do this. I just couldn't get into that bed with Fiona. I wanted to, ached to, had secretly desired to ever since I'd first seen her. But where would it lead? A night of filth, but then what? Would it end there? Did I want it to? Or would I want to do it again? Did I actually want to be with her – and Oliver and Amelia? Because they came as a package, and a damaged one at that. And what about Dora – a new life, a fresh start, sunshine, beaches, paradise even ...?

There was no way round it: I was confused. Except about the one thing I had to do next. Not that I was relishing it.

Fiona was lying as I'd left her. 'Ah.' She smiled. 'I was starting to think you'd done a bunk.' She pulled back the duvet for me to climb in.

I took a deep breath. 'Look, I'm really sorry, Fiona, but I don't think I can do this.'

'Eh?'

'I'm just ... I just don't think it's such a good idea. I'm sorry.'

A moment of incomprehension, then she gasped with surprise. No – make that shock. I ploughed on.

'It's just going to complicate things, and it's so soon after Martin's death and—'

'Right. *That* hideous, am I?'

'Don't be silly, you're gorgeous. It's just ...' I reached out to stroke her hair but she swatted my hand away.

'It's just *nothing*,' she hissed. 'What d'you think I am – some sad, drunken cow who ... who chucks herself at anything in trousers?'

'No, of course not.'

'I can count the men I've had on one hand – without the thumb!'

'Look, it's not about you. It's me. I'm—'

'Oh puh-lease. At least do me the favour of being original. Bloody hell ...'

She turned her head away and I struggled in the painful silence to find the right words. I didn't.

'Look—'

'Just go. Go on.'

So I did. Back to my sofa bed, sure I'd made the right decision but churned up about what would come next. Because hell hath no fury like a woman scorned, and Fiona had been. Again. Big time. By me.

Chapter Thirteen

Anxiety is like a gas. At low levels it can go undetected; at higher levels you start to notice the smell; and left unchecked it can build and build till – BOOM. Like when you're deeply asleep, then suddenly alert and full of dread. Dreadful.

It happened to me three times that night. I'd dropped off soon after going back downstairs, only to jolt awake a couple of hours later, instantly aware that I was in trouble. But it wasn't Fiona who jumped into the frame – it was Valeria and her hospital bill. Would I really have to pay it? What if she got sicker? What if she *died*? I could be destitute. If this was karmic retribution it was pretty bloody harsh. Having to sell my house just because I wanted to catch a mugger? You cannot be serious …

The next thing I remember was checking the time on my phone at just before four – *ushitora* – and wondering how much the house was worth and should I get up and read or make a cup of tea or write a will or surf the internet for legal advice and would we still be here for Christmas and what did that mean anyway if you didn't have a family to celebrate it with and what a bizarre collection of myths and customs it was anyway I mean what did Jesus have to do with Father Christmas and eating turkey and anyway he was invented by Coca-Cola his red and white costume was in an ad campaign and how bloody grim it must be to do Christmas if your dad's just topped himself and …

Then it was dawn, and futile to try to go back to sleep – I'd have to be up soon. At which point I fell into a black pit of slumber. And then my alarm went off.

07:00.

And so another day and another tense, uncomfortable breakfast. Fiona and the children came down together and it was clear in a blink that she'd joined the 'avoid eye contact' club. Any contact, in fact. She busied herself with cereal bowls and mugs of tea and responded to my wary question about how she'd slept with a brisk 'Fine.' Even Dave could sense the atmosphere. The family ignored his usual exuberant morning greeting and, rebuffed, he went to lie quietly by the front door, waiting for the release of the school run.

I was worried about Amelia. She was drawn and listless, with tired panda eyes, and refused breakfast with a silent shake of the head. I tried to encourage her but Fiona broke in.

'Leave her,' she snapped. 'If she's not hungry she's not hungry.' She stroked Amelia's face. 'I'll make a marmalade sarnie, OK? You can have it at break if you're hungry then.' Amelia gave a grateful nod and Fiona retreated to the kitchen. I checked my watch.

'Leave in ten minutes? I'll just have a quick shave and—'

'No, it's fine. We'll take a cab.'

'What? But that's—'

Fiona appeared in the kitchen doorway, butter knife in hand. 'Don't worry, really. We've imposed enough.'

'It's no imposition. I'm happy to do it. And it's going to cost—'

Fiona's tone hardened. 'We're taking a cab – all right? It'll be here in fifteen minutes.'

So this was my punishment. Cold war, the freezing of relations, even if it meant laying out £20 for a cab there and back. Twice a day would be forty quid, two hundred for the week ... Nuts.

'Right,' I said, 'I'll have a shave and get out of the bathroom before you go.'

Fiona shrugged – I'd been demoted to irrelevance, clearly – and returned to her sandwich-making. Oliver glanced up from his Coco Pops with a glint of quiet triumph, then picked up the bowl and drained the chocolate milk, noisily.

It's very upsetting to feel shut out in your own house, especially if you're trying to help, for God's sake. But, I decided while shaving, the whole situation just reflected my own lack of clarity. So if this arrangement was going to continue I had to explain things clearly to Fiona, come clean about Dora and Barbados. Which meant I had to sort them out in my mind first. But how?

Bernie. He'd know what to do. He was a man of the world. And finding Martin's body had created a unique bond between us.

There was a knock on the door: Oliver, wanting to brush his teeth. I vacated the bathroom and hovered around in the kitchen till the cab arrived.

'You coming straight back or...?'

'Dunno,' said Fiona. 'Things to do, you know.'

I didn't but I got the message: drawbridge up, portcullis down. 'Well, you've got a key.'

Fiona gave a curt nod and pulled the door hard shut behind her.

I called Bernie at once. He was surprised to hear from me but said I could come over any time; he'd got his tools back but work had completely dried up and he was filling his days trying to encourage various friends and family who were also going through the mill.

'Don't want any more Martins, eh? Not if I can help it. And if you wanna feel good, my son, you gotta do good, in't yer? Cause and effect.'

I said I'd be there later – after my meeting with the restorative justice man.

My first sight of Greg Turner did not fill me with confidence. He had a ponytail and a beard, both grey. And wore faded blue jeans, with a faded suede leather waistcoat over a faded blue denim shirt. And a pair of faded white trainers. Everything about him suggested lost decades at music festivals, smoking dope in soggy fields. But I was wrong. He turned out to be a former prison officer from Newcastle who, like many of his colleagues, had grown jaundiced at seeing the same old faces passing round and round the system.

'So how'd you get into this side of things?' I asked.

We were sitting in his tiny office in the bleak sixties office development that overlooked the constant traffic on the Watford ring road. Stuffed lever-arch files surrounded him on all sides – on the shelves, the filing cabinet, his desk, the window-sill – giving him the appearance of a perky rodent in its nest. He'd taken me through what to expect during my meeting with Big Boy/Carl Macer and what I wanted from it – an explanation, an apology and a promise he'd never do anything like it ever again – and now I was curious about his own story.

'Well,' he said in his soft Geordie accent, 'it was this old lag I'd been bumping into, on and off, for twenty years in different jails, from when he was in Feltham as a juvenile. But this time he weren't inside: he was a visiting speaker on restorative justice, how it'd put him straight, saved his life, supposedly. Here we go, I thought when he started, cos I knew he'd been trying to play the system for years – you know, get some advantage from all the schemes on offer and that. But what he said …'

He shook his head, still surprised.

'What was it?'

Greg laughed. 'This guy'd been a druggie since about fifteen – right? Anything he could lay his hands on basically: dope, pills, crack, heroin. Glue. And tricky – you know, devious, always looking for an angle. But one face-to-face with this old biddie he'd burgled … he was a changed man! He'd never been confronted with one of his victims, you see. And I don't know what it was she said exactly but he took courses, got skills – a job even, when he got out, with this drugs charity. And that was prison done for him, for good. What could I say? I wanted to know more. So I read stuff, talked to people, and after a time all me scepticism just faded away. Eventually I jumped ship and haven't look back.'

'So you're a convert?'

Greg grinned. 'Aye. Man with a mission, me.'

I left his office reassured that if an old cynic like him had faith in the process perhaps some good might come of it. But the encounter was now very real and I was getting nervous. No, let's be frank – scared. Not that Big Boy might attack me or anything; that would be madness and anyway Greg was going to be there throughout. No, the real fear was how I'd react. I might smack *him* in the face, for all I knew. Or go into one of my uncontrollable meltdowns. How embarrassing would that be?

I couldn't back out now though. Except why not? It was all voluntary. I could postpone it till I felt ready, and if his conscience was bothering him – tough. Let him squirm.

But then it'd be hanging over me, too, my antennae for-ever twitching in case I ran into them again, my stomach muscles tightening whenever two black lads came towards me in the street. How long did I want to live like that?

I was still chewing things over when I pulled up outside Bernie's house, a pebble-dashed and satellite-dished semi in the backstreets of Neasden, within spitting distance of the noisy North Circular. The tiny square of front garden had been turned into a car park for his van and a half-restored Harley Davidson: 'Labour of love,' Bernie explained when he opened the door; while the back garden accommodated a cement mixer, a pile of rough planks, a scaffolding tower in bits, an old boiler and a dozen cast-iron radiators, two aluminium ladders chained to the cement mixer, and three large piles of discarded wood off-cuts.

'Don't normally have all this crap here,' said Bernie as he made us mugs of tea in the kitchen. 'Move it around from job to job. The missus is well pissed off – killing all the grass.'

'Is she here?'

'At work, thank Christ. Least we got one person earning.'

I looked out at the garden. 'What's with the radiators?'

'Bought them for this geezer in Hampstead – a renova-tion. 'Cept he did a flit a few days after Martin checked out. It never rains, eh? Sugar?'

I declined and followed him into the sitting room with a mug of scalding, brick-red tea. He sat in a large leather armchair set in the bay window, king of all he sur-veyed, while I perched on the sofa opposite the glowing, coal-effect gas fire. In the alcove to the left of the fireplace bubbled a large aquarium, a solitary goldfish swimming in and out of the murk behind algae-stained glass. Above it hung a portrait of Bobby Moore, badly painted from a photograph, holding aloft the World Cup. A small book-case snuggled into the alcove to the right of the fireplace. On it stood Bernie's Buddhist altar and, on the shelf below, a bell, beads, candles and incense.

The shock was on the next shelf down – the middle of three framed photos. To the left was an elderly couple and to the right a middle-aged woman, his parents and wife, I guessed. But between them ... I got up to make sure my eyes weren't deceiving me. Yep – a group of skinheads, snarling and yelling at the camera as they threw a Nazi salute. In the centre of the group was a young Bernie. I pointed, shocked.

'What's this?'

Bernie took a sanguine drag on his roll-up.

'A reminder – for whenever I think someone can't change. And what might happen if I stop practising.'

'Bloody hell. With your Buddhist stuff?'

'Of course – from the mud grows the lotus. Anyway,' he said, taking a loud slurp of tea, 'what's up with you?'

I sat down again and told him: about Fiona and Dora and *There you are* and Barbados; and Valeria and Barry Raymonds and how I might lose Bladon Street; but how that might not be such a disaster because I felt totally stuck and all of a sudden it looked like I had a choice; except I really didn't know which way to go. And throughout it all Bernie listened with a frown of concentration, apart from a couple of times when I thought his eyes were starting to glaze over.

'So,' he said, when I finally stopped, 'torn between two lovers.' He started to make another roll-up.

'Sort of. Only it feels bigger than that, as if – I don't know – the universe is trying to tell me something. Or something.' I explained the significance to me of Piers's experience with Rachel.

Bernie snorted. 'Well, that's guff.' He saw my surprise. 'Yeah, Piers and Rachel could be relevant, but d'you honestly think the universe could give a toss about who you're going to knob?'

'Well, of course not. I just meant—'

'It really bugs me when people talk crap like that.' He pinched a stray shred of tobacco from his newly made cigarette.

'Why?'

'Why? Cos it shows they don't understand, that's why. Life's plastic.'

'Eh?'

'Plastic, bendable, not fixed. It changes the whole fucking time. So do you. So what you see's down to you – your life condition. You must know that.'

'I do. But—'

'And life's what you make it. So the past only sets your future if you let it. That's called *honga' myo*, "from this moment backwards": you see what's happened to bring you to now, this moment, then just project it forward, so the future's basically a continuation of the past, yeah?'

'OK …'

'But look "from this moment forward" – *honin'myo* – and whatever you've done in the past, however crap or fucked up, *this* moment, right now, can be the start of something new, and better – like that.' He pointed at the skinhead photo.

'All right. Except the past is still there, isn't it? You can't just ignore it. I mean, Dora coming back is the past … you know, reappearing in the present.'

'Fine. But that don't mean you got to get back together, any more than you got to get together with Fiona just cos you think you might have had a shag in a past life.'

'You're such a romantic, Bernie.'

He grinned. 'But you already worked that one out, which is why you hit the pause button – right?'

Was that right? Maybe, at some level. But it didn't get me anywhere. I could feel a wave of hopelessness rising in my chest.

'Well, that's great,' I said, 'in theory. But the thing is … I just don't know what to do – about anything.'

Bernie lit his roll-up and squinted at me through the smoke. 'You think about death at all? Not topping yourself,' he added quickly, seeing my uneasy look. 'Just generally.'

'Not if I can help it, no.'

'You should,' he said. 'Do you good.'

I snorted. 'Yeah? How?'

'Deathbed regrets – you never played that?' I shook my head. 'Come on, then, we'll play it now. Close your eyes.' He leaned forward in his chair. I frowned, suspicious. 'Nothing's going to happen – just close your eyes.' He waited till I complied, reluctant. 'Right. Now imagine you're dying, OK?'

'OK …'

'It's … ooh, let's say thirty years from now, you're all alone in a room in some council-run hospice, a miserable old git with no friends or family.' I opened my eyes in protest. 'Just go with it, trust me.' I sniffed my displeasure but closed my eyes again. Bernie continued. 'Right, so you're on your deathbed, looking back over your life, key moments – stuff you did, stuff you didn't do – and you got this one big regret, this one thing you wished you'd really gone for while you could, when you were still healthy and had thirty years ahead of you. Got that?'

'Uh-huh.'

'Right. So what is it – your one big regret?'

I thought. And thought. Then opened my eyes.

'I don't know.'

Bernie leaned back into his leather throne. 'Well that, my son, is your problem. Find what you'll most regret *not* doing – then do it. And everything else will fall into place.'

I didn't stay long after that. I was shaken. What Bernie had said was so blindingly obvious I just felt … stupid. Why hadn't I seen it? If he'd asked that question ten years ago I'd have been able to answer in a shot: my greatest regret would have been to die without writing the book I knew I had inside me. But I'd been there, done that – so now what?

I drove back to Watford under dark skies that threatened yet more rain. Back to the big black hole at the centre of my life, the hole I'd been trying to plug for years, in one way or another; most recently with copious amounts of red wine. In fact, was that the real reason for my interest in Fiona and Dora – they were just another plug for the hole? And why on earth were they even remotely interested in me, unless …? I groaned. Like attracts like, so they must have a big black hole at the centre of their lives, too. Dora had admitted how lonely she was and Fiona was obviously all over the place; had been even before Martin's death. I mean, to seriously consider shagging me to get back at him, while he was sleeping it off across the landing …

Still, at least I now knew what the real problem was. And maybe, if I sent in the truffle hound, I'd even find out how to solve it. By the time I turned off the M1 my spirits had started to rise – something I couldn't often say when approaching Watford.

My good mood didn't last long. As soon as I opened the door to 15 Bladon Street Dave started to bark. He never barked, he was a good dog. But here he was, running around, in and out of the furniture, up and down the half-dozen steps at the bottom of the staircase, yapping as if my entry had thrown him into an ecstasy of excitement. Something was up.

I found Fiona in the bedroom, packing.

'We're going,' she said, barely glancing round as she folded a grey silk blouse and laid it in the suitcase open on the bed. 'Get out of your hair.'

'What – now?' I felt as if I'd been punched in the stomach.

'Taxi's coming at two.' It was just past one.

'But what about the kids?'

She nodded at the party wall. I took a couple of steps along the landing and looked into the spare bedroom. Oliver and Amelia, still in their school clothes, were diligently packing a bag each. They studiously ignored me. I went back to Fiona.

'I don't understand. Has something happened?'

Her mouth twisted into a bitter smile as she continued to fold her clothes with deft, practised movements. 'What, you mean apart from Martin, and losing the house and all our money and everything we own? Well, yes: Amelia was bullied is what's happened, and Olly stood up for her, and there was a fight and I … I just decided – that's it, I'm not having it.'

Her face was taut, her anger directed into her packing.

'Where are you going?'

'Home.'

It took me a moment to understand. 'What, you mean … Ireland?'

'Yep.'

'Today?'

'Uh-huh. Got last-minute tickets from Luton, Ryanair.'

'But I thought you and your parents didn't—'

'You never heard blood's thicker than water?' For the first time she turned to face me. 'And where else is there, hmm?'

'Here. You don't have to—'

'No.' She cut in hard, definite. 'There's only so much humiliation a person can take, you know.'

'Fi, that was—'

'No!' She raised a hand as if to push me away, though I'd made no movement towards her. 'And I'm not Fi, I'm Fiona – to you. OK?' She stared at me, letting the cold sink in. I drew back, dismayed. But I also knew that I'd brought this on myself.

'OK, if that's what you want … But at least let me drive you to the airport. '

'There's no need.' She turned back to her folding and packing.

'It'll save you thirty quid.'

Silence. I was at the top of the stairs before she answered, from the bedroom doorway.

'All right. Thank you.'

'What time's your flight?'

She hesitated. 'Nine fifteen.'

'*Nine fifteen?*'

Another kick in the stomach – she'd been hoping to be away before I got back.

'There's the check-in and we've got all the excess baggage and, you know …' At least she had the decency to look embarrassed.

'Well, we *can* go at two if you really want to spend half a day at the airport. Or later. Up to you.'

I plodded down the stairs, where Dave greeted me as if I were still the best thing that had ever walked into his life. But I felt numb. This was just so sudden. Yes, we'd agreed to them staying no more than a week but they'd been here only three days and there'd been no warning, no discussion …

I fought off Dave's love-bombing and went through

to the kitchen to make a desultory cup of coffee. As I waited for the kettle to boil I remembered finding the note Chris had left propped up against it, and realised that he'd gone without warning too. So had Vanda. And Constanza and Bella. And Rachel. And Valeria from the hospital. In fact, since that fateful lunchtime when I'd stopped to pick a warm, ripe blackberry, my life had been a series of abrupt encounters and departures, of people appearing and then being ripped away; of situations starting, like the job at Hillview, and then – bang – the next minute it's all over. Bloody hell, even Martin had gone like that, in the most brutal, final way possible. Everything that had been settled – stuck – was in turmoil. And I was starting to feel lost. And tired. And so pathetically sorry for myself that I could feel a hard, painful lump of self-pity rising in my throat. I'd tried to help Martin and failed. I'd tried to help his wife and kids and that was in the process of going pear-shaped. And my attempt to help the general good by bringing two muggers to justice might lose me my house! I was starting to feel I was cursed.

My phone rang: Dora. How was I, how was 'the family'…?

'Good,' I lied, forcing a laugh. 'It's just been, you know, hectic. That's why I haven't called you.'

'Don't worry,' she said. 'I know you've got a lot on your plate right now, and I don't want to hassle you. I just wondered if I could ask a small favour.'

She was clearing her flat for the new owners and had various things to take to the recycling centre – old furniture mainly. Piers had offered his van on Monday afternoon but another pair of arms would help.

'Sure,' I said. Monday morning was my 'conference' with Big Boy, so a debrief afterwards with Piers and Dora, plus a bit of manual labour, sounded a good idea. We made a time and I ended the call, just as Fiona appeared in the kitchen doorway.

'I cancelled the cab,' she said, 'but I don't really want to hang around here, if that's OK. All on top of each other. And it'd be good to get Dave out of the house.'

He was right behind her, staring up at us, sensing action.

'He's OK to go on the plane?'

'Ah, sure, he'll be fine. He'll just lie down under our feet, between the—'

'No, I meant – do they allow it? Only I don't think I've ever seen a dog on a plane.' There was a faint flicker of doubt in her eyes. 'Does he have a ticket?'

'No,' she snapped. 'He's a dog.' But behind her irritation I could see a rising panic.

'Better check,' I said, pushing past her into the sitting room and opening up the laptop on the table. 'Don't want to get to the gate and—'

'Yeah, all right – I get the picture.'

She peered at the screen over my shoulder as I sat and googled. The answer was almost instantaneous: no animals except guide dogs. I glanced round. The blood had drained from Fiona's face.

'We can't leave him.'

I glanced down. Dave was watching us closely, tail wagging, grinning in anticipation of some imagined adventure. I did some more googling.

'Well, the good news is there are no rules about taking him into the country, but the bad news is Ryanair don't do refunds. Use 'em or lose 'em, ticket-wise, I'm afraid.'

Fiona groaned and dropped into the armchair. Dave padded over and rested his muzzle on her leg.

'We can't not go,' she said, digging her fingers into the thick black curls on his head. 'That was the last of my money. And my parents ... Just calling them took ...

Wasn't easy. And they actually sounded, you know, happy – to hear from me, that I was coming back. They've never seen the kids even …'

She was almost in tears.

'Mummy, what's the matter?' Amelia was standing on the stairs.

'Nothing, darling – I'm just being silly,' said Fiona. She opened her arms and Amelia ran down into them. 'But I've been a really silly mummy, because I've made a silly, stupid mistake.'

'What?' Amelia looked alarmed.

'Well, I've just found out that Dave can't come on the plane with us.'

'Then I'm not going!' said Oliver, who had come down the stairs unseen and now rushed over to Dave. He fell to his knees and flung his arms around the dog's neck.

'Me either!' declared Amelia, pulling away from Fiona to join Oliver in strangling Dave, who turned his head from side to side in an attempt to lick them both. Fiona's eyes met mine, desperate. There was no alternative.

'That's no problem,' I said. 'He can stay here while we sort it out. Should only be for a couple of days, I imagine, then I'll take him wherever he has to go and he'll be whisked over to you. How's that sound?'

'Really? You're sure?' Fiona sounded so relieved – and grateful – I thought she was going to hug me. But Oliver was dismissive.

'He doesn't like you.'

'Oh, don't be silly,' said Fiona. 'Ed takes him for walks. They get on fine.'

'But he'll be lonely,' said Amelia, 'and scared.'

'Not with Ed,' said Fiona.

'No, I mean when Ed whisks him. He'll be all by himself.'

'Oh, he'll probably sleep most of the way,' I said. 'And he'll have his toys with him – his squeaky bone and everything. He'll love it.' I had no idea, but Amelia seemed reassured.

'Don't worry, Dave,' she said, pressing her forehead against his. 'You'll be all right.'

Her brother wasn't so easily mollified. He looked up at me and scowled.

I discovered what his problem was with me at the airport.

I'd managed to jam their eight very full bags into the Civic and then, with Dave perched on a holdall between the children on the back seat, I'd coaxed the car up the M1 as the heavens opened. Even with the wipers on manic I could barely see the road. We soon slowed to a crawl, then the traffic just stopped. Not that it mattered, as we had hours in hand, the kids seemed content to coo over Dave in the back, and Fiona and I got the chance to talk. She apologised for her earlier frostiness, and I apologised again for the previous night.

'Well, you probably did us a favour,' she murmured, 'the amount of wine we had.'

We exchanged a glance, both knowing that there was something between us but neither of us sure quite what. We edged on a few yards, then stopped again, the rain beating on the roof. I glanced round at the kids; Oliver had plugged into a game and Amelia was dozing off. I turned back to Fiona.

'You are sure about this – taking them out of school, Ireland …?'

Fiona sighed. 'I'm not sure about anything any more, to be honest. I mean, fancy not checking about Dave. God knows how much the shipping's going to cost.'

I'd emailed a couple of companies to get a quote but hadn't heard before leaving. 'Well, you could always collect him when you come back for the funeral,' I said. 'I really don't mind having him for a while if you can wait; and the kids.' There was something about her silence that triggered a sudden thought. I shot her a glance. 'You *are* coming back for the funeral?'

She looked away, out of the window. 'Dunno,' she said. 'We'll see. Probably.'

It was still chucking it down when we finally reached the airport, which meant going straight to the terminal to avoid getting soaked – and a thirty-minute parking limit. I couldn't hang around.

We piled the bags onto two trolleys and sprinted with them to the terminal building, where Amelia promptly announced she needed the toilet. Fiona took her hand, leaving me in the entrance with Dave (who wasn't allowed inside), the bags – and Oliver. He pulled out his game console, pressed a button and stared at the screen as it chirruped into life. I decided to try to make contact.

'Would you like a drink or something? I could give you the money.' He didn't move. 'Oliver?' He shook his head, eyes still on the game. 'You know, we don't have to be like this, Oliver. We could be friends, you know.' He shook his head again. 'Why not?'

'Cos you're such a loser.'

His eyes didn't leave the screen.

An hour later I was home. With Dave. Amelia had given him firm instructions to be good and not to worry as they'd only be apart for a few days. Fiona had thanked me again for sorting out his travel arrangements; and Oliver had buried himself in his game. Fiona and I brushed cheeks… Then I dashed back to the car, Dave at my side. He didn't give so much as a backward glance.

Bladon Street felt cold and empty. Yes, I had Dave for

company but, if anything, he just underlined the absence of his owners. I turned on the heating and took him out to the corner shop to buy some dog food (and wine), then decided to turn the excursion into a long walk; the rain had eased off and anyway, that's what dogs are for. Plus I couldn't face going back to a cold house.

We walked up to Cassiobury Park, where Dave romped around making friends with the other dogs till we reached the canal, then turned back down the towpath towards Long Valley Wood. Eventually we found a track across the fields, then a bridleway that after a mile or so took us to the end of Vicarage Road, past the hospital and football ground, and finally, in the dark, home – a two-hour circle. Dave was in heaven; he'd probably not had such a long workout since Martin's death, and I certainly hadn't. He wolfed down a can of food as soon as we got in, then settled in his basket under the dining table and instantly fell asleep.

I envied him. Eating, sleeping, long walks, even short walks – it didn't take much to keep him happy. Throw in regular nasal encounters with his canine pals and some head patting and Dave seemed perfectly content. I gazed at him, his flank rising and falling as he dreamed his doggy dreams. I didn't suppose he'd have any deathbed regrets. OK, he'd been neutered and wouldn't live that long, but did he ever fret at the thought that he'd never sire a litter of pups or see past his fifteenth birthday? Of course not. Ignorance is bliss. And if he never saw Oliver and Amelia and Fiona again, would he regret that? Did he even remember them? Or was his memory wiped as soon as he turned away – out of sight, out of mind – and they would snap back into existence only if he saw them again?

Not out of my mind, though. I missed them, even Oliver. I missed the life they brought to the house. The problems. The surprises. The see-saw of emotions, including mine.

And I didn't know if I'd ever see them again. I'd drop off Dave at the pet-shipping company, a credit would appear on my bank statement when Fiona eventually reimbursed what I'd forked out, and that would be that. Especially if she didn't come back for the funeral. Amazing that she might not, for the father of her children. But that's anger, I guess. Or grief. Or the confusion of the two. Anyway, at least Barbados was still an option.

I glanced at my watch. I should chant, wrestle with what Bernie had said, but regret was something I didn't want to look at – not yet. Ignorance *is* bliss and the night was young. I opened a bottle of red.

Such a loser.

Chapter Fourteen

I spent the rest of the night drinking. I knew I was being stupid, that it wouldn't help, that I was indulging in avoidance and self-pity, self-debasement even, but for some reason I couldn't stop myself. A voice in my head just said, 'Fuck it – why not?' So I drank. It was if I'd been taken over by an alien that wanted me to obliterate all thought.

Next morning an email arrived with a price for air-freighting Dave to Ireland: £800. It was such a shock that I more or less snapped out of my hangover in that instant. I called Fiona but got her voicemail and left a message. A little later she sent a text: 'Jesus – no way! Nothing cheaper? Fx'.

I tried to call the second company – no reply – so I googled some more till I found a couple who did regular pet runs around Europe and could take Dave door-to-door for £600, which was starting to sound cheap. They had good references and seemed legit, so I texted the link to Fiona. She could have been doing all this herself, of course, but – well, she had her hands full with family stuff and anyway love is blind. Not that it was love. I just wanted to help.

She didn't reply for hours. I was starting to wonder if she'd simply decided to abandon Dave to my care when a text arrived: 'OK. God. Expensive mistake or what? Fx'.

And so, on Saturday morning, Dave and I said goodbye. I took him for a final nose around the damp leaves of the cemetery and returned just as a large silver Mercedes van pulled up outside the house. I handed over his basket and bowl and squeaky bone, as he clambered trustingly into one of the cages in the back; then I patted him one last time, the cage was fastened, the van door slammed – and off he went. Another wrench.

That afternoon I went to a football match. Watford were playing Reading, the ground was just around the corner and the prospect of being cooped up alone in the house …

I stopped by the Red Lion for a couple of pints before the game. It was heaving with Watford fans, clad to a man in the club's sun-yellow shirt – no true believer would wear a coat or jacket, despite the damp November weather. They were a cheery, beery lot, erupting every few minutes into sudden bouts of clapping and chanting, as if cued by an invisible hand. We had several bursts of '1–0 to the Golden Boys' and 'Watford! (clap-clap-clap)'; 'You are my Watford', sung to the tune of 'You Are My Sunshine'; and, to the tune of 'The Wild Rover', the ever-popular:

> And it's Watford FC,
> Watford FC are great,
> We're by far the greatest team
> The world has ever seen.

After each eruption they would stop as abruptly as they'd started, and continue their drinking and hollered conversations. It was all very mysterious – and fascinating.

Ditto the behaviour of one of the fans inside the ground later. I was in the upper tier of the Rous Stand and a few seats below me, in the front row, sat a middle-aged man with neatly parted hair and a greying, trimmed moustache.

271

He wore a tweed jacket, cardigan and buttoned-down shirt, with a yellow and red Watford scarf knotted carefully under his chin. He could have been a fifties' bank clerk on his day off.

Except that every ten minutes or so he'd leap to his feet and unleash a torrent of puce-faced obscenity at the referee or one of his assistants. The slightest perceived injustice and Mr Tweed would jump up as if jabbed with a cattle-prod.

'No way! No fucking way,' he screamed – at a *throw-in* awarded to Reading. 'You fucking dozy fuck-head! You fucking blind useless fucking wanker!'

The assistant referee was sadly out of reach, so Mr Tweed sat down hard, arms folded in fury. A few minutes later the referee waved away an appeal for handball in the box by a Reading defender. Mr Tweed was on his feet in a flash.

'Cheat! You fucking cheat!' He leaned over the balustrade and thumped the metal advertising hoarding. It clanged. 'Fuck me! How much they bunging you, you fucking cunting corrupt cheating fucking bastard!'

This was too much for those close by, whose muttered disapproval now found a champion. A balding dad in the row behind Mr Tweed leaned forward and muttered into his ear.

'Oi, you – button it, right? There's kiddies here, families.' A young lad was sitting beside him, white with shock.

'Fuck you,' said Mr Tweed, over his shoulder.

'You what?' Balding Dad hauled himself to his feet. He was a big man. 'You wanna say that again?'

Mr Tweed whirled round – to see the burly figure towering over him. He gulped.

'Just … supporting our boys, that's all.'

'Well, you want to use "language", you go in the Rookery with the rest of the animals.' He stabbed a finger at the sea of yellow in the stand behind the goal to our right.

Mr Tweed clamped his mouth shut for the rest of the half, and didn't return to his seat after the break – which was a shame, because I was intrigued. The instant transformation from mild-mannered bank clerk to frothing berserk was at first alarming, then amusing and, finally, baffling. There was nothing much at stake – three points in a mid-table clash – so why all the passion? Unless the club was his *honzon*, his anchor, the thing that gave his life meaning and identity. That's why every transgression against it was felt as a personal affront, almost a physical assault. And why he had to fight back, defend himself.

Luckily for Mr Tweed, Watford came away with a draw; his self-esteem could stand intact for another week. But at least he'd found something to fill his black hole – a nine-month drama with forty-six episodes and a clear ending. And then, after a brief rest, it would start all over again. Very Buddhist, I mused, as *Match of the Day* swum in and out of focus that evening through a thickening haze of Cabernet Sauvignon. The beginning of the season was birth, the end of the season death; the teams that earned the most points would be reborn into a higher division, and those with the least into a lower one. And while they'd all be reborn with a clean slate – zero points – they wouldn't be equals. From the off, some teams would be more blessed – with stronger players, more money and better facilities carried forward from the past. Karma.

Martin paddled into my addled thoughts. He'd tried to bale out of the leagues all together – but you can't escape the universe, right? So did that mean he'd start his next season in a semi-pro division, hobbled with a points deduction or a whacking great fine? *If* he was coming back. If any of us are … I had polished off the second bottle by then, plus a couple of very large brandies, so couldn't really be expected to think straight. Or even stand straight. I woke

273

up at midday on Sunday with the hangover from hell and a large bump over my right eye – I must have fallen over at some point on my way to bed. Pathetic. I wouldn't be able to act like this when Dora and I got back together. But then, I wouldn't want to, would I?

Monday morning came around. Buttered toast and some strong coffee. And then, finally, I forced myself to chant, for the first time since Fiona and the kids had left. I didn't want to – it would mean having to look at myself – but very soon I'd be sitting opposite Big Boy, Carl Macer, and I needed some courage. At least, I thought I did, because after ten minutes I realised it wasn't courage I lacked – it was hope. This encounter wasn't going to make any difference to either of us, so what was the point in going?

I called Greg's mobile. He answered at once.

'Hello, Ed. I was wondering if you'd call.'

'Oh? Why's that?'

'People bottle out – you know, last-minute doubts.'

'Ah. Well, I was just ringing to check I'd got the right time: nine thirty?'

'Aye, that's it.' I couldn't tell if he believed me or not.

'OK. Well, see you later then.'

After all, what was the worst that could happen – a wasted morning?

We were booked into Conference 2, a small room down the corridor from Greg's office. The walls were covered in grey-blue hessian, four low wooden armchairs were grouped around a Formica coffee table, the window looked out over the roof of the indoor market – and that was it. Impersonal, functional, colourless. Pretty much how I felt. Greg brought me a black coffee, then went to fetch Carl.

As I waited I wondered why I did feel so empty. It was as if the bender of the past two days had drained me of emotion; almost as if I'd purged myself for the showdown: 'The warrior must be still in mind and body.' Or perhaps I was just knackered.

Then Carl came in – and everything changed. He looked sheepish, nervous, but my stomach churned, just like when I'd seen Smiler on that ID video. Carl was wearing a black puffer jacket and baseball cap, baggy low-slung jeans and brand-new, sparkling white trainers. And his diamond ear-stud. He couldn't have looked more like a gangsta if he'd tried. Ridiculous. A surge of anger welled up in me.

Greg closed the door and gestured to the armchairs. I slung my fleece round the back of one and sat down, arms crossed. Carl sat opposite, still in his baseball cap and puffer jacket, hands thrust deep into the pockets, and lean-ing so far back I thought he'd tip out of the seat. He's scared, I realised. Good. It was a small payback for what he'd made me suffer. I had a flashback to his stare when he was climb-ing the hill towards me, rock in hand ...

Greg took the chair between us and smiled a welcome.

'So – thanks very much both of you for coming here this morning to take part in this conversation, cos that's what it is, basically, a space for you to talk about the crime, what exactly happened, what led up to it, how you feel about it – especially you, Ed – then what happened after, and what you'd like to see going forward. OK?'

'Sure.' I looked across at Carl. He nodded to Greg but wouldn't meet my eye. Greg continued.

'Great. Couple of bits of housekeeping. This is a voluntary process but it's based on honesty, listening, mutual respect and confidentiality, OK? What's said in here stays in here, unless you both agree to share it outside.' Carl and I nodded that we'd understood. 'Also, let's try to focus on behaviour and not get personal. And I'm not here to adjudicate, just to help the conversation, all right?' We nodded again. He referred to a folder of papers. 'Right. So, let's start with you, Carl. You pleaded guilty to committing two street robberies on August the twenty-fourth this year, one in Harrow against a Mr Patrick Walters and the other—'

'Against me.'

I wanted Carl to acknowledge my presence, to engage, but he just flicked me a wary glance and locked eyes back on Greg, who continued without breaking stride.

'Right,' he said. 'So, Carl, take us through that lunchtime. What happened?'

Carl shifted in his seat. He cleared his throat, leaned forward – and spoke to his trainers.

'Fing is, what we done, right, you know it's like it's … we shouldna done it, right. And we know that now, so …' He looked up at Greg, who pointed to me.

'Talk to Ed.'

Carl dragged his eyes round to mine but they skittered away almost at once.

'Yeah, well, that's it really, like I said, we was out of order innit and doing that fing weren't right, to you and that other man, and we … we ain't doing it no more and that's a promise, right? On my life.' He paused and looked up from his trainers to gauge my reaction. I stared at him. His hands were still in his pockets. Not acceptable. He shifted uneasily in his chair.

'Why me?' I said, after a long pause. 'And the other guy.'

'You had a bag innit. Both of yous.'

'Ah. That all?'

'Yeah. Like I said, it weren't right but that's, you know, that's the way we was. Then.'

'Right. But now you've changed?' Carl nodded. 'And that's because you know it's wrong or because you got caught?' I didn't even try to keep the cynicism out of my voice.

'Both.'

'And you didn't know it was wrong before – robbing people in the street, beating them up, threatening them? Cos I'm not your first victim, am I?' Carl squirmed. 'Well?'

'No comment,' he said, and looked away.

That did it: the red mist came down. 'This isn't a bloody police interview, Carl!' My voice was shaking, my body rigid with anger. 'If you can't be honest you'll never change! You'll just keep lying – to yourself and everyone else. You want that?'

Carl jumped in his seat, shocked. He looked to Greg for help: was I allowed to talk to him like that? But Greg just raised his eyebrows in a silent 'Well?' And waited.

'OK,' I said, taking deep breaths, '*I'll* be honest with you. You scared me on that road, really scared me. I thought you might kill me.' Carl looked taken aback. 'Yes, with that rock. Bash my brains out. And I had bad dreams, flashbacks, for weeks. In fact, I had another one just now, sitting here looking at you.' Carl shifted uncomfortably in his seat. 'And endless replays of it, only this time I was beating you to a pulp, both of you. And seeing you again in the mall ... I was scared shitless.'

'We wasn't doing nuffing,' Carl muttered, peeved.

'How was I to know that? To me, you and your brother are just a couple of thugs. Carl and Kevan, the Mugging Macers. Your mum must be proud.'

He froze, his eyes snapping on to me; the same cold stare he'd held me with before the attack.

'My mum's dead,' he said. 'When we was little.'

'Oh.' My righteousness deflated in an instant. 'And your dad ...?'

'Never seen him. He's in Africa. Some businessman.'

'So who looked after you?'

'We was in children's homes, and fostered.'

'Right ...'

I was thrown. In a few words Big Boy and Smiler had gone from random muggers stalking their prey to orphan brothers struggling in a hostile world. This time it was me who looked to Greg for help. He was frowning, but why I couldn't tell.

'Look,' I said to Carl, 'I shouldn't have talked about your mum like that and—'

''S'all right.' He pushed himself to his feet. Greg looked worried. 'I need a slash, yeah.'

'Turn right, through the swing doors, it's on your right.' Greg indicated the route with his hand but didn't look happy.

'Think he's doing a bunk?' I asked when Carl had left.

Greg pulled a face, then sprang out of his seat. 'Excuse me. Back in a moment.'

'If it's because of what I said about his mum ...'

But he was gone. I got up and poked my head out into the corridor. At the end, through the swing doors, Greg and Carl were locked in an intense discussion. Carl moved out of sight and Greg followed him. I went back to my seat and waited. And waited. And before long, had wandered off into a meandering stream of consciousness about how I came to be sitting here: because of Greg and the police and the court case and the mugging ... and Martin. If he hadn't stopped Carl and Kevan wouldn't have run off. If he hadn't seen them at the bus stop we wouldn't have followed them, caught them. And Valeria wouldn't have danced on the desk and broken her arm. And I wouldn't be facing the loss of Bladon Street. Or thinking about Fiona and *There you are* ... or Dora even. Because without Martin I wouldn't have got back into the whole Buddhist thing. She'd have returned from Barbados, found the same old me and never made the invitation back into her life. So, one way or another, I owed Martin a lot …

I got up and crossed to the window. Looking out over the jumble of Watford town centre I was reminded of Dora's story about walking along the beach and seeing the rocks offshore. Up here was like swimming at high tide, looking down on the rocks below. But you couldn't swim for ever, even if you wanted to. You had to live down among the rocks, where there was danger, jagged edges – but challenge too, varied, fascinating.

My mind drifted back to Martin, here one moment and then, suddenly, gone. Like a swimmer thrashing around in the smooth sheen of ocean until, without warning, it decides to fold him under, stretching serenely to the horizon as if he'd never been. And already, the ripples from Martin's death were fading.

Greg came in, sat down and grabbed his folder of papers. I noticed he'd left the door open.

'And?'

'He's thinking about it,' he said, leafing through his notes.

I sat back down. 'So was it the dig about his mum?'

Greg looked up. 'Yes and no. He'll explain, if he comes back. And I know there's lots of emotions and anger and stuff, Ed, but I did say these meetings go best if you don't accuse or have a pop. Just try to say how *you* feel without—'

Carl entered before Greg could finish his sentence. He closed the door and sat down with the air of a man who's finally made his mind up to face the dentist.

'So,' said Greg, smiling at him, 'thanks for choosing to keep the process going. Because it is a process, not a straight line … But I believe there's something you wanted to say, Carl, to clarify the situation?'

Carl nodded, opened his mouth – and closed it again. Silence.

'Actually,' I said, trying to change the mood, 'could I ask a favour: that you take your jacket off, and your cap? Then I won't think you're about to leg it any moment.'

Carl considered this, then removed his jacket and baseball cap and tossed them on to the spare armchair. He leaned forward as if about to speak, but the words still wouldn't come. He started to clench and unclench his fists.

'No hurry, Carl,' said Greg. 'Take your time.'

Carl glanced at him, then at me. 'Stays in this room, yeah?' We both nodded. He took a deep breath to steady himself, then launched into the speech I guessed he'd been wrestling with.

'Right, well, my mum – she ain't dead. Except she is to me, yeah?' He threw Greg a challenging look – happy now?

'Oh,' I said. This was unexpected. 'Can I ask why?'

'Cos she's an idiot.'

'In what way?'

'In every way. Smackhead, crackhead, weed, pills, booze – from when we was little, babies almost.'

'Right.'

'She's had a lot of problems,' said Greg.

Carl scoffed. 'She *is* the fucking problem.'

'Your dad?' I asked. Carl shrugged and looked away. 'D'you know him?'

Carl shook his head, staring at the floor. 'Guys …' He made a slow sweeping gesture with his arm, as if to indicate traffic passing through his mother's life. 'You know?'

I caught Greg's eye. He gave the slightest shake of his head – don't go there.

'OK. And the children's homes, foster parents …?'

'Ah no, that's honest, bruv, cos my mum …' He shook his head at the thought of her. 'Like, with Kevan, yeah? He's slow, right, cos they said when she had him she wouldn't stop doing none of it – you know, the booze, the pills, nuff-ing. That's the total idiot she is.'

'You mean when she was pregnant with him?'

'Yeah.'

A realisation hit me. 'Ah – Smiler.' Carl looked puzzled. 'I called him that because he smiled the whole time you were mugging me. You were Big Boy.'

'Right.' Carl took this in. 'Well, yeah, he smiles cos of what he's got innit.'

'What's that?' Carl shrugged again. 'You don't know?'

'He's never been diagnosed,' said Greg. 'Fell through the gaps somehow – not surprising, I suppose, considering.'

'Fing is,' said Carl, growing more animated, 'two days after we done you was my birthday, right? Eighteen, not a juvenile no more. So if we'd done you just two days later I'd be in the Scrubs now or somewhere, doing twelve months, yeah? And Kevan, he'd be … there'd be no one looking out for him right? And that can *never* happen, bruv, no way. So that's why I come here. Summink's gotta change innit and … I dunno what to do.' He suddenly looked very miserable. I almost felt sorry for him.

'OK,' I said carefully. 'At the start of this conversation Greg talked about respect and honesty – right?' Carl held my gaze and nodded. 'Right. Well, coming back to what I asked earlier then: was I your first victim?'

Carl hesitated. 'In this room, yeah?' Greg and I nodded again. And so the real conversation began.

It was extraordinary. For the next hour Carl told us everything: about his troubled schooling, his years of truanting and shoplifting, his two failed attempts at burglary – he couldn't get into either house – his early introduction to booze and marijuana, and recent experiments with other drugs, which he knew was a no-no, especially as Kevan was following his example; his graduation to street crime – he thought he'd committed 'about eighteen, twenty' muggings in different parts of London. And all this against the churn of foster parents and children's homes, always with Kevan under his protective wing, and so far – amazingly – all out of sight of the police. Till they met me and Martin and their luck ran out.

'Except,' I said, 'perhaps it didn't run out. Perhaps that's when it started.' Carl knitted his brows, confused. 'Well, you said it – you only just missed prison. And Kevan probably would have wound up there as well, eventually.'

Carl accepted this with a slow nod. And so the conversation continued. By the end of the hour my anger towards him had evaporated. He was just a lost teenager. But he'd still done some pretty unpleasant things, and when I suggested he think about how he might begin to repair some of the hurt he'd caused he looked at me as if I were mad.

'What, like, find everyone and say sorry?'

'That'd be a start,' I said. 'Though you still haven't said sorry to me.'

He looked shamefaced. 'Well, I am,' he muttered. 'I didn't even fink about people after, you know?'

'I know. But thank you.'

'Ah man, you shouldn't be fanking *me*!'

Greg suggested that Carl write me a proper letter of apology and he agreed, but he had trouble with the idea that he could also say what changes he was going to make towards some positive goal. He was concerned about Kevan and finding somewhere to live; now he was eighteen his current foster parents were on the point of kicking him out. But beyond that he had no positive vision for his life at all – because nothing positive had ever seemed possible.

'You must have some secret dream,' I said, but he just shook his head. 'Nothing?'

He thought for a moment. 'No.'

'OK,' I said, 'let's play deathbed regrets.'

'What?'

I explained, acutely aware I'd not done it properly myself yet. But Carl was keen, and Greg intrigued.

'Right,' I said. 'So close your eyes and imagine you're about to draw your last breath.' Carl closed his eyes. 'Now, what's the one thing you really wish you'd done if you had your time over again?'

'And Kevan's OK, yeah?'

'Yes, he's fine. This is just for you. You're on your death-bed, full of regret, saying I wish I'd ... what?'

Silence.

'Run a sandwich shop,' said Carl. 'With loads of different fillings.'

I came away from the encounter sensing that something significant had happened. I didn't know what exactly but I felt oddly...satisfied. Carl had repeated his promise to write a letter of apology and had added that as soon as he got some money he'd pay me the £25 the court had ordered, which I'd forgotten about, and nudge Kevan to pay up, too. I had no idea if he'd keep either promise, but he seemed sincere. In fact, it was the personal pledge that had seemed to motivate him, the desire not to let me down. We'd ended on a handshake and he'd thanked me. I'd asked what for and he'd shrugged.

'Dunno. Just ... you know.'

And I did know. I'd been his victim on that empty lane in the summer; he'd terrified me. Yet it had become clear as we'd talked that he was desperate for help, so desperate that in his honesty he'd made himself completely vulnerable. He'd offered his trust, and that was something I had to carry with me.

I realised, as I drove down the motorway towards Dora's, that I felt strangely privileged.

Piers was already there when I arrived and – a pleasant surprise – so was Bernie. He'd come along to give a hand but also to see if there were any pickings. So far he'd relieved Dora of the full-length mirror that had hung by the front door, and the old upright piano she'd bought soon after the start of our relationship. Piers and I had risked serious injury heaving it up the four steep flights to her flat, and now we were being asked to heave it down again. At least we had gravity on our side this time. And Bernie.

'What are you going to do with it?' I asked as, with a final gasp, we lumped it into his van. But he just tapped the side of his nose, locked the van doors and disappeared back inside the house. Piers followed him but I took a moment in the fresh air to recover, and reflect.

Dora's rediscovered passion for the piano had been intense but brief, an attempt to grow a side of her that had lain dormant since school. She'd found a teacher, booked lessons, applied to take her Grade 4, and she still had her old sheet music for practice. But after a flying start other things had once again begun to take precedence – work, Buddhist activities, me – and before long the piano had fallen silent. My risked hernia had been in vain. And when Dora had nagged me about not chanting, her failure to practise the piano had been my favourite counter-attack. 'You've got to want to do it!' I'd yell. 'Like you and the piano! The moment it becomes an obligation it's dead!'

So the upright came with a story, baggage. And humping it back down the stairs and packing it off in Bernie's van was – well, unsettling. In fact, I found the whole process of decanting the remnants of Dora's flat into two vans and off-loading them at the recycling centre deeply disconcerting. I'd shared her space for five years and every piece of crockery and cutlery, the toaster, the microwave – everything came with a memory attached. And now it was being discarded it stirred emotions I didn't know I had: attachment, longing, regret, sadness. Why, when I had in my hand an open invitation from Dora to start over again in a tropical paradise?

By late afternoon I knew the answer. We'd made two trips in both vans to the recycling centre and the flat was now empty. The only thing left was Dora's brass bedstead – she had a buyer who couldn't collect till later in the week – so we couldn't even make a farewell cup of tea.

'No problem,' said Piers. 'Got to rush anyway – I've got a Skype call with Constanza. First time since she left so ...' He crossed his fingers.

We wished him luck, he made Dora promise to get in touch whenever she was back in London, and he hurried off. Bernie followed soon after. Throughout our exertions he'd made no reference to anything I'd told him during my visit and he left simply wishing Dora all the best in Barbados.

'And if ever there's any building work you want doing, m'darling, don't hesitate to send me the air fare and I'll be out in a flash.'

Dora laughed. 'That's very big of you, Bernie, thanks.'

They hugged, he shook my hand, and then there were three: me, Dora and the bedstead. I gazed at it fondly.

'Happy memories.' Dora gave my arm a slap. 'Seriously,' I said. 'I hope you got a good price for it. Great suspension, steady runner, loads on the clock.' Dora smiled – sadly, I thought. 'You're off when?'

'Thursday.'

'And what – you're staying with Cedric till then?' Her brother.

'Uh-huh. They're coming out at Christmas.'

'Right. That'll be nice.' There was a pause, an awkward one, just long enough to signal the elephant in the room. 'Look, Dora—'

She didn't let me get any further. 'It's all right, Ed – I know. You're not coming.'

'Wha... How did you—'

'Fiona. That's who you want, isn't it?'

I was even more surprised. 'Fiona? Fiona's gone back to Ireland.' I told her about the sudden departure and the Dave debacle but not, of course, about the preceding night. Dora's gloom seemed to deepen.

'Ah. So it's just me then.'

'No, not at all!'

'This was last week?' I nodded. 'And you didn't share it till now? So what does that say – about us?'

I looked at the floor, silent. I could hardly tell her I'd been on a bender, not least because it would sound as if Fiona's departure had torn my heart out.

'The thing is,' I said, 'you've got a reason to be out there, a mission – and I haven't. I'll be trailing around after you, trying to find something to do. And I do want to save the world, just...'

'Not yet.' I smiled. 'It's OK, Ed, you don't have to explain.'

'But I want to,' I said. 'I mean, it's a lovely thought, really flattering, but – well, to be honest, for me, for my life, it feels like running away.'

Dora searched my face, then sighed. 'And to be honest on my side, I think I knew the answer when I first said it. I just blocked it out.'

'Oh?'

She smiled. 'You know at Christmas when you give someone a present? You can tell the moment they unwrap it what they think of it. Their eyes light up – wow, what

286

I always wanted! Or there's this look of disappointment, then a forced smile – thank you. Or best of all, total surprise and joy – that's amazing! I didn't even know I wanted it myself! And then there's the look I got from you. Ee-oo – what am I supposed to do with this ...?'

She was right. And the sadness and regret I'd been feeling while clearing out her flat had been my gut recognising that this marked the reality between us: not a new beginning but the end, once and for all.

'I'm sorry,' I said. And I was.

'Oh don't be, my darling.' She leaned forward and kissed me softly on the cheek. 'At least the answer's clear.'

'And? Then what?' Darren was agog.

We were at Piers's for the December discussion meeting. Traditionally it was a time for reflection on the year just gone, an accounting of challenges surmounted (or not) and a declaration of determinations for the year ahead. The sitting room was crowded: the usual faces, who were starting to feel like real friends, plus a couple of guests. Darren and Aidan and Bernie and Jenny; and Piers of course. Still no Constanza, but he was hopeful – a Christmas visit to Barcelona had been agreed, not least because the baby was due around then.

'High stakes, though,' he'd warned. 'There are more murders at Christmas than at any other time of the year, so ... Anyway, we'll see.'

Luis was there, too. Quietly, out of sight, he'd overcome his initial doubts and was now giving the practice both barrels; he was talking about getting his own Gohonzon and had brought along his brother, Gil, who was on a work recce from Portugal. Jenny had brought a guest, too – Maria, a pretty young nurse from her local veterinary practice. Right now they were all staring at me, eager to hear the end of the story I'd been telling about me and Dora.

'Well,' I said, 'there were tears – from both of us – then we said goodbye, with a hug, and I went home and chanted. Send in the hounds – the truffle hounds. That's how I imagine it working,' I explained to Gil and Maria. 'I'm snuffling around in my life, trying to find the answer, the treasure, and dig it up.'

Maria nodded while Luis translated into Gil's ear. '*Interessante*,' he murmured.

'And at the same time I played deathbed regrets on myself – you know, if I was dying what would be the one thing that I really regretted not having done.' I acknowledged Bernie with a nod but he didn't react, just continued to stroke his beard. 'It wasn't easy but, finally, I realised that I'd really regret thinking when I died that somehow I hadn't made a difference; that, basically, it wouldn't matter if I'd never existed. I don't mean saving the world or anything, but that's why the whole thing with Carl just …' I searched for the right words. 'I felt I made a difference. He's written to me to apologise for what he did and sent me a fiver towards what he owes me. And he's talking about going to college to do business studies or maybe catering – whatever he needs for his sandwich shop. And that makes me feel good. It's not huge but at the same time it is – for him, maybe. And definitely for me, because I've decided that's what I want to do more of: work with young people. Maybe young offenders, maybe teaching in prison. Or maybe just proper teaching, stop farting around with what I'm doing and get a proper qualification – you know, commit to it. So that's for next year. And I don't know which path yet exactly but, well, it'll become clear. Me and my truffle hound. Oh – and try to cut down on the red wine, too. *Alors. Fini.*'

I looked around the circle of faces – all smiles and nods, except from Aidan.

'One question. What about Valeria and the insurance?'

'Thanks for reminding me.' I pulled a sheet of paper from my back pocket and unfolded it. 'I got a letter this morning from the school – St Catherine's.' I scanned the text and read. 'Blah blah blah ... "Following a detailed investigation by the loss adjusters, our insurers have today contacted us to say that they have decided to meet the cost of Mr and Mrs Adamoli's claim in full."' There were murmurs of surprise around the room. '"In light of this, we now consider the matter closed and would like to wish you all the best for Christmas, the New Year and your future career." No apology or mention of a reference but still – result.'

'Ha! That's pretty bloody amazing,' said Piers. 'What happened?'

'No idea,' I said. 'I did think of trying to call Barry Raymonds – the loss adjuster – but decided, you know, don't look a gift-horse in the mouth. My guess is he's trying to help Fiona. Maybe he thinks she's still living with me. I don't know and, quite honestly, I don't care. I'm just extremely grateful.'

'Protection,' said Jenny. 'You did the right thing and the universe responded.'

I glanced over at Bernie. He smiled.

I was surfing the web the other day when I came across a video of a speech that Steve Jobs made to students at Stanford University in 2005. Since I'd found it via my Mac I thought I'd give him a few minutes and I'm glad I did, because it's all about understanding life through death, and turning poison into medicine – and joining the dots. One line really struck me. 'You can't connect the dots looking forward,' he says. 'You can only connect them looking backwards.'

Meeting Martin on that August day had seemed like an amazing coincidence, but that was looking forward. Now, looking backwards, I'm not so sure; because, somehow, it's pushed me in the right direction. It sort of makes sense. Which means, maybe, that being mugged by Carl and Kevan, Big Boy and Smiler, was also no coincidence. They were always in my life, unseen, waiting for the moment when our paths would cross – and change things for all of us.

Later I decided to drive up to Hillview, just to have a look. St Catherine's had broken up for the Christmas holidays and the area was still and quiet under a dark December sky. A cold wind was blowing over Watford, under the hill to the west.

The site was boarded up, exactly as we'd left it, except that now there were no leaves on the trees. I wondered about the carpet, slowly rotting in the back garden; about the suicide in the basement and what effect it might have on the house or its future owners. And I wondered if the house would ever be finished and sold.

My phone pinged: a text, from Fiona. Martin's funeral had been set for 4 January, in Durham, and I'd be welcome.

There you are…

I hadn't said it at the Buddhist meeting – it felt too personal and I didn't want to risk it getting back to Dora – but my deathbed regret had thrown up something else, something equally unexpected. It was that I'd regret not having a family, being a dad. Which was a shock, as I'd always seen myself as an independent person. But I realised that when Fiona and the kids left my place, and Dave, that's what I really missed: family. Whether it's that particular family … well, I don't know – yet.

I texted back saying I'd be there, and wishing a very happy Christmas to her and Amelia, and Oliver and Dave, and to her parents. I was about to get back into the car when the sun burst through the clouds and suddenly I was in a Turner painting again, like the time I was in the garden fighting with the brambles. A finger of gold seemed to be pointing at Watford – of all places. It's a sign, I thought, with a cynical grin – then caught myself. Why 'of all places'? Why not Watford? Surely there's gold there too. There's gold everywhere, if you look hard enough.

The clouds shifted and in a moment the sun had gone. But not really. It was still up there, burning away – constantly, day and night, summer and winter, spring and autumn, rain or shine. Or snow, which looked to be on its way.

I read Fiona's message again: 'You'll be welcome.'

I got into the car and set off down the hill for home.

Enjoy life. Win.

About the Author

Edward Canfor-Dumas is a novelist and an award-winning TV scriptwriter. He was educated at New College, Oxford and after a spell as a comedy writer and performer started writing for popular television series such as *The Bill* and *Kavanagh QC*. His TV work includes *Tough Love*, *Pompeii: the Last Day* and *Supervolcano*. He took a lead role in establishing the All-Party Parliamentary Group on Conflict Issues, launched in February 2007, and in 2011 co-founded Engi, a social enterprise that works with businesses, civil society and government to reduce conflict. He is the author of *The Buddha, Geoff and Me* and is a practising Buddhist.

The Buddha, Geoff and Me
A Modern Story

Edward Canfor-Dumas

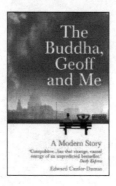

Ed is having a hard time – at work, in his love life and, well, generally. Then he meets an unlikely Buddhist – who drinks and smokes and talks his kind of language. Bit by bit, things begin to change...

Ed doesn't always take Geoff's advice. Or, when he does, he lapses at the crucial moment. His path to understanding is not a straight one, especially as life keeps throwing more stuff at him. Often he fails – like most of us, in fact. But sometimes he manages to get it right. And when he does, surprising things begin to happen.

A novel by award-winning writer Edward Canfor-Dumas, *The Buddha, Geoff and Me* is for anyone who's ever begun to wonder what the whole damn thing is all about...

ISBN 9781844135684